HUMMINGBIRD

BOOK ONE OF A CHARADE OF MAGIC

HELEN HARPER

Cover created by Clarissa Yeo at Yocla Designs

❀ Created with Vellum

For Molly, Rachel and Zara x

CHAPTER ONE

ONLY THE DESPERATE VENTURED OUT AFTER DARK. OR THE MAD. It was entirely likely I was both. It was illegal to set foot outdoors once the sun had gone down, but for once it wasn't fear of the Mages that ensured most people toed the line. The streets weren't safe for anyone at night.

The screwed-up message in my pocket with its shaky writing had been more than enough to draw me out, however. I knew I was taking an incredible risk but I didn't have much choice.

I pulled into a shadowy alcove underneath the row of darkened tenements by the river and looked at the message again. *I need you, Maree.* She'd spelled my name wrong. It was how I knew the message was from her, and not a lure or a cruel trick.

Isla had never been much of one for paying attention to her letters. My old bedmate wasn't stupid – far from it – but her heart lay with numbers and equations. She had no interest in the written word, no matter how often the matron unlocked the sturdy oak drawer in her study and taken out her thin cane in a bid to 'teach' Isla the error of her ways. Even at a young age she had been too stubborn to do as she was told and keep her head down, and nothing had changed in the intervening years. But she was also too stubborn to ask for help when she needed it – usually. Things had to be desperate; Isla wouldn't have sent the note otherwise.

I stuffed the message back into my pocket and peered out at the dark street. The moon was obscured by heavy clouds, so there was barely a sliver of light to illuminate my way. That was probably for the best.

I rubbed my arms, as much to comfort myself as to gain any defence against the cold, then I ducked out into the open again, weaving down the pavement, my eyes darting from side to side as I checked for any lurking shapes or signs of life. If ever I needed some luck, it was now.

I maintained a steady pace for several minutes, ignoring the damp hem of my skirt as it flapped around my ankles, and the pinching pain from my too-small shoes. The less time I spent in the open, the better. I adjusted my bag, switching it from one shoulder to the other, without pausing. I was making good time. Maybe there was hope after all. All I had to do was get across the river and I'd be almost there. As long as Rutherglen Bridge was clear, I'd make it. I could already see the crooked rooftop of St Mags. It was practically within touching distance.

I crossed the street, keeping low as I passed the warehouses that lined the river. It was more exposed here, and the breeze skittering across the water to sting my cheeks wouldn't let me forget it. I steeled my stomach. Not far now. Five minutes, tops.

Jogging up a small rise, I raised my head to scan the bridge. It looked empty. I fixated on the intricate Mages' ward etched into the centre. It was designed to protect passers-by from whatever might be hiding in the murky depths of the river below, but it didn't always work, even in daylight. And at this hour, it wasn't just the swirling black water I had to worry about.

2

I bit my bottom lip hard enough to draw blood, but it was fine. The bridge was clear; nothing was there. I pushed ahead, pausing only when I reached the start of the bridge itself. Three minutes, I estimated; if I sprinted, I could get across in three minutes.

I straightened my shoulders. *Come on, Mairi. You've got this.*

I stepped onto the bridge. On a count of three, I decided.

One.

Two.

Thr–

Shite.

I bit back a cry and threw myself to the side. Four of them. Four of the Afflicted were heading this way from the opposite side of the bridge. Fear roared through my veins. Had they seen me? What should I do?

I debated running. I could twist away and flee in the opposite direction – but then they'd definitely notice me and I'd be moving further away from my goal rather than towards it. My heart hammered against my chest until it felt as if my whole ribcage was thumping. I gulped in a breath of air and tried to calm down. Panic wouldn't help me.

When a guttural groan reached my ears, it was enough to galvanise me into action. I glanced right, spotted the point under the bridge where the water met the land and dived towards it, sliding down the muddy slope until I was beneath it. I could hunker down here. Unless the Afflicted marched off the bridge and turned towards the riverbank, they wouldn't see me.

A chilling thought struck me and I sniffed my clothes and armpits. They might not *see* me but they might possibly *smell* me.

I swallowed. It was too late now, I had to stay where I was. With shaky hands, I slid my umbrella out of my bag. It wasn't much of a weapon, but it was all I had.

It seemed to take an age. I waited and waited, until I began to think that they'd changed their minds and headed in a different direction. That was when I heard the snuffling, followed by yet another groan. They were directly above my head.

My fingers tightened round the umbrella handle and I pressed my spine against the cold stone, trying to make myself invisible. *Nothing to see here, folks. Carry on your way.*

One of them snorted, a loud sound that seemed to ricochet off the stone bridge, and the faint smell of rotting meat tickled my nostrils. The tension in my shoulders eased slightly. I shouldn't have worried about my personal stench; the Afflicted would never be able to smell my skin over their own reek.

I held my breath and listened as the four of them shuffled off the bridge and turned to the right. Curiosity overtook my fear and I peeked out. I couldn't see their faces because they were already facing away from me, trudging downstream with a slow, uneven gait. All four were barefoot, with ragged clothes and dirt-streaked skin. It was too dark to make out the pockmarks and scars that marked them as Afflicted. The nearest one had long hair hanging down his back in ratty clumps; judging by the body shape and broad shoulders, that one was a male.

Suddenly there was a screeching yowl from somewhere further down the road. A cat, probably. The Afflicted reacted with lightning speed, moving from a slow shuffle to a sudden sprint in a split second. I realised that they were going after the animal. They needed meat. If they'd seen me, I'd have been a far tastier – and more satisfying – prospect. I licked my dry lips and breathed out. That had been close.

I waited another minute or two to be sure I was safe, then ducked out and scrambled up the bank. The Afflicted had gone, and the bridge was empty once again. I was safe for now. And St Mags was in sight.

TEN MINUTES LATER, I raised my fist and knocked gently on the wooden door at the back of the orphanage. A beat passed, then another. As I reached forward to knock again, the knob suddenly turned. With a jarring creak that made me wince, the door opened an inch. I could just make out a small grubby face – a boy, eight years old, maybe nine.

'Who are you?' he asked in a too-loud whisper.

I stared at him, nonplussed. I hadn't been prepared for anyone other than Isla to open the door. My hands fluttered as I gestured helplessly.

He must have been prepared for that because he nodded and opened the door wider. 'She's upstairs,' he told me. 'In the squinty room.'

I knew exactly where he meant. It was nine years since I'd last stepped inside this building, but those sorts of memories don't fade. All the same, I allowed the lad to lead me through the old kitchen and up the worn stone steps to the second floor. Our feet barely made a sound.

Nothing had changed here. The walls of St Mags still reeked of loneliness and desolation and neglect. The children inside were safe from the Afflicted, but monsters weren't the only things that could kill a person. Or a child.

We turned down the corridor and tiptoed to the end of it. The boy paused outside a door and scratched it lightly with the tip of his index finger before pushing it open. It was indeed the squinty room, with its uneven floor and misaligned windows.

I crossed my fingers and hoped I wasn't too late.

There were a dozen narrow beds, each one containing hunched figures curled up two to a bed. At the far end of the room, close to the first window, a woman was bending over a bed. She straightened up and her face altered as soon as she saw me.

'You made it. I wasn't sure you would.' Isla's relief was palpable. I hoped her trust in me wouldn't prove misplaced.

I nodded at the boy, indicating he should go. He turned away, silently leaving the room to return to his own dorm. I slid my bag off my shoulder and moved to Isla.

'Did you have any trouble getting here?' she asked.

I shrugged. That would depend on how you defined trouble, but this wasn't the time for those sorts of stories.

Isla frowned slightly, then sighed and pointed at the thin body in front of her. 'Her name is Meg. She started getting sick this morning.' Her worried voice took on a bitter edge. 'They refused to call a doctor. Now I'm afraid it might be too late.' Some things never changed, and the orphanage at St Magdalene's was one of them.

I placed a hand on the girl's forehead. She was soaked in sweat and her skin was burning. She let out a shuddering breath when I touched her, and her chest rattled. Whatever was wrong with her, it wasn't good.

Isla's voice was low. 'Is it—?'

I shook my head quickly. No, she wasn't Afflicted. There were none of the marks that indicated the start of the terrible disease that turned men into monsters. However, that didn't mean I knew what the problem was.

A small voice spoke up from the bed next to us. 'She's scunnered, ain't she, miss?'

Isla spoke firmly. 'She'll be fine. Don't worry.' She raised her eyes to mine, anxiety reflected in them together with a question. I gestured in response and Isla tracked the movement of my hands.

We'd shared a bed for five years here at St Mags, topping and tailing until the day of my sixteenth birthday when I'd been sent to Belle and Twister. When Isla turned sixteen the month after me, she'd remained at the orphanage and gained a place as scullery maid. Even now, years afterwards, neither of us was sure who had got the better deal. But we knew each other well enough to communicate without words – we'd developed our own method.

Isla breathed out and her shoulders sagged slightly. 'Okay,' she said quietly. 'Okay.'

I delved into my bag. I didn't know exactly what was wrong with the wee girl, but that didn't mean I was out of options. I had elderflower, white willow bark and echinacea, all gathered during my few precious moments of freedom before being dried carefully in my room. I took several pinches of each, humming softly to myself as I mixed them. Then, while Isla left to fetch some hot water, I took some peppermint oil and massaged it gently into Meg's palms and the soles of her feet. She twitched and murmured uncomfortably. I hummed some more until she calmed.

When Isla returned with a steaming cup in her hands, I dropped the herbal mixture into it and added a tiny pinch of belladonna. I lifted Meg into a sitting position and placed the cup to her lips.

'Drink up, Meg,' Isla murmured.

Meg moaned, but her mouth remained resolutely closed. I bent my head and hummed a single note for comfort. My hand at her back was already clammy from her sweat. I rubbed her spine and she let out a soft sigh, then parted her lips and drank.

'Good lass,' Isla said. 'Well done.'

I waited until she'd finished the entire concoction – it was important that she drank it all – then pressed some more of the herbs into Isla's hands.

'Are you sure? Is this your entire supply?' she asked.

It was, but that didn't matter. Everything I had might not be enough to save Meg, but people like her were the reason I spent so much time gathering and collecting. It wasn't easy to find what I needed in a city like this, even with all its parks, but it was necessary. Meg proved that. Without the orphanage's support, there was no money to pay for a doctor or visit an apothecary. This was all she had; *I* was all she had.

I scribbled down instructions and made sure that Isla understood my messy notes. By the time I'd finished, Meg's breathing seemed to have eased even though her temperature was still raging. She was little more than skin and bones. It was possible that I was already too late, or the few herbs I'd been able to give her wouldn't be enough. She might still die, and sadly there was little else I could do.

'You've worked your magic,' Isla whispered. 'She's already breathing more easily.'

I shook my head, my expression filled with warning. Meg wasn't out of the woods. And Isla shouldn't use that word. It wasn't magic. Women didn't use magic.

There was a rustle of blankets. From one of the beds on the opposite side of the room, a pair of bare feet emerged followed by a small figure in a nightgown. A tiny girl with large dark eyes and a tear-stained face padded towards me. She slipped her hand into mine. 'Will Meg be alright?'

'This is Alice,' Isla told me. 'She's usually Meg's bedmate.'

I crouched down in front of Alice and brushed her mussed hair away from her cheek as I tried to look reassuring.

Alice continued to stare at me. 'Thank you,' she whispered.

She shouldn't have thanked me, not yet, but I managed a smile. Alice nodded in return. I thought she understood – I hoped she did.

'You should stay until dawn,' Isla said. 'It's not safe to go back out there yet.'

It wasn't safe in here either, not for me. Even though I was an ex-inmate of St Mags, there would be hell to pay for everyone if I were spotted by one of the matrons. Besides, if I didn't get back to Belle and Twister's by the time the sun rose, I'd receive several smacks to my head as punishment. Dawn wasn't far off now.

I'd made it all the way here in the dark so I could make it back. The hardest part was already over.

I shook my head at Isla and she pursed her lips, though she didn't argue. She knew better than that. 'How are things going over there?' she asked.

I pulled a face. There wasn't any need to elaborate; Isla understood the score. I pointed at her, throwing back the question. Her expression was similar to mine. 'No different.' She looked down at Meg. 'As you see.' Her face darkened. 'A baby went missing last week. The first one in a long while.'

My eyes narrowed. I signed towards her. *A girl?*

'Yeah.' She glanced round and tugged on her earlobe. I nodded and we walked out of the squinty dorm room and into the corridor, away from the small ears of nosy children. 'There was a Mage here,' Isla said quietly. 'The night the baby vanished, there was a Mage.'

I gave her a warning look and Isla sighed. 'You know I wouldn't tell anyone other than you. I'm not stupid.' Her jaw tightened. 'But I don't know where the baby's gone and I don't know if the Mage took her. I can't pretend it didn't happen.' Her voice was very low but it didn't hide her note of desperation. 'Can I?'

I couldn't understand why a Mage would take a baby, but if they had the child was already lost. The Mages' power was absolute, and there was no gainsaying their actions. Isla knew that as well as I did.

I delved into my pocket and drew out a short length of purple thread that I'd picked up during Belle and Twister's most recent delivery of tartan. I tied it round Isla's wrist. It wasn't much but it would remind her that she wasn't alone; I'd always be with her.

I reached for her hands and squeezed them tight. Isla squeezed back. We remained like that for a long moment, two old friends seeking comfort in each other. Finally, by unspoken agreement, we both pulled away. The real world, in all its grimness, was beckoning us back.

CHAPTER TWO

IT WAS STILL DARK WHEN I LEFT ST MAGS, WITH NO SIGN OF THE impending dawn. At this time of year, the nights were painfully long – at best you could only hope for seven or eight hours of daylight, although the reverse was true in the summer. Still, people adjusted. In my experience people always adjusted. They adapted their lives and spent more time indoors where it was safe, then made up for lost time when the days grew warmer and longer. This was living. Apparently.

I took my time scoping out the river and Rutherglen Bridge. This time there were no signs of life so I darted across with my heart thumping until I reached the other side. There were no heavy grunts or groans and no sign of the group that I'd narrowly avoided on my first journey. All the same, as I skirted the shadows and wove my way from the Clyde river towards the narrow streets beyond, I continued to keep a wary eye out for more Afflicted. I couldn't let my guard down, even though other anxious thoughts were troubling me.

A baby girl missing. How long had it been since the last one? Six years, probably, maybe even seven. It used to happen with far more chilling regularity. The year that I'd turned ten, three babies went missing from St Mags alone, and I heard that at least twelve more vanished from homes around the city. It was always girls, never boys. Sometimes the children reappeared with no explanation; sometimes they never returned. The Afflicted were blamed. There were whispers that the Mages were involved, though nobody dared to accuse them outright. There was never any proof – and what on earth would the Mages want with squalling children? Maybe Isla had been mistaken and imagining things, or the Mage had been at St Mags for a completely different reason. But who else could have taken the babe?

I grimaced. Even thinking about it chilled me to my core. It wasn't as if I could do anything about it; I was a nobody with nothing. Somehow, that made it worse. I sighed. At least with wee Meg, I'd been able to try and I hadn't been completely helpless. I sighed again, more loudly. And then I felt the back of my neck prickle.

I didn't falter or stumble but I veered closer to the walls of the houses on my left, hugging the shadows to make myself invisible. The strange sensation didn't disappear; someone – or more likely some*thing* – was behind me.

I resisted the temptation to turn my head. I couldn't hear anything, and I knew that the Afflicted were rarely silent or stealthy. The night belonged to them, so they had no need to keep quiet. But I couldn't shake the feeling that I was being stalked.

I suppressed the shiver that ran down my spine and considered my options. Even if I ran all the way, it was still a fifteen-minute journey back to the relative safety of Belle and Twister's shop. I was already bone tired and I doubted even an adrenaline rush could help me to escape any but the slowest of pursuers. Fleeing wasn't the answer, so either I found somewhere to hide or I prepared myself for a fight. But nobody would open their door to me, not at this hour. I was on my own.

Squinting through the darkness, I spotted a narrow wynd to the left. I had no way of knowing where it led, but it was better than staying out on this wide street. I ducked my head and took slightly longer strides while maintaining the same speed. I didn't want to alert whatever predator was behind me; I didn't want them to know that I was aware of their presence. Not yet. It was only about thirty steps to the wynd. One thing at a time, I decided. Get there first and then worry about my next move.

I passed a butcher's shop, and the hanging slabs of meat visible through its window did nothing to ease my state of mind. As I slipped past an ironmonger's, I glimpsed knives and tools and thought of my pathetic umbrella. I should have come better prepared. I could have taken the old carving knife from the kitchen. Its blade was dull, no matter how often I worked it against Twister's whetstone, but it would surely have been better than a damned brolly. I was a complete fucking numpty.

Twenty steps. Fifteen. Ten. I held my breath. Almost there. I drew level with the wynd and glanced down it. It was narrower than I'd expected and bone-chillingly dark.

I heard a thump from behind me, perhaps only thirty feet away, and wasted no more time. I spun left, sprinting into the wynd and away from whatever was trailing me, tugging the umbrella out of my bag at the same time. *Run, Mairi. Just bloody run.*

I made it less than ten feet before something grabbed me by the scruff of my neck. Momentum carried me forward for a second, but my escape was well and truly thwarted. I hissed as hot breath scalded my cheek and strong hands twisted me round.

I gripped the umbrella with both hands and brandished it, waving it in the air as if it could save me.

A dark face loomed forward. 'Now what good is that going to do you?'

I swallowed and stared at him. He was tall – at least a foot

13

taller than me – but he was muscular rather than lanky. I registered dark hair, piercing eyes that shone with an emerald-green colour that was far too bright to be human, and curling tattoos across his sharp cheekbones. My eyes rose and I saw his pointed ears and the coiled horns rising a few inches from either side of his skull. I'd thought I was scared before, but now I was rigid with terror. A daemon. This was a damned daemon.

He was wearing a long black cloak over black trousers and a shirt. The metal collar round his neck glinted, and I knew there would be matching metal cuffs round his wrists. He was one of the Mages' creatures; only they had the power to control a daemon like this one. My stomach sank to the bottom of my damp shoes. I would have been better off with the Afflicted.

'Don't you know how dangerous it is to be out at night?' the daemon asked. He had a strange accent. 'What could be so important that you'd risk your life to be out here?'

I stared at him. He tilted his head, curiosity in his gaze. 'Cat got your tongue?' he enquired. 'Or are you damaged in the head?'

Somewhere deep inside me something tightened.

I raised the tip of the umbrella a fraction and smacked him on the side of his tattooed face. Surprised rather than hurt, he released his grip on me. I didn't waste my chance: I twisted round and started to run for my life.

This time I got less than three feet. He grabbed my upper arms and pushed me against the wall, pinning me so that I couldn't attempt a second escape. His face dipped towards mine and I caught his scent: spicy with cinnamon and cloves – and something else.

My chest heaving, I gulped in air. *Shite. Oh shite.*

'Why would you do something like that?' he asked. He didn't sound angry; if anything, his tone was mildly inquisitive. 'You won't get away from me.'

My fingers tightened on the umbrella handle, but the

daemon caught the movement and adjusted his grip until I was forced to drop it. It fell to the ground with a clatter.

I raised my knee sharply, aiming for his groin, and he blocked me easily. 'There's no need for any of that,' he chided. He peered into my face, his green eyes glittering. 'Who are you?'

My mouth was bone dry. There was no way out of this, not now.

The daemon tilted his head and examined my face intently. 'So,' he murmured, 'it's not that you won't talk but rather that you *can't*. Interesting.' Something flashed in his eyes. 'Your hair is the colour of fire.' He inhaled. 'And you smell like honey.' He smiled slightly. 'Good enough to eat.'

Oh hell. I licked my lips, then I tilted my chin and met his eyes. *Make it quick. Go on. Just make it fucking quick.*

There was a shout from somewhere on the main street, and both the daemon and I jerked in surprise. It came again. 'Nicholas!'

I blinked. Nicholas? Was that the daemon's name? It wasn't as foreign to my ears as I'd imagined it would be.

'Nicholas! Where are you?'

The daemon muttered something. Whatever he said, it wasn't English. He leaned in even closer. 'If you value your life,' he whispered, 'do not move.' He stepped back and released his hold on my arms.

I thought about bolting again. Third time lucky, right? But something about the look in the daemon's eyes made me stay where I was.

He gave me a single approving nod and lifted his hands. '*Ashgaroth var.*' He grinned. 'Good luck, sweetheart.'

'Nicholas!'

'I'm here,' he called as he bent down and picked up my umbrella. He placed his index finger against his lips then turned as a figure appeared at the entrance to the wynd.

The newcomer's scarlet clothes were a dead giveaway: a

Mage. Could things get any worse? He strode into the wynd. 'Well?' he demanded. 'Where is she?'

Uh... I was right here. I wasn't exactly hard to miss.

Nicholas swept an arm out. 'You tell me.' He pasted on a baffled look, which seemed out of place on his tattooed features.

'You cursed creature! How difficult is it to get hold of one human female?' The Mage looked towards the end of the wynd. He was less than a metre from me and hadn't once looked in my direction. What was going on?

'She dropped this,' Nicholas offered. He held up my umbrella. 'Perhaps you can use it to track her.'

'Eejit. You know my skills don't extend to that – and even if they did, I wouldn't expend that sort of magic on a damned woman.' The Mage rolled his eyes. He wasn't bad looking but his skin was sallow, suggesting he didn't spend much time outdoors. Thirty years old, maybe slightly more.

'She was obviously up to no good. Nobody would come out here at this hour if they meant well.' He sniffed. 'The sun won't rise for a while yet. You didn't catch her, but I bet the Afflicted will. It'll serve the bitch right. The law is clear. We've told those idiots over and over again not to come out at night.'

'You have indeed,' Nicholas said.

The Mage's head whipped towards him, his eyes narrowing. 'Are you making fun of me? Because I can still make your life hell, you know. Just because the Ascendant trusts you, it doesn't mean that I do.'

There was an odd flicker on the daemon's face, but he merely bowed politely.

I stared at him and at the Mage, then stared down at myself. My skin was shimmering and I felt a tingle up and down the length of my body. He'd done something to me; the daemon had said those strange words and done something, and now the Mage couldn't see me.

'Shall we head back, sir?' Nicholas asked.

The Mage grunted. 'Might as well.' He gazed towards the other end of the wynd again. 'Stupid woman,' he muttered. He clicked his fingers. 'Come on then.' As he turned on his heel, his scarlet cloak flared out and the hem scraped against my cheek. The Mage didn't look round. Nicholas didn't glance at me, either. He simply walked after the Mage. Within moments, the pair of them had disappeared.

I poked my arm. It felt solid: I was still here. I waved my hand in front of my face and wiggled my fingers; my skin continued to shimmer, but it was visible – at least to me. I took a step and the tingling grew stronger. I held my breath and took another step, then another. Gradually the shimmer dissipated and the strange tingling ebbed away. I poked myself again. I felt fine. But was I fine?

What the hell had happened there? It made no sense. I rubbed my arms where the daemon had held me. I could still feel his imprint. He'd done something – he'd performed some kind of magic and concealed me from the Mage. I had no idea why a daemon, of all creatures, would do such a thing.

I couldn't ask him why he'd done it and I couldn't hang around here with dawn approaching. I shrugged. Maybe I'd imagined the entire thing. Or maybe, as the daemon had suggested, I really was damaged in the head. At that moment, it felt like anything was possible.

CHAPTER THREE

Five days later, I'd stopped wondering what on earth had happened in the wynd and was spending more time wishing I still had my umbrella. It was not a huge amount to ask for, not in the great scheme of things, and I could have bought a new one at any number of places. But when it was the choice between having enough food to fill my belly and getting wet, it was no contest.

I trudged down Buchanan Street with its colourful hawker stalls and unending traffic of horses, carriages and bikes. The icy rain continued to pelt my exposed head, while the tips of my ears turned numb and freezing droplets snaked their way down the back of my neck, no matter how much I pulled up my collar. It was no surprise that the refrain was pattering through my head: I really, really wished I had my damned umbrella.

At least Isla had managed to send word that wee Meg was past the worst and on the mend. I'd already started the slow process of replenishing my stock of herbs. With luck, they wouldn't be needed again any time soon. A small knot of anxiety still remained in the pit of my stomach, though. Isla hadn't made any mention of the missing baby girl but I doubted she'd forgotten about her. I certainly hadn't.

'Long day?' Marsh called out as I passed him and narrowly avoided stepping in a dirty puddle.

I nodded and raised my hand in greeting. He was one of the kinder stall holders, so it was the least I could do. When I had enough coin to rub together to buy fresh food, he often threw in a few extra scraps of meat whilst I pretended to look the other way. Unfortunately today was not one of those days so, although I acknowledged him, I didn't stop to listen to his natter. Besides, if I'd had enough money for a meal and dallied to buy one, Twister wouldn't be happy. He was waiting on the message in my pocket, and I knew how things would go if I was late bringing it to him. The soft inner flesh of my palms still tingled after the last time.

I skirted round Santorini's, doing my best not to inhale. Even in this weather, the yeasty smell of his wife's bread was enough to drive a person insane with hunger. The diversion forced me onto the road and I had to duck and dive to avoid the speeding bikes.

'Ho!'

I jumped to my left as a three-wheeler sped up behind me. It whizzed forward, its front wheel dipping into another puddle that was congealed with muck and faeces and goodness knows what else. The dirty water splattered, staining my cloak. I cursed but I couldn't do anything about it. I didn't have the time.

I hopped back onto the pavement, paying no attention to the dark spires and grim, forbidding steps of the City Chambers, and scurried faster. I could see the bell tower ahead and its clock hands were edging their way towards four pm. Twister's shop was only round the corner.

The beady-eyed raven that flapped down to take cover didn't

make my steps falter. Let the Mages watch, if they wanted. I wasn't doing anything worthy of their attention – not today, anyway.

'Nay so braw weather today, hen,' Ma McAskill called from the other side of the street.

I grinned, despite my discomfort. Ma McAskill could always be counted on to state the obvious. *Och aye. Nay so braw at all.*

Shaking myself and rubbing at my stained cloak in a vain attempt to clean off the worst of the muck, I pushed open the door to the shop and ducked inside. Twister was in conversation with a customer. He glanced up, only the faintest tightening of his thin mouth registering my presence – until the reek of my cloak reached his nose and I saw the thick hairs in his nostrils quiver with disgust.

Alarmed, he shooed me away. 'My apologies, my lady,' he said, bowing to the woman in front of him.

'For what?' she enquired, as I scooted round the back of them, down the narrow corridor towards the dusty rear of the shop.

I untied the offending cloak and hastily dumped it with the rest of the dirty laundry that awaited my attention, then I smoothed down my skirt and did my best to make myself presentable.

Their voices drifted back in my direction. 'My assistant's hygiene is not always as good as it could be,' Twister replied.

I rolled my eyes. 'Assistant' was pushing the description of my status to its limits; indentured servant would be far more appropriate.

'It's not easy to find good workers these days,' the woman said.

'Indeed, my lady. Indeed.'

I walked back out and stood primly behind Twister. He liked it when I hovered meekly, awaiting orders, especially when the shop had potential customers with money to spend. He believed it made him appear more successful than he really was. I had other tasks to be getting on with, and this delay would only extend my already long day, but I knew my place and the futility of failing to meet Twister's expectations.

The woman looked to be around fifty, although her skin had the smooth, unmarred complexion of someone far younger. I cast a practised eye down her clothing. The material of her dress was heavy and expensive, and the string of pearls round her neck looked real. Then she moved to her left to finger the dark tartan on the counter and I spotted her shoes peeking out from under her petticoat. They looked scuffed and cheap.

More interested now, I raised my head and examined her features again. Somehow, I didn't think Twister would be making a sale today after all.

'This,' she said. 'This is close to what I require but it's a little too sombre. Do you have anything slightly lighter?'

'Of course,' Twister answered. 'In fact, we have a mauve version that I'm certain will delight.' He snapped his fingers but I was already moving to the shelf, pushing up on my tiptoes and carefully sliding out the material. I placed it on the counter and returned to my original position, folding my hands on top of each other.

The woman's mouth puckered as she lifted a corner of the fabric and held it up to the dim light. 'This is more suitable,' she agreed. 'But it's not quite what I'm looking for. The weave is somewhat unimpressive. Perhaps you'll permit me to browse the shelves myself?'

My heart sank. There was a reason why we usually fetched the tartans ourselves and displayed them on the counter rather than allowing customers to retrieve them. More than once I'd been forced to spend several hours removing grubby finger-prints from the more delicate samples – and I had yet to encounter a customer who could re-fold the material correctly.

Of course, Twister bowed. 'You are more than welcome to do so, my lady.'

The woman gave him a perfunctory smile. As soon as her back was turned, he frowned at me. I was tempted to pretend that I didn't understand but I'd only suffer for it later. I dug into my pocket and passed the folded message to him. The paper was light and inexpensive so that it could be easily destroyed, if needs be. If I had been stopped in the street by the wrong person, namely one of Twister's competitors, that's what would have been expected of me. Whether I'd have done it or not was another matter.

Twister's nimble fingers fiddled with the note. He was desperate to break the seal and read what it said, but the presence of the woman was holding him back. It had been a slow day; unless sales had picked up considerably after I'd departed on my orders this afternoon, he still needed to boost the till's takings.

'Oh, how charming,' the woman cooed to herself, stroking a particularly garish tartan. 'It's *almost* perfect – just not quite perfect enough.' She slid along and examined the next shelf. 'No,' she tutted. 'Not this. Or this.'

I was fascinated by her commentary, not by what she was saying but that she was speaking aloud. Did she find it easier to choose a fabric by discussing it with herself? Was she aware of what she was doing? My eyes followed her around the shop.

Twister nudged me sharply in the ribs, managing to push his elbow into the same spot where a bruise was forming thanks to his wife's irritated kick on Tuesday. I'd been on my hands and knees scrubbing the shop floor and got in her way. I hissed softly in pain, but I was already moving.

The woman clicked her tongue against her teeth. 'Well, this one certainly won't do,' she said disapprovingly, touching a pretty red-and-green tartan. Then she jumped and turned her head as she sensed my presence at her side.

Twister didn't notice; he was already thumbing the seal of the message, using his nail to crack the wax so he could get at the contents. The woman's eyes drifted briefly towards him before snapping back to me. 'Fetch that one for me, will you, girl?' She pointed upwards. 'The one with the green weft.'

I nodded and pulled the ladder towards me, placing it so that I could reach the tartan she desired. I scampered up and pulled it out.

'No. Not that one.' She frowned and shook her head. 'The one next to it. To the right.'

I reached for the material, heaved it down and placed it in the woman's hands. The weave on this sample was tighter so it weighed considerably more than the others, but if she noticed she didn't comment.

She stroked it a few times while she considered it. 'I need to see it in a different light,' she announced. 'It's far too gloomy here.'

While the interior of the shop was indeed dark, especially at this time of day, I couldn't let her take it outside to check it for imperfections. The last time that had happened, the would-be buyer had sprinted off and Twister took the cost of the sample out of my already meagre allowance.

Fortunately, the woman took it to the counter rather than towards the door. That didn't make sense; she was now further from the windows so there was even less light. Still, the customer was always right.

Twister, whose attention had been wholly absorbed by the message in his hands, blinked when she put down the material.

'Tell me,' she commanded. 'Is this too rough for a young girl to wear? I'm looking for a tartan suitable for my entire family and my niece has very delicate skin. I do not wish for her to get a rash.'

Somewhat reluctantly, Twister put the message down and

glanced at the tartan. 'Rough? My goodness, no. You'll never find a more forgiving or gentle fabric.'

The woman peered at him. 'My dear sir, this is tartan. Not silk.'

Twister forced a smile as he conceded the point, although I know that he despised silk. And linen. And cotton. Truthfully, he considered any material that was not true tartan to be horribly inferior. 'Fair enough,' he said mildly, the burr of his accent growing more pronounced as his emotions intensified. 'I must agree it is not silk, but it is a fine and gentle tartan.'

'Hmm.' The customer leaned over the counter to pick at the frayed edges on the far side. Her ample bosom was so close to Twister's face that his nose was almost buried in her cleavage. I suppressed a smile. It was as well that his wife would be taking her daily nap upstairs at this hour of the day.

'I'll have to think about it,' she said eventually, as I'd suspected she would. 'I will return in a day or two.'

No-one who said they would come back another time ever did. Twister knew it as well as I did, and he launched into full salesman mode in a bid to change her mind. 'As you wish, my lady, as you wish. This particular tartan is of limited supply, of course, and we do have another customer who is interested in it as well.' He smiled at her benevolently. 'Hopefully, it will still be here when you come back, or you may have to choose another instead.' He allowed himself a wistful glance down at the material. 'It is beautiful, is it not? Those colours complement any complexion.'

'They are passable,' the woman returned briskly. 'I thank you for your time. With another being interested in this fabric, it's fortunate that I am never tardy in my decision making.' She sniffed. 'I am sure I shall see you again in a few days.'

Twister made a face as soon as her back was turned, then nodded at the tartan. I hastily took it off the counter and walked back to the ladder to return it to its rightful place on the shelf.

As I moved, I hummed the first few bars of the ditty that had been worming its way through my ears all day. The woman, who had already pulled the door open and was stepping outside, stopped and turned her head.

I continued humming. I might have been tuneless, but she was leaving and the shop was due to close. The only person I could irritate now was Twister, and his attention had returned to his message and whatever it contained. The woman paused for another beat, then continued on her way. The door swung shut behind her.

Twister didn't look up when the door closed. Instead he threw back his head and bellowed, slipping into vernacular now that the need to maintain a polite veneer had passed. 'Belle! Fetch your skinny arse doon here!'

There was no immediate response and both of us glanced upwards. I knew that any second now Twister would order me to rouse his wife. I wanted to tell him to let sleeping dogs lie, but I didn't. Obviously.

Fortunately, on this occasion I was spared the trauma of waking Belle. There was a creak from above, followed by the familiar groaning of the floorboards as she heaved herself out of bed. A smattering of dust from the loose plaster in the ceiling pattered down. Twister scowled and opened his mouth, but I was already reaching for the broom in the corner to sweep it up.

By the time I'd moved on to repair the disarray to the shelves that the woman caused, Belle had made her way downstairs. Her hair was askew; strands of tawny brown were escaping from her bun, and various curls and wisps sticking up at all angles. She must have been a handsome woman once, but her years of yelling and scolding and maintaining a façade of proud matron had taken their toll. Now her appearance was akin to that of a grouchy fishwife rather than the lady of the manor.

'I was sleeping, you bampot,' she growled, her mouth puckering in disapproval at her husband.

He paid her complaints no mind. 'Forget sleep.' He waved the message at her. 'It's come.'

Belle immediately dropped her frown. 'And?'

Twister's face was shining. For a brief moment, I glimpsed the innocent cheerful young boy he had once been. 'We're in.'

Belle's eyes widened, then a slow smile spread across her face. She lifted her heavy skirt and her feet began to tap out a dance. 'We're in?'

Twister nodded. 'We're in.'

Belle pirouetted, losing her balance halfway round before falling into Twister's arms with a bark of delighted laughter. He hugged her. 'This could be the making of us,' he whispered, pressing his mouth to her temple.

'We're no' there yet,' she warned. 'It's only an audience, not a commission.'

He wagged his finger at her. 'But our foot is in the door. That's the hard part over with.' He held up the message. 'Have a keek.'

Belle snatched the note from his hand and scanned it, while Twister rubbed his thumb and forefinger together. 'It's going to be spondoolies from now on!'

I wouldn't hold my breath; this wasn't the first money-making scheme the couple had embarked upon in recent times. And I doubted that any spondoolies would come my way, no matter how much over-priced tartan they sold.

I finished folding the last of the tartan and hopped down the ladder. I would have liked to wipe down the counter and dust the shelves behind it, but I couldn't while they were standing there. I watched them, hoping they'd repair to the lounge so I could finish my work before I started the laundry and prepared the evening meal, but Belle's face was falling. It didn't look as if she'd be going anywhere soon.

She dropped the piece of paper onto the counter and glared

at Twister as he gave her a hopeful smile. Without missing a beat, she reached across and backhanded him.

'Ow!' He clutched his cheek. 'What was that for?'

'We don't have our foot in the door, you bampot! We don't have anything in the door. The Mages are coming to us, not the other way around. And that's only if the bursar can persuade them to take a detour. They're no' in the market for new clothes!' She spat at the now-crumpled message. 'This is nothing!'

'Hardly anyone gets into the City Chambers, love, you know that. The bursar will definitely bring them here, though,' Twister protested. 'I bribed him enough. More than enough! And look,' he snatched up the message again, 'he's talking about the Ascendant. The Ascendant is coming to *our* shop!'

Belle's lip curled and she swiped at him again. This time Twister managed to duck, but she still caught the side of his head. 'Our wonderful shop.' She swivelled round, her arm extended. 'Our glorious department store.'

'It's hardly a market stall,' Twister objected.

Belle sneered. 'If you think *this* will impress the Mages enough to place an order and give us a Mage Warrant, you're an even bigger eejit than I thought.' She turned on her heel, then glared in my direction as if noticing me for the first time. 'What are you gawking at, lass? Don't you have work to do?'

Twister, fully deflated now, watched her as she stormed out with her skirts billowing behind her. His bottom lip jutted out and I wondered if he would sob. Instead he shook himself and, in the absence of any other convenient target, sent a kick in my direction. 'Well?' he snarled. 'You heard the lady! Get back to work!'

Despite Belle's conviction that Twister's plotting would come to nothing, he ordered me to prepare the shop front for the Mages' supposedly imminent arrival. I scrubbed the floor until the flagstones were cleaner than they'd ever been and polished the wooden counter and shelves until they gleamed.

The smell of beeswax, which was normally pleasant enough, mingled with the powerful reek of bleach to create a potent mixture that made my nostrils tingle. As a result, Twister sent me back out in the rain to find some fragrant foliage to improve matters. The best I could come up with was a bunch of drooping lavender that I stole from one of the window boxes hanging outside the Grand Central Hotel.

The bellhop spotted me as I yanked it free and he set off in hot pursuit, his fist raised. He was no match for me and I fled easily from his angry shouts and slow feet. All the same, I'd have to avoid passing in front of the hotel for some time to come. From what I'd heard on the street, the upmarket hoteliers didn't take kindly to thieves, even when they pilfered something paltry. They'd called in the Mages when they caught a house-maid helping herself to one of the bed turn-down chocolates. Apparently, her resulting screams shook the hotel's very foundations.

Once the lavender was displayed in a crystal vase on one of the higher shelves, I made a start on the interior of the windows, ridding them of smears and streaks. I'd almost finished when Belle reappeared, demanding to know when her supper would be served, so I nipped to the kitchen and did my best to whip up a quick stew of mutton, carrots and onion. Without much time to simmer, it would be as tough as old boots to chew on. Even so, there wouldn't be enough leftovers for my plate.

I was guaranteed porridge for breakfast and nothing beyond, except what scraps I could find once Twister and Belle's needs were taken care of – and those were few and far between. I chomped on a few carrot ends as I took care of the laundry, however, so things could have been worse. I thought of Meg and missing babies and dangerous daemons in dark wynds. Things could always be worse.

When I finally escaped to my little room, located high in the draughty rafters of the building, I was bone tired. I couldn't afford to sleep, though. Although it had been necessary, my expedition to the orphanage had lost me valuable hours that I needed to make up.

I headed straight to my battered lockbox and gazed at its contents. Nothing had changed since the last time I'd opened it, but my heart still sank. I estimated that I only had about four evenings' worth of light remaining.

With a heavy sigh, I took out the squat candle and placed it in its holder on the tiny desk by the porthole window, then struck a match and lit it. An hour, I decided; I'd allow myself an hour. That should be enough time to wrap my head around at least some of the basic points about carboxylic acid.

I flipped open the textbook, which was hopelessly out of date but which I'd spent the better part of six months saving up for, and found the section I'd studied last. The scholarship exam was less than a month away. I knew I'd never be accepted as a trainee doctor, because at some point doctors were expected to speak to their patients and that would be something of a stumbling block for me, but I was sure I could gain entrance to Apothecary Studies.

Only a tiny number of candidates were invited to take the scholarship exam each year. I had waited until now to apply because it was a one-shot deal. I had to be sure that I would pass if I sat the exam.

I didn't care that I would be older than the other university entrants. I didn't have parents willing to fund my education, so I'd had to take the snail's route. I had dedication and most of the knowledge, I just didn't have the money. Pass the scholarship exam, however, and I had the chance to get out of this life and make something of myself.

I was not confident enough or imaginative enough to dream of my own little apothecary shop far away from Twister and Belle's melodramas. Not yet. But I was getting tantalisingly close.

CHAPTER FOUR

MY LIPS FELT DRY AND STICKY. A TRAIL OF DROOL HAD LEAKED from my mouth, and there was a painful crick in my neck. That was what happened when you fell asleep on a chair over a book. The only saving grace was that I'd been sensible enough to blow the candle out before I succumbed unwillingly to sleep. I didn't remember doing it, but enough of the wax and wick remained to prove I had – either that, or some helpful house brownies had done it for me.

I smiled faintly at the idea and massaged away the worst of the ache. There was a pink glow coming from the window, indicating that dawn was approaching. I needed to get the fire started and the water boiling. I had a feeling that Twister's excitement about a few Mages possibly visiting the shop would encourage him to rise early.

By the time I'd cleaned out the ashes from the fireplace and filled the water pot, I could hear Twister's heavy footsteps plodding down the creaking staircase. He walked into the kitchen rubbing his palms together and grinning broadly. Suddenly, I was hopeful. Maybe today would be a good day.

'This is it, lass,' he beamed. 'This the day when all our

fortunes will be made. Just you wait and see.' He grabbed me by the waist and spun me round. 'Belle might still be a wee bit crabbit but pay her no attention.' He spun me again. 'Today, lass, we win.'

As much as I disliked him, his enthusiasm was infectious and I smiled back. And who knew? If he did win a contract with the Mages, maybe it would mean a bonus for me. Stranger things had happened. He gave me one last turn and backed off, but his grin remained so wide that it split his face in two, just like a melon.

'Make me a jam piece,' he instructed. 'Then I'll...' His voice faltered and his smile vanished. 'What?' He looked me up and down. 'What are you wearing?'

The same damned things that I wore every day: heavy cotton breeches that were shabby but clean, and a white unembroidered blouse. It was exactly what Belle had pressed upon me when I'd started work nine years ago after I left St Mags. The sizes had changed as I'd grown taller and filled out, but the style of the clothing hadn't altered.

I realised there was a smudge of ash from the fireplace on my right cuff. I didn't bother rubbing at it – I'd only make it worse. It would come off easily with a damp cloth.

Twister clicked his tongue. 'You cannae wear that in front of the Mages.'

I pursed my lips and shrugged. That was okay with me; I certainly didn't mind staying out of the way if they appeared. Given my recent close encounter, it would be a good thing to avoid them entirely. I quashed down the surge of rising hope that I might be able to sneak away to my room and study some more; the last thing I wanted to do was pre-empt fate.

He stepped back and examined me with a critical eye. 'You ken,' he said, 'you're a bonnie lass underneath it all. We might be able to work with that.' The furrows in his brow deepened. 'I might have just the thing. Dinna move.'

I stayed where I was until he left the kitchen, then jumped to it and started cutting the bread for his jam sandwich before preparing the oats for my porridge. He'd only complain later if I didn't do it now. By the time Twister returned, most of my early-morning chores were completed.

'Here,' he said, thrusting a dress towards me. It wasn't one that I'd seen before, though I recognised the tartan immediately. It had been co-opted by the Argylls when their youngest son got married the previous year and we had a lot of it left over. I was certain there was still a heap in the back storeroom. However, this version felt rougher.

I peered at it. It was definitely an older weave and there was the faintest scent of mothballs clinging to the fabric, but it was still pretty. Unfortunately, I couldn't say the same about the cut of the dress.

Twister noted my expression and glared. 'You will wear this,' he told me, 'or you'll see the back of my hand – and then you'll still put it on anyway. I won't have your clatty appearance ruining this for me. You should be pleased! I thought you women liked to dress up!'

The man was as mercurial as the moon, and as mad. I took the dress reluctantly and shuffled upstairs to change.

'Don't take long!' he yelled after me. 'There's still work to be done!'

Yeah, yeah.

IT TOOK LONGER than I'd anticipated to put on the dress. I was unused to such a design, so I struggled to pull it over my body and not end up tangled in the fabric. Then there were stays around the waist that required a series of contortions to tighten and tie. When I was satisfied that I had everything on the right way round and in the right place, I found I was shivering. The dress made me feel cold and exposed. I glanced down. It was incredibly low cut, and I wasn't used to seeing my cleavage like this.

I hoisted the upper half of the dress as far as it would go. The dress offered the dubious freedom of displaying skin, but it was incredibly constricting to wear. I sincerely hoped that once the Mages' visit was over – assuming it happened – I could return to my usual garb.

I walked warily down the stairs, afraid that I would trip on the hem and plunge headfirst onto the hard tiles below. By some miracle, I made it to the ground floor again.

Twister was already busying himself in the shop. When I appeared, the look on his face was one of surprise. 'Well, well, well,' he murmured. 'Who knew?'

Before he elaborated, Belle strode in. She looked round the shelves and gave a wet sniff. 'You ken they won't come.'

'They will come. Just wait and see.'

She sniffed a second time. 'The arrangement is all wrong. The blues are the most expensive, so they should be at eye level. The Mages have more coin than they know what to do with. If they *do* show up...'

'They will.'

She gave her husband a hard stare. 'If they *do* show up and actually make a purchase, we want to make sure they buy our best.'

Twister nodded fervently. 'Yes, Belle.' He glanced at me. 'Move them around. Blues at eye level.'

As I bobbed my head and turned, Belle grabbed my bare arm. Her sharp nails dug into my skin. 'That is mine,' she hissed. 'That is my dress. Where did you get it from? You ... you...'

'I gave it to her, Belle,' Twister soothed. 'We need everyone to look their best for the Mages – even her. There's no harm in showing off all our goods.'

My eyebrows flew up my forehead. Surely he didn't count

me as one of those goods? I realised he was referring to the tartan itself. I didn't relax – the fury on Belle's face didn't allow for that – but I didn't feel quite so alarmed. Twister was an arsehole, but he wasn't a complete tyrant.

'It's mine,' she spat.

'Darling,' Twister said, without paying enough attention to his words, 'it's a young woman's dress. You don't want to look as if you're mutton dressed like—'

Belle howled with rage, grabbed the folded tartan samples from the nearest shelf and threw them at him, one after the other. He ducked a few but at least three smacked directly into his face. 'You mad bampot!'

'She can't have it!' Belle shrieked. 'It's mine!'

I was already heading for the door, quite prepared to change back into my normal, far more comfortable, attire. Unfortunately, Twister was standing his ground for once. 'The lass is pleasing on the eye, Belle. She'll charm the Ascendant and soften him up enough that he might be more inclined to part with his silver! We need to use every tool at our disposal!'

Belle dropped the tartan she was holding and put her hands on her hips. 'How will she charm anyone? She doesnae even speak!'

Twister managed a smile. 'Some men prefer their women that way,' he muttered under his breath. 'Most men, in fact.'

Belle's eyes narrowed. 'What was that?'

'Nothing, dear.'

She kicked at one of the fallen wads of fabric. 'Fine,' she said eventually. 'Fine. If that's the way you want it, then that's the way it will be. But the dress is coming out of her allowance.'

My stomach dropped. No. She couldn't do that.

'Grand.' Twister nodded. 'She can pay it back in instalments.' He reached for his wife and put an arm round her waist. 'Let's go and eat breakfast.' He waved at me. 'Mairi, clean yon mess up. Quickly now.'

I scowled at their departing backs. I'd have to hope that they'd both forgotten about the dress by the time the end of the month rolled around. I put up with a lot in return for a roof over my head and safety from the Afflicted who roamed the streets at night, but I was reaching the end of my tether. The scholarship exam couldn't come quickly enough.

THE REST of the morning was an exercise in pure misery. As the hours dragged by, Twister's good mood dissipated. The bell above the shop door only jangled three times: once for a delivery and twice for browsers who departed without buying so much as a scrap of tartan. On each occasion, hope flared in Twister's face – and on each occasion, when it was apparent that the customers were not Mages, that hope died.

By early afternoon, he was growing desperate. Every hour or so, Belle popped her head round the door and heaved a nod of grim satisfaction; she seemed pleased that her pessimism had been proved right, rather than Twister's dreams coming to fruition and their little shop being granted a Mage Warrant that would set it above their competitors.

Despite the squalling wind and driving rain, he ordered me to prop open the front door so that he could see out and ensure that any passing trade was aware we were open for business. When it blew closed for the third time and I was wedging a stopper firmly underneath it to prevent it from slamming shut again, I noticed a figure on the opposite side of the street keeping shelter under Ma McAskill's doorway and watching me intently. It was the female customer from the day before.

I tilted my head and stared at her. She stared back. I almost raised my hand in greeting, although I couldn't say why I had the urge to do so. Then there was a loud caw. Raven, I thought. The woman hastily turned away as three massive black birds flapped overhead. One settled its clawed feet onto the sign over my head, whilst the other two assumed positions nearby. Well, well, well.

I turned around, thinking I should catch Twister's attention and let him know. He was sitting behind the counter on a stool, his head back, his eyes closed and his mouth wide open. I coughed politely, but my only answer was a loud, rumbling snore.

The woman bustled in behind me, shaking off droplets of rain. 'Goodness me,' she exclaimed. 'What terrible weather!'

Twister woke with a start and blinked rapidly. When he saw her, his shoulders sank then he remembered himself and stood up. 'Welcome back,' he boomed, as if he'd been expecting her all along. 'I take it you have decided, then?'

'Actually,' the woman said, 'I would appreciate a second look before I make up my mind.' She glanced round, her brow creasing slightly. 'Have you rearranged your stock?'

Twister opened his mouth to answer while I attempted to signal frantically in his direction. He frowned at me. 'Mairi, what are...?' He didn't get the chance to finish his sentence. A trumpet sounded and the three ravens cawed in unison. Twister jumped, delight crossing his normally glowering features.

'My lady,' he said quickly. 'Unfortunately, we are expecting some other customers. Can I suggest you visit us later? Perhaps tomorrow?'

The woman drew herself up sternly. 'I most certainly will not. I came out in this poor weather particularly to visit your shop. I will not get in the way of your other customers, I assure you.'

Twister would have manhandled her out of the door if he could have, but there was no time. As soon as he stepped out from behind the counter, a long shadow fell across the doorway.

I held my breath as five hooded men swept inside. One was wearing a black cloak, and the others were dressed in scarlet.

None was the Mage whom I'd seen in the wynd the other night. Thank heavens for small mercies.

Even so, I backed into the corner to keep out of their way. Mages were actually here, in this shop, next to *me*. With a brief flare of panic, I suddenly wondered if any of them could read minds. What if they looked into my head and saw that I'd been scuttling around the streets in the middle of the night less than a week earlier and had narrowly avoided being caught by one of their brethren?

As they pulled back their hoods and revealed their faces, I realised I had nothing to worry about. Their expressions ranged from boredom to nothing more than mild curiosity, and none of them were looking at me. I was a nobody. I'd never been happier about that fact.

Twister flinched but didn't let his anxiety get the better of him. He bowed obsequiously with far greater flexibility than I'd ever seen before. 'Gentlemen! Thank you so much for gracing us with your presence! I welcome you to our humble shop and—'

The door behind the counter burst open and Belle threw herself through it, pushing past me and then her husband. She came close to knocking Twister over in her enthusiasm. She thrust herself in front of him before dipping into a low curtsey. 'My dear sirs! Welcome to our wonderful store. We have all the tartan you could ever wish for, and I can assure you that the quality of all our stock is beyond compare.'

The nearest Mage, who looked to be the oldest and who was wearing black rather than scarlet, untied his cloak and held it out to her. 'See that this is dried and hung up. And some hot refreshments wouldn't go amiss.'

Belle nodded vigorously but didn't move. After several painful seconds, the Mage frowned and gazed down at her, his arm still outstretched with his dripping cloak still waiting for attention. 'Go on, woman! Do as you're told!'

Belle cleared her throat. It was the first time I'd ever heard her sound nervous. 'Uh ... begging your pardon, sirs, but I can't get up.'

She was frozen in her low curtsey. I pressed my lips together and sent an alarmed glance at Twister, then I spotted the face of the other woman, who had also moved into a corner. She looked like she were trying hard not to laugh. It was almost too much, and I had to clamp a hand over my mouth to prevent a nervous giggle escaping.

Twister rushed forward and hauled Belle back up to a standing position. He waved urgently towards me and I smoothed my face into a blank before nipping up and taking the Mage's cloak. It was heavier than I'd expected and obviously of remarkable quality. I draped it over my arm then moved round the other four, taking each of their cloaks in turn.

'Dry the cloaks, Mairi,' Twister said. 'And bring us some tea.'

I couldn't have been more grateful to be dismissed. I took the heavy cloaks and raced out of the room as fast as I could.

CHAPTER FIVE

CONSTRICTED BY THE DAFT DRESS, IT TOOK ME LONGER THAN IT should have done to get hold of Belle's best china and brew the tea. As I carried the heavy tray back up the stairs from the kitchen, I had the horrible conviction that I was going to tangle my feet in my hem and fall flat on my face. There was one particularly hairy moment when my foot almost missed the final step, but I regained my balance and made it without incident although I knew my cheeks were burning with the effort of staying upright.

The shop was even busier now. Instead of five Mages, there looked to be at least ten of the buggers. The latest arrivals had left their wet cloaks in a pile by the door. There was no more room to hang them downstairs by the fire, so I pretended not to notice them and looked dubiously at the tea tray instead. There weren't nearly enough cups.

I pulled a face, staggered forward and set the tray on the counter. Fortunately, Belle caught sight of me and, desperate to place herself front and centre, quickly took over. That allowed me to slip back into the shadows so I could quietly observe the proceedings.

'We have tea!' Belle declared in a loud but slightly shaky voice. 'Would anyone care for a hot drink?'

The old Mage, who seemed to be in charge, nodded. 'Three sugars,' he said with a flick of his wrist.

Belle paled slightly. Sugar was a precious commodity these days. I didn't know anybody who put sugar in their tea, let alone three lumps. If all the Mages wanted such sweetness, there would be no sugar left until spring. Luckily for her, none of the others seemed particularly interested in a drink. Not from her, anyway. I spotted two of the Mages swigging from small hip flasks when they thought nobody was watching.

'Will the Ascendant be joining us?' Belle asked, her hand trembling slightly as she poured the tea.

The response was curt. 'Not tonight. He's in Edinburgh this week meeting the other city Ascendants.'

I glanced at Belle's expression. It was difficult to tell if she was relieved or disappointed. I knew how I felt; entertaining this many Mages was bad enough and the last thing I wanted was to have the Glasgow Ascendant here too.

Twister was holding court in the centre of the room, a vivid array of tartan spread out in front of him. He waxed lyrical about each sample and, surprisingly, several of the Mages were being attentive.

It wasn't only the Mages who were listening; the woman was still there. She'd drawn herself into an alcove and was pretending to flick through a heavy book of samples. From the way her mouth twitched at different moments, however, her focus was on the Mages' conversation rather than the tartan itself. That was interesting.

'Hello.'

I jumped half out of my skin and jerked round to meet the eyes of yet another Mage. This one was younger than the others, with soft brown eyes and an easy smile. I blinked several times before I remembered my position and managed to smile politely.

'With such a fabulous dress as that one,' he murmured, nodding at what I was wearing, 'you must work here.' He looked at Belle and Twister. 'Are they your parents?'

As if. I shook my head and kept my expression bland.

'Uh-huh.' He moved a bit closer. 'But you do work here?'

I nodded. What was he doing? Why was he talking to me?

His smile grew and he held out a hand. 'I'm Noah. And I'm very pleased to meet you.'

I stared at him, then took his hand and shook it limply. I felt a faint tingle when my skin touched his and drew back in surprise.

Noah didn't seem to notice and dipped his head towards mine. 'This is where you tell me your name,' he said.

I swallowed.

His smile didn't falter. 'You don't have to be afraid of me. I might be a Mage, but that doesn't mean I'm scary. Magic isn't scary.' He held up his right hand and crooked his pinkie. 'Quite the contrary, in fact. It can be very gentle indeed.' He paused before deepening his voice. '*Mazni.*'

A strange breeze sprang up from nowhere, ruffling my hair and brushing against my skin with a warm caress. I started, but Noah only gazed into my eyes, the expression on his face matching the soft heat of the breeze. 'See?' he whispered. 'There's nothing to be afraid of.'

I felt myself leaning in towards him almost involuntarily... Then another voice broke in – and this one was chillingly familiar. 'She won't talk to you.'

'Fuck off, Nicholas.'

The daemon stepped to the side so I could see him. He didn't glance in my direction; instead he inspected his fingernails and sighed. 'She doesn't talk. She can't.'

A crease appeared in Noah's perfectly smooth forehead. 'Don't be ridiculous.'

'I see things that you cannot. And I know that you're wasting your time with this one.'

Noah glared at him with surprising hatred before turning his attention back to me. 'Go on,' he murmured. 'What's your name?'

I gave a tiny squeak, which was pretty much the best I could do. Noah's frown deepened. Out of the corner of my eye, I saw Nicholas stiffen.

'You! Girl! Come over here! I need some help with this!' a voice said imperiously. I looked round and saw that the woman had abandoned the shadows and was now perched halfway up a ladder, trying to retrieve some folded tartan from one of the higher shelves.

She wobbled precariously; it looked as if she were going to topple backwards onto the group of Mages who were still crowded round Twister. Shite. If she fell onto them, I'd probably get the blame. I squeezed out from between Nicholas and Noah and darted towards her. Within seconds I was behind her on the ladder, holding her steady before helping her down. By the time we reached the floor, every damned eye in the shop was watching us.

'Who is *she*?' asked the lead Mage, his voice dripping with disdain.

Belle wrung her hands together. 'Er, sir, that's Mairi. She works for us.'

But he wasn't looking at me. 'Not her. The other one.'

The woman might not be very skilled at climbing ladders but she wasn't afraid to speak up. She lifted her chin and met the Mage's eyes. 'I am a paying customer like you, sir,' she said. 'I'm here to purchase some tartan for—'

The Mage turned away. 'Get rid of her.'

Belle stared at him, but he obviously wasn't going to repeat his words. He simply folded his arms and waited.

'Uh, Mairi?' Twister squeaked.

I took the woman's elbow and tried to steer her towards the door.

'Why don't you come back tomorrow, my lady?' Twister suggested. 'We'll be able to help you then.'

For a horrifying moment, I wondered if she was going to refuse to leave. I dreaded to think what would happen if she did. Fortunately, she allowed me to lead her round the damp discarded cloaks, out of the shop and onto the street. The three ravens were perched on the guttering across from us, their glistening dark eyes watching our every move.

As I let go of the woman's elbow and prepared to return inside, her hand shot out and encircled my wrist. 'Walk me to the end of the street, hen,' she said, using her free hand to open her umbrella to shield us from the weather. 'I'm not sure how to get home from here and I need directions.'

It wasn't her first time here – surely she knew where she was? But I wasn't in any particular rush to return to the scene inside the shop, so I ignored the rain in favour of shuffling down the street with her.

She didn't say a word until we reached the first crossroads. Then her grip on my wrist tightened and she turned her head towards me. 'You fool,' she hissed. 'Much more of that and they'd have realised what you are. I was already risking everything by being there. You could have ruined it all!'

Uh ... what?

'How you've survived this long with wits like that is a bleeding mystery!' She clicked her tongue in anger, then peered at my face. All at once, her expression changed. 'You don't know, do you?' she breathed. 'You don't know what you are.'

I wrenched my wrist away from her. She was freaking me out. Everything about this was freaking me out.

'You have to come and find me,' she said, her words vibrating with urgency. 'Sauchiehall Lane. Ask for Fee, and someone will show you where I am. You deserve to know the truth, hen.' She gave me a meaningful look. 'You'll end up dead if you don't.'

She jerked her head back down the street. One of the ravens had taken flight and was heading towards us. 'So,' the woman said loudly, 'turn right and I'll end up at Buchanan Street? Thank you, hen. You get yourself back into the dry.' She twisted away and plodded off, avoiding the muddy puddles in her path.

I stared after her as I rubbed my wrist where she'd grabbed it. She was as mad as Belle and Twister. She had to be. I shrugged and then returned to the tartan shop as she had told me. There was no chance I'd seek her out again. No chance at all.

I'D BARELY SET foot inside the shop when Twister flapped his arms at me. 'The Mages are leaving!' he barked. 'You need to fetch their cloaks! It'll be dark soon and they need to get back to the City Chambers. We can't have them running around the streets while the Afflicted are out there!'

'Indeed,' I heard Nicholas say. 'That would be madness.'

I stared at him. He smiled benignly at me before turning to engage a Mage in conversation. I couldn't stop myself from shivering, but I nodded obediently at Twister and dashed off to retrieve the cloaks. To my dismay, they weren't dry. There was nothing I could do about it, so I picked them up, raced back and handed them out with downcast eyes.

'Mine is still damp,' one of the Mages complained.

'At least yours wasn't left in a pile on the floor,' said another.

It was on the floor because that was where he'd dropped it. I lowered my head further so he wouldn't notice my expression.

'Stop fashing yersel,' Noah said, lapsing from a clipped

Mage's accent to a rougher Scot's. 'I'll dry those cloaks off in a jiffy.' He raised his head. '*Belzair!*'

There was a rustle, and an odd vibration ran through the air. The cloak in the Mage's hands slowly changed colour as the dampness seeped away into the ether. I only just prevented my jaw from dropping open.

'Showing off, Noah?' Nicholas asked, clearly still bored.

The young Mage looked at me and winked. 'Maybe I am. Maybe I have good reason.' He smiled.

Twister hustled forward. 'Thank you so much for your visit, kind sirs. Please feel free to drop in again any time. We can expedite any order, and I can do you a very good price. Mages' special.' He gave a self-deprecating titter and bowed so low in front of the lead Mage that his forehead almost scraped the floor.

'We'll be in touch,' the Mage said curtly as he fastened his cloak and swirled away. The others followed suit. Noah waved at me as he left. Nicholas glowered.

Once the door had closed behind them, Twister clapped his hands gleefully. 'Whit's fur ye'll no go by ye,' he crowed. What will be, will be. He beamed at Belle. 'We did it, love. We really did it.'

'They've no' ordered anything yet,' Belle said, but she was smiling and her cheeks were pink with excitement.

'They will,' Twister declared with unwavering confidence. He pointed at me. 'Come on, you, tidy this place up! It looks like a hurricane's been through here.' He held his arm out to his wife. 'You and me are going upstairs to celebrate.'

Belle giggled, then together they waltzed out of the room.

CHAPTER SIX

'WE SHOULD HAVE PAID FOR A CARRIAGE.'

'We don't have enough money, you bampot,' Belle snarled.
Twister's confidence was unshaken. 'We will. Once the
Mages take these tartans off our hands, we'll have enough spondoolies to travel in style wherever we go. We should get our
own carriage. Brand it on the side, like the proper shops on
Buchanan Street. In fact,' he added thoughtfully, as if it were a
serious consideration, 'we should get two carriages. One to
transport us and one to transport the tartans.'

'Away an' bile yer heid!' Belle scoffed.

'You reckon we ought to get three carriages, darling?'

Belle reached across and smacked him on the arm. 'What
about the rent? And the bills? And the fact that we owe Grubb
all that money for the dyes last month?'

Twister's response was soothing. 'We'll pay all that off in a
jiffy. The lass is carrying enough tartan back there to sort all
that out, and then some.'

Belle's head twisted round and her piercing eyes fixed on
me. I didn't cower under her sharp gaze; frankly, I could barely

see her face over the towering pile of material in my arms. I shifted my grip. It wasn't far to the City Chambers, but the tartans were heavy. I could only imagine what disaster would befall me if I dropped the precious bundle.

The Mages had put in an order for a good amount of material, all of it high quality and incredibly expensive – nothing but the best for our magic masters. It had taken all of Belle and Twister's resources and cunning to get it together in such a short space of time, and I'd been up till the wee hours folding and packaging so that it could be transported on foot.

I'd had neither the time nor the energy to crack open a book for days, and the scholarship exam was fast approaching. Invitations to participate would be sent out any day now. Tomorrow was Sunday, however; the shop would be closed and I'd have several free hours to catch up. I could do it. I knew I could.

Belle looked away and snorted. 'Let's hope for all our sakes that they give us a good price and pay up quickly.'

'These are the Mages, not a bunch of arsehole chancers. By nightfall we'll be rolling in it. We'll no have to worry about bills ever again.'

I'd believe it when I saw it. I adjusted my grip and sucked in a breath. There wasn't far to go. I could do this. Five more minutes. Tops.

A sudden high-pitched screech sounded from the other side of the street. 'Belle! Whit like? Whit ye doing?'

My heart sank. A chance meeting with one of Belle's gossipy cronies was all I needed. She wouldn't be able to resist the temptation to stop and show off.

'Lacey!' Belle called. 'As I live and breathe!' She turned to Twister and muttered under her breath, 'Watch that eejit's face when I tell her where we're going.'

Lacey held up her skirts and picked her way over to us. I gritted my teeth. My arms were aching and beads of clammy sweat were popping out across my forehead. I was starting to envisage passing damp, sweat-soaked tartan over to a stern-faced Mage who would get his pet daemon to eat me for breakfast as punishment. Chomp chomp, slurp, and then goodbye Mairi.

'So where are you two headed on such a braw day?' Lacey inquired, her desperate curiosity entirely undisguised.

'City Chambers,' Belle announced.

'City…' Lacey's mouth dropped open. She glanced over at me and the pile in my arms and looked back at Belle. 'The Mages put in an order?'

'That they did,' Twister boomed. 'That they did.'

'Blimey. So ye'll be getting a Warrant, then?'

'Aye. I reckon so.' Pride vibrated through every word. 'We'll be moving to better premises on Buchanan Street before you know it.'

Lacey shook her head. 'Well, I never. It couldn't happen to a more deserving couple.'

'You're nay wrong,' Belle said. 'It's no' been easy all these years. It's about time we got some proper reward. You know me, Lacey, I'm no greedy. I only want what I deserve.'

'Indeed, Belle,' Lacey replied. 'Indeed.' She leaned in and lowered her voice. 'You take care in there, mind? I hear there's an execution scheduled for this afternoon. You dinna want to piss off the Mages and join whichever poor fucker is swinging later on.'

Belle forced out a laugh. 'You're too funny, Lacey. As if the Mages would execute us!'

'Just a wee joke, that's all. Mind how you go.' Lacey picked up her skirts once again and tripped away at high speed, no doubt keen to pass on Belle and Twister's good fortune to anyone who would listen.

As soon as she was out of earshot, Belle cursed and spat on the ground. 'Executed? Who does she think she is? Just because

we're trying to make something of ourselves, that bloody
woman—'

'Hush, love,' Twister said. 'Forget about her.' He grinned.
'Let's get to the City Chambers and prove to the likes of Lacey
McKinnon that nothing will stop us.'

I nodded fervently. Yes. Let's get there now before my
damned arms fall off.

Belle sniffed. 'Very well. She'll be laughing on the other side
of her face soon.'

'That she will, love,' Twister soothed. 'That she will.'

THE CITY CHAMBERS WAS AN IMPRESSIVE, albeit intimidating,
building. I'd passed it almost every day of my life and often
wondered what lay beyond the forbidding grey stone and
ornate exterior. I had never thought I'd get so much as a glimpse
inside, though. From the way Belle and Twister were gazing at
the domed towers, arched windows, heavy balustrades and
elaborate columns, they felt much the same.

I counted at least twenty ravens perched along the roof,
blinking down at us. I hoped they knew we were here by invita-
tion – I didn't fancy getting my eyes pecked out.

Even Twister suddenly seemed nervous. 'Are we supposed to
go through the front door, do you think?' he asked. 'Or is there
a rear entrance we have to use?'

'We're no' servants,' Belle snapped. 'We might be providing a
service, but it's a valued service. I'm no' skulking in the back
door like I've done something wrong. They told us to come
here.' She paused, before adding with less certainty, 'Go and see
if there's a side door.'

I swallowed. The heavy folded tartan in my arms was beginning to slip and I'd have to put it down sooner or later. Probably
sooner. It would likely take Twister several minutes to circle the

building in search of a side door. I knew in my heart of hearts I couldn't hang on for that long.

I coughed, attempting to alert them to the situation. Twister was already moving away, but Belle glared at me. 'Don't you go getting your germs all over the tartan, lass!'

I gave her a pointed look and nodded down at the packages, attempting to let her know that they were going to fall if I didn't put them down soon. For once she caught my drift and paled slightly. 'Get back here, Twister! We're going in the front.'

'Are you sure, love?'

She clicked her fingers at him. 'Of course I'm sure! Come on.'

We started up the steps. Fortunately, the rain had held off for a few days so there was little chance of slipping on a damp patch; that was helpful when I couldn't see my own feet. I trudged upwards, sending occasional wary glances towards the line of ravens. None of them twitched and I heard no angry caws. Perhaps the damned birds were merely lulling us into a false sense of security. I wouldn't have put it past them.

We reached the top step without incident – and without anyone rushing towards us or sending out a bolt of magic to stop us. I peered round the tower of tartan at the front door. Most of it was made of a dark, burnished wood – mahogany, perhaps – with swirls of black iron fretwork set into gleaming glass on either side. It was firmly closed, but Twister pulled back his shoulders, marched towards it and raised his fist to knock.

Before he made contact, it swung open without warning. Startled by the sudden movement, all three of us jumped. It was probably the first time I'd been in sympathy with my two employers; we were all feeling the same.

I did my best to suppress the cold shudder that ran down my spine and followed Belle and Twister inside, where a stern-looking woman was waiting. She had the sort of thin face that could have passed for thirty or fifty, or anything in-between.

Her hands were linked together and her expression was disapproving – she immediately put me in mind of several of the matrons from St Magdalene's. Given her job, I couldn't blame her for not cracking a smile. I doubted I'd be grinning from ear to ear if I had to work for the Mages.

'You are the tartan people, yes?' she enquired in a tight voice that only bore a faint accent.

Twister recovered first and bounded forward with his hand outstretched. 'Aye! I mean, yes! It's a pleasure to meet you. We weren't sure if there was another entrance we were supposed to use, but—'

Without taking his hand, the woman held up her palms to stop his babbling. 'The material is all there?' she asked, glancing at the packages in my arms.

Twister bobbed his head vigorously, as if his nervous enthusiasm couldn't be contained. 'Aye! It's our very best, and everything the Mages asked for. The tartans there are soft and supple and the most expensive on the market. We have not shirked on quality at all. You will find nothing finer. The very spirit of the Highlands, if you will. In fact—'

The woman sighed deeply and Twister fell silent abruptly. She strode forward and took the heavy packages from me. It was a blessed relief to be free of them, but I still felt an underlying unease that I couldn't quite explain.

She turned to a table and carefully piled the packages on top of it, then she glanced at Twister and raised an eyebrow. 'You may go now,' she said.

Twister swallowed and his Adam's apple bobbed in his throat. 'Thank you, ma'am,' he said. He nudged Belle and she hastily reached into her bag and pulled out an envelope. 'The invoice is here. It's all in order, and we added a special discount for the Mages. It cost us a lot to get hold of everything they wanted at such short notice, and we have to pay our suppliers, so we would appreciate it if you could, uh, make the payment now.' He wrung his hands together. 'If you wouldn't mind.'

The woman stared at the envelope in Belle's outstretched hand but made no move to take it. Something flickered in her grey eyes. Oh no: I could have been mistaken, but it looked like sympathy. 'It's best,' she said, 'if you post the invoice directly to the bursar. He will deal with it in due course.'

'In due course?' Twister asked. His expression took on an anxious slant. 'Do you know how long due course takes?'

'I do not.'

'The thing is,' he persisted, 'we really do need the money in order to—'

She interrupted him. 'If you are relying on the payment, it would be wise to seek alternative financial support in the meantime. It may take … a while before your invoice is processed.'

Both Belle and Twister blanched. We all knew what she meant; we all knew *exactly* what she meant. Payment would not be forthcoming, not now, not soon, not ever.

Twister's eyes darted to the piles of tartan on the table. If they'd been destined for anyone else, he'd have ordered me to scoop them up again and marched out without a second glance. But you didn't cross the Mages. Even Twister was too smart to try to take back his goods.

Belle was shaking, and I wasn't sure if it was with rage or fear. She lifted her chin and met the grey-eyed woman's gaze. 'I completely understand,' she murmured, playing the game. 'Payments such as these can take time.'

'Indeed.'

'We would hope, however, that in the absence of immediate remuneration we can receive a Mages' Warrant. We would be proud to display to everyone in the city the fact that we have served the Mages.'

That was a wise move on her part. Belle and Twister could ill afford to lose so much expensive tartan, but the Mages'

Warrant would go a long way to softening that loss. Other potential customers would take note and business would improve.

'Certainly,' the woman said. 'You can apply for a Mages' Warrant once you have provided goods and services to the Mages for a total of five consecutive years.'

'Five...' Twister spluttered. 'Five...! This can't be right! This —' His voice was rising. From beyond the grand hallway, a door to the right opened and a frowning Mage stalked out, his expression indicating that the sound was disturbing him. I recognised him immediately as the Mage who'd complained about his cloak being left on the shop floor.

'What's going on? What's all the shouting about?' He glared at the woman. 'Ailsa? Is there some kind of problem?'

She immediately dipped her head and dropped her shoulders, the perfect picture of subservience. 'I apologise, sir. I did not mean to disturb you.'

The Mage swung towards Twister. 'You? Are you the one creating all the commotion?'

Poor Twister looked terrified. 'No, sir. I mean, yes, sir. It's just that I've brought all the tartan ordered by your kind self and the other Mages and—'

'And what?'

'Well, it's proven quite costly to source—'

The Mage snorted. 'I should think so too! We can't be seen walking around the city in rags. We have a reputation to maintain. What is good for the Mages is good for you, too. I should have thought that a businessman like yourself would understand that.' His eyes grew flinty. '*Do* you understand that?'

There was an odd twang in the air; it felt similar to the atmosphere I'd felt when I'd run into the daemon in the wynd in the middle of the night. I looked down and saw flickers of blue around the Mage's fingertips. My stomach tightened. If Twister answered wrongly, things were not going to end well.

I reached forward and touched his elbow in warning. Twister jerked and frowned at me, then he glanced back at the Mage and saw what I had seen. His body sagged. 'Aye, sir,' he whispered. 'I understand.'

'Good.' The Mage sniffed. 'Now get the fuck out of here.'

CHAPTER SEVEN

I DIDN'T HAVE THE HEAVY PACKAGES OF TARTAN TO CARRY, BUT that didn't mean the trudge back to the shop was any lighter. Belle and Twister didn't say a word to each other for the entire journey. Their shoulders were slumped and their steps were slow. I didn't have to glance at their faces to know that their expressions were tight and pinched.

The closer to home we got, the more oppressive the atmosphere became. It was unnerving. Despite my own condition, I was unused to such discomfiting quiet.

I'd been expecting the recriminations and shouting to start as soon as the shop door closed behind us. Belle turned to her husband and opened her mouth, and I prepared to scuttle down to the kitchen to get out of her way. Instead of yelling, however, her words came out as little more than a mumble. 'I'm going to lie down.'

Twister nodded mutely. I could only stare at them both. Raising their voices at each other was the norm; they sniped and spat all day long, and arguments arose over the smallest of matters. This silence was more terrifying than any amount of yelling.

Twister and I watched Belle leave the room. He remained where he was while the floorboards creaked as she made her way upstairs. There was a brief moment where everything went quiet, then a single sob from directly above our heads rent the air.

I winced, but Twister didn't react. 'Go and boil some water, Mairi,' he said quietly. 'We could do with a cup of tea.'

I almost ran out of the room to do his bidding. The explosion might not have happened yet, but I reckoned the delay would only make it worse when it inevitably occurred.

When I returned to the shop floor with the tea tray, Twister was no longer there. I set it down on the counter and glanced upwards, assuming he'd gone upstairs to attend to his wife. I decided to allow a couple of minutes before I interrupted them. As much as I disliked both my employers, they were still human beings; they'd need some time to themselves to re-group.

I wasn't party to the shop accounts, but I knew the loss of all that expensive tartan without any hope of payment would be devastating. And I knew that in the end I would feel that loss as much – if not more – than either Belle or Twister. It was good that I had an exit plan.

I reached behind the counter for a duster, having decided that I might as well make myself useful in the interim, when the bell above the shop door jangled. I glanced round, expecting to see one of the locals wandering in to get the lowdown about what had happened at the City Chambers. When I saw who was standing nervously on the threshold, the blood in my veins turned ice cold.

Wee Alice was pale. Although she was now appropriately dressed, rather than in the nightgown she'd been wearing when I'd seen her before, she looked just as small and vulnerable. When her dark eyes fell on me, her relief was palpable. 'You're here! I wasn't sure you would be but Alistair said I had to try. He said I had to find you.'

I was by her side in a heartbeat, kneeling down so that my face was level with hers. I took her hands and squeezed them urgently, hoping I could convey the urgency I needed to. It had to be little Meg. Had she taken a turn for the worse? Had her fever returned? It couldn't be anything else. I swallowed hard and gazed at the child for answers.

She blinked several times and gulped. 'They came for her this morning as soon as the sun was up.'

What? Who?

'One of them hit her in the face and they put her in shackles.' Alice's voice wobbled slightly. 'They dragged her away. Matron Campbell said it was her own fault. She'd been asking too many questions and she should have kept her mouth shut, but ... but ... but...'

No. Oh no. Nausea was already rising from the pit of my stomach. It couldn't be. I did everything I could to keep the terror from my face and nodded at Alice to continue. She *had* to continue.

She drew in a shuddering breath, but she also lifted her chin and I spotted a steely defiance in her red-rimmed eyes. She couldn't be more than nine years old, but she possessed more inner strength than most grown men I knew.

She licked her lips and spoke again. 'Isla was only trying to find out what happened to the baby,' she whispered.

For a moment the world around me spun and blood roared in my ears with a heavy, pulsating thump. Alice let out a tiny squeak and I realised I'd tightened my grip on her hands. I let go immediately. She offered me a tremulous smile that didn't reach her eyes, as if to say that she wasn't hurt and it didn't matter.

'Alistair said they were taking her to George Square. I don't know why they'd do that. He said I had to find you. He said I had to find you and tell you.'

I was already reaching for my cloak. There was no time to waste.

'You're going there?' Alice asked.

I nodded.

'Will you rescue Isla?'

My mouth was dry. Yes. No. Maybe. I had to try. I had to fucking try. I nodded again.

'Can I come?'

Absolutely not; it was not the place for a child. I shook my head vehemently. Alice had to get back to St Mags, and I had to get to George Square. Immediately, before it was too late.

I was so focused on Alice and what I had to do that I didn't hear Twister come in behind me. 'What's going on, Mairi?'

I jerked and looked round. His gaze drifted from me to Alice and back again. 'Ask a stupid question,' he muttered, 'get a stupid answer.' He pointed at the tea tray, which still lay on the counter where I'd left it. 'You need to bring that upstairs to Belle.'

I couldn't do that. I turned away from him, tied my cloak strings round my neck then reached for the door.

'Mairi!' he said sharply. 'Get back here!'

Alice looked at him defiantly. 'She can't. She's going to George Square.'

'George Square? Why the fuck—' His voice drifted off as, belatedly, realisation dawned. 'Oh no. You'll get back here now, lass, and do what you're told.'

I ignored him and opened the door. Twister reached for me, his large hand circling my arm. He yanked me backwards and spun me round. 'You will not go there,' he ordered.

I shook my head.

'I will smack you halfway to fucking Dundee if you take another step!'

I wrenched my arm away.

'Leave her alone!' Alice cried.

I moved to the door again.

'Can't you get it through your stupid, mute head?' Twister

59

hissed. 'They'll kill you too, if you get involved.'

I paused for half a beat, then my mouth tightened. So be it.

MA MCASKILL WAVED at me cheerily from the other side of the street, but this time I didn't pay her any attention. I had only one focus – to reach George Square as quickly as possible. I had zero idea what I would do once I got there, but I would do something. There was no other choice.

The closer I got, the busier it became; crowds were always drawn to these things. Call it a sick fascination or the need to be part of something, or simply the desire to bear witness to the Mages' continuing control. It could have been all of those or none – humans were strange creatures – but there was certainly a reason why the Mages made events like this public. Everything they did was for a reason.

I pushed forward, my mouth set into a grim line and my shoulders tight. I jostled my way through, ignoring the mutters and few sharp elbows sent my way. I had to get to the front; I had to do something.

I continued to move forward, finding gaps in the crowd where I could. I prayed to whoever or whatever might be listening that Alice was wrong, that this wasn't what I thought it was going to be. Deep down, I knew it was a false hope.

I squeezed through the last available gap. Only a few people were in front of me now and I had a clear view of the scaffold. A Mage was already standing there, his hood pushed back and his face visible. Purple robes: this was the Ascendant.

I stared at his hard eyes and bristling moustache, unable to quell the surge of hatred that flowed into my bones and settled deep in the centre of my chest. He took a step forward and I saw his lips move; a moment later, his voice boomed around the square, magically amplified to reach us all.

'It gives us no pleasure to be here,' he intoned, though he didn't appear particularly distressed. If anything, he seemed happy that so many people had turned out. 'But there are things that must be done to maintain the peace. You can rest assured that what occurs here is for no other reason than to keep you safe.

'It is thanks to my position as Ascendant, and the Ascendants in the four other cities in the country, that we can enjoy such joyous levels of freedom. Make no mistake, however. We live in dangerous times and there is no telling what could happen if order is not maintained. We are on a knife's edge and, in these days of woe and hardship, we have to work with each other, not against each other.'

A gaunt man in a threadbare suit who was standing next to me hissed under his breath and shook his head. 'What woe and hardship do those fucking Mages experience?' he muttered. 'Tell me that.'

The woman next to him looked at me nervously and nudged him in the ribs. 'Wheesht yourself.'

'He can't hear me.'

'Maybe not, but others can.'

I turned my head, trying to indicate that I wouldn't speak even if I could. I didn't care about the man or the woman, I only cared about what was about to happen on that damned scaffold.

Two more Mages ascended the scaffold, followed by three heavyset men wearing the livery of the Mages' servants. They were accompanying a group of hooded prisoners. My gaze swung desperately across them, but all of them were wearing shapeless shifts and their faces were obscured. All I could tell was that two were female and one was male – and there was no way of knowing if either of the two women was Isla.

The Ascendant spoke again. 'These three citizens have been found guilty of sedition, the punishment for which is death.' He beckoned to the first guard and the male prisoner was thrust forward. The Ascendant whipped off the prisoner's hood, revealing a middle-aged man with terrified eyes. He looked about as dangerous as a mouse in a house full of cats.

'This is a mistake,' the man mumbled. 'This is all a mistake. I didna do anything wrong!'

The Ascendant shrugged. He looked bored. He jerked his hand and a female prisoner was brought forward. I held my breath. Not Isla, I prayed. Please don't let it be Isla.

He pulled off her hood. The instant I saw curly grey hair, I gasped with relief. It wasn't her. Then I saw the woman's petrified expression and immediately felt the stain of dark, heavy guilt. She wasn't Isla, but she was someone.

The woman stared out at the crowd as if she were looking for someone in particular, then her expression altered and her fear changed to something akin to defiance. She lifted her chin, hawked up phlegm and spat it at the Ascendant.

His lips were already moving before the spittle left her mouth, and whatever magic words he uttered were enough to make her attempt fail. Her spit hit an invisible barrier.

'At least she tried,' muttered the man next to me.

'Much fucking good it did her,' the woman replied.

The Ascendant looked unconcerned. He pointed at the third prisoner and she was brought forward. I knew it was Isla before her hood was lifted. Maybe it was the way she was standing, or some kind of sixth sense, but I wasn't shocked when her face was revealed. Instead, I was filled with a sudden rage that rose from deep within my chest and threatened to choke me.

Isla didn't look scared; if anything, she looked proud. I shook my head. That didn't make sense. What was she doing? Missing baby girl or not, what on earth had happened to make her end up here?

'They're taking babies!' she yelled. 'The Mages are taking babies and killing them!'

The Mage next to her rolled his eyes. '*Vair al,*' he said, and

Isla's mouth snapped shut.

For some reason, it was the act of silencing her that made me move. My feet, which had been frozen to the spot, marched forward.

The man next to me jerked. 'Hey!' he hissed. 'What are you doing, you eejit? Get back here!'

I elbowed one woman out of the way and side-stepped another. It was only a couple of metres to the scaffold and few people were now in my path. The guards were already looping nooses around the necks of Isla and the other two helpless prisoners.

No: it wasn't going to happen. I tilted my chin and Isla finally looked down. Her eyes met mine and, for the first time, panic crossed her face. I realised with dull horror that she wasn't afraid for herself, she was afraid for me.

I wouldn't watch her die. I'd stand up for her even if it meant my death too.

Isla started to shake her head, her alarm obvious. I gritted my teeth and attempted to push past the final person who stood between me and the scaffold. It was a burly man who seemed determined to keep his front-row position. Not today, mate. I was getting past him, come hell or high water.

I moved to his left, hoping to squeeze past and somehow get to the scaffold. As I did so, something – or rather some*one* – grabbed hold of my arm in a vice-like grip and yanked me backwards.

A voice murmured in my ear, 'I wouldn't do that, if I were you.'

That fucking daemon.

The people around us, including the couple I'd been standing next to, shuffled away in alarm. Daemon attention meant I was a tainted being; for their own protection, they were determined to keep away from me.

I tried to shake him off but his hand tightened round my

arm. Up on the scaffold, the nooses were being tightened. No no no no no no. I struggled against Nicholas's grip. I had to get up there. I had to do something – *anything*.

'You can't help her,' he told me in a low whisper.

Fuck him. I couldn't help and I couldn't talk, but I could damned well scream. It would draw attention and might delay the execution. I took in a gulp of air – then his hand clamped over my mouth and he started to drag me to the side, away from the crowd and the horrific scene about to take place.

'You don't want to watch this, sweetheart.' He paused. '*Meshar al.*'

The air crackled and, without warning, my entire body went limp. My legs and arms flopped, my brain unable to control them. I tried to make a noise – any noise – but nothing came out.

Nicholas removed his hand from my mouth and moved it to my waist, holding me against him. From the scaffold, Isla's eyes met mine for one final time. I could feel Nicholas spinning me round, away from the terrible view. No: I resisted with every ounce of energy I had. I gasped, and a tiny squeak emitted from my mouth.

The daemon dropped me as if I'd burned him, and immediately the sensation of control returned to my limbs. Praise be. I whirled back to face the front and lunged forward to storm the scaffold, but he grabbed me again.

'No.' This time both his arms encircled my body. Futile as it was, I still tried to fight. He sighed in my ear. 'Bear witness if you must. The nightmares afterwards will be yours to deal with alone. But you cannot stop this. It is too late. It will be quick for her, I can promise you that.'

Isla looked at me and I looked at her. The purple thread I'd given her dangled down her wrist. And then the trapdoor beneath her feet dropped open and my mouth opened in a silent scream.

CHAPTER EIGHT

EVERYTHING BECAME A BLUR. NICHOLAS PICKED ME UP IN HIS arms and pushed his way out of the crowd, away from the scaffold and George Square. I was dimly aware of a Mage blocking our path and questioning him, and I heard the daemon say something about a fainting fit. I tried to protest by waving my hands, but all they did was flutter uselessly in the air. Then I was being hauled down a narrow side street and through the first open doorway.

Nicholas muttered something and the door slammed shut behind us. Only then did he release me and drop me to my feet.

I swung my hand back and punched him in the face. From his expression, the only pain I'd caused was in my own fucking hand.

He reached forward, his large hands cupping my face and his emerald eyes piercing me, as if he were stabbing my very soul. 'I didn't save you the other night, sweetheart, so you could commit suicide by Mage.'

Hot scalding tears were running freely down my face as I glared at him with all the hatred I could muster. Chances were I would have died, I knew that. But I deserved the opportunity to try. Nicholas had taken that choice away from me. He worked for the Mages – he was their creature. For all I knew, Isla had been executed on his say so.

Rage swelled up inside me again and I struck out. He pushed me against the wall with ease, quelling my pathetic attack in an instant. 'Your physical strength is no match for mine. You cannot beat me like that.' Suddenly his eyes glinted. 'But you are far more powerful than you realise.'

My chest was tight and I felt like I couldn't breathe. I kept seeing Isla's face and, coupled with Nicholas's proximity, it was becoming too much. I raised my chin and shoved him in the chest with both hands. He barely twitched, but he did step back and give me the breathing space I desperately required.

'I am sorry about her. She was your friend?'

I didn't react. I wouldn't give him the satisfaction of responding in any way, shape or form.

He sighed and nodded as if he understood – except someone like him could never understand. 'If I could have done something to prevent it from happening, I would have,' he said. 'Believe me.'

I snorted in disgust and looked away. He was part of the system that had caused Isla to die.

Nicholas held up his hands, indicating the metal cuffs around his wrists, then pointed to the matching collar round his neck. 'Look,' he said. 'These limit my powers and bind me to the Mages. I cannot raise my hand against a Mage, no matter how much I might wish to, and I cannot gainsay a direct order from them. You are bound by their magic and so am I. We are simply enslaved through different means.'

I didn't know whether to believe him or not, but I didn't really care about the truth of his words. He didn't matter to me. Isla had mattered to me – and now she was dead at the Mages' hands for reasons I didn't understand.

The realisation that Isla was dead slammed into me. It didn't seem true, but I knew it was; I'd seen it with my own eyes. Oh God. My one friend was no longer breathing; never again would she laugh or cry or joke or tease. The children she looked after at St Mags would never see her again and neither would I. My knees buckled and I sank to the floor.

The door opened and a man walked in. He stopped in his tracks when he saw us.

'Get out,' Nicholas ordered.

'But – but – but I live here.'

'Get. Out.'

The man backed away and stepped outside. Nicholas reached down and pulled me to my feet. 'You can't stay here,' he said. 'You should go back to your little tartan shop and stay there. Mourn your friend, keep your head down and survive. That's all you can do.'

I gazed into his face. No, it wasn't all I could do. He'd said I had power, and that woman – Fee – she'd said the same thing. I thought about how Nicholas had backed off suddenly in the crowd: he'd sprung away as if I'd scalded him. Something I had done had achieved that. I didn't know what and I didn't know how, but there was something in me. If I could take that something and turn it against the Mages, make them pay for what they'd done to Isla – what they'd done to all of us – then maybe my life wouldn't be in vain.

I wiped my eyes furiously with the back of my sleeve and lifted my chin in defiance.

Nicholas raised an eyebrow. 'Don't do anything stupid.'

What I did or didn't do wasn't any of his business. I met his eyes and offered a brief nod – not in acquiescence, and certainly not in gratitude for his interference – but as an acknowledgement of what he'd done.

He gave me a long look filled with foreboding, then he

stepped back so I could pass by him. A moment later, I was out on the cold street once again.

I DIDN'T KNOW what I'd been expecting when I trudged back into Belle and Twister's shop, but it certainly wasn't the pair of them holding hands over the counter and looking at me, white-faced, when I walked in.

'Mairi. Lass. You made it back.' Twister opened his arms expansively as if preparing to hug me. The man had never given me a hug before in his life; I'd worked for him for nine years and the only physical contact I'd had from him was a blow when I didn't do what he wanted. 'How did it go at George Square?'

I stared at him blankly. He knew I wasn't going to answer him, so why bother asking?

Then Belle stepped forward holding a letter. 'This came with your name on it,' she said. 'I opened it for you.'

I rarely received any post. The fact that she'd read a letter addressed to me should have angered me – on any normal day, it would have enraged me. Instead, I simply took it from her and read the contents.

'This is a good thing,' Belle said. She even smiled. 'I had no idea you had applied.' She nudged Twister. 'A scholar under our own noses all this time! I always thought you were up to some-thing strange in your room, and now I know what.' She took my hand in hers. 'I want you to know, Mairi, that we will support you wholeheartedly. If this is what you want to do, then we will no' stand in your way.'

How very magnanimous. No doubt she'd spent the after-noon looking at the books and decided, upon reflection, that the shop could no longer sustain my employment. Despite my pitiful wages, the loss of all that tartan to the Mages likely meant my meagre existence was too much.

I looked again at the letter.

Your place at the scholarship examinations for Apothecary Studies is confirmed for February 2nd. We look forward to welcoming you and warmly wish you all the best with your endeavours.

I knew that I could pass the exam with flying colours. I'd studied enough, despite the time I'd lost in recent weeks, and achieving my lifelong dream was in my grasp. Isla would be so proud.

The carefully printed words swam in front of my eyes. I sniffed, then I ripped the letter into several pieces and tossed them onto the floor. Both Twister's and Belle's jaws dropped. I ignored their expressions and walked past them, heading up to my room.

'Mairi!' Belle yelled. 'What are you doing?'

'This isn't a good time, love,' Twister said to her. 'Maybe give her a moment first.'

'And who the fuck will give us a moment? Hmm?'

A second later Belle came after me up the stairs. 'Things have changed,' she said. 'What happened with the Mages this morning is a setback for us. It'll be tight living around here for a wee while, and it's no easy having you here. You have to under-stand you're another mouth to feed.'

It wasn't as if they ever gave me much food, so I wasn't much of a burden to them. I shrugged and walked into my tiny bedroom, glanced round and located the small bag at the foot of my bed. I scooped it up and began stuffing in clothes. I couldn't take much but, there again, I didn't need much.

'Stop what you're doing and listen to me!' Belle snapped. She paused. 'What *are* you doing?'

I shoved in some underwear, then looked at the heavy apothecary book that had cost me so much, and which I'd spent so much time studying. I turned away from it and picked up my spare pair of shoes instead.

'You're leaving now?'

Round of applause to the bitch in the tartan dress. I pulled the drawstring on the bag and slung it over my shoulder.

'You cannae go *now*,' Belle said. 'You can stay for a week or two yet.'

I headed for the door.

'You've still got tonight's supper to make.'

Uh-huh.

'And I want you to clean down the shelves before you go. We need to make the most of our stock now there's no' much of the good stuff left.'

Sure thing, Belle. You go do that.

'Mairi! You ungrateful bint!'

I walked down the stairs and into the shop. It wouldn't be long before the sun set. I'd have to hurry.

'Er, what's going on?' Twister asked.

I stopped and turned my head. They were both staring at me. As I looked at their faces, I wondered if their own hardships had been less severe, they might have been kinder. I'd never know.

Without smiling, I raised a hand in farewell then I walked out of the door for the last time.

IT WAS a wonder I made it to Sauchiehall Lane. There wasn't any real conscious thought to my journey, I simply put one foot in front of the other, ignoring all the passers-by, the spinning three wheelers, the occasional carriage and the many dirty puddles. Normally, I would step out of the path of oncoming folk, politely moving aside to give them right of way but, on this occasion, people moved out of my way. Maybe it was the blank expression on my face. Maybe it was nothing more than expediency.

Either way, my pinched feet found themselves at the edge of

Sauchiehall Lane by the time the sun was sinking behind the tenements and people were starting to rush to get indoors. Only then did I consider the wisdom of my actions – but it was either remain outside and face the dangers of the Afflicted or continue on my course.

A plump woman with apple cheeks and a friendly face stepped out of the doorway and shook out a small rug. When she saw me standing nearby, she squinted. 'Can I help you, hen?'

Shite. Fee had told me to ask for her once I got here, but for me that was easier said than done. I bit my lip, nodded at the woman and gestured towards the end of the street with a questioning shrug.

Her gentle smile faded slightly as she gazed at me in confusion. 'You're gonna need tae gie me a bit mair than that. Who do you want?'

My lips formed the words, although no sound came out. *Fee. I want Fee.* Fortunately, that seemed to be enough. 'Fiona?' she asked. 'You want her?'

I shrugged again. Presumably Fee was short for Fiona. I guessed I'd find out soon enough.

The woman's eyes shifted left and right, as if she were afraid that a Mage would spring out from behind a nearby stall. She held up a finger, indicating that I should wait a moment, then turned back into her house to drop the rug. She quickly reappeared with a scarf, which she wrapped round her head and knotted beneath her chin before beckoning me to follow her.

'You're one of them, ain't you?' she asked in a low voice.

Was I? I didn't know.

'You don't say much.' Her mouth tightened. 'That's a good thing.' She took my arm and picked up the pace. 'Come on. We don't have long before the sun sets.'

She led me down Sauchiehall Lane without pausing. I'd been there several times before on errands for Belle. It was a good place to pick up second-hand goods, and the long line of small shops with competitive prices were perfect for finding a bargain. Unlike the posh, more well-to-do stores, haggling was the norm and there were still shoppers arguing cheerfully with the shopkeepers and stallholders, even at this late hour.

It seemed all wrong to me. Isla was dead. She'd been executed less than two hours ago and her body was likely still warm. Yet here life was going on as normal. Rationally, I understood that these people didn't know her; their hearts weren't aching with her loss and they couldn't feel the burning rage that I did. All the same, an irrational part of me felt that they should be marking her passing with grief and respect, regardless of their ignorance. Isla had died and, as far as I was concerned, the world should stop turning even if only for a moment. It didn't though. And it wouldn't.

The woman kept going until we reached a drab door next to a tiny second-hand bookstore. She gave me a meaningful look then knocked tentatively. No sooner had her hand dropped to her side when the city bells rang out, indicating the light would fail within the next five minutes and everyone should get indoors. Almost immediately the narrow street became a flurry of activity as people stopped what they were doing and hurried home.

'I have to go,' the woman said, flicking a nervous look at the darkening sky. 'Fee is in there. She'll answer the door soon, I'm sure.' She picked up her heavy skirts and darted away.

I waited for a long minute, debating whether to knock again or leave and find somewhere to hide out. Doubt was beginning to creep in. Given the hour, Fee would have little choice but to allow me to stay the night and she might not want to do that. We were still strangers to each other. Despite what she'd said to me about visiting her, she might not want to be forced into helping me.

I shifted the bag on my shoulder and turned to go. That was

when the door opened and Fee's face appeared. She stared at me unblinkingly, then she suddenly grinned.

'Finally!' she exclaimed. 'I thought you'd never come. I thought I'd been too harsh on you and scared you away.' She reached out and grabbed my shoulder. 'Get in here quick, hen, before it's too dark to see.'

CHAPTER NINE

THE SMALL HOUSE SMELLED OF LEMON AND BEESWAX. ALTHOUGH the floorboards creaked and there were several ominous-looking cracks in the old plasterwork, it was clean and tidy and had a warmer atmosphere than I'd ever experienced at Belle and Twister's.

Fee led me to the kitchen. A young woman was attending to the dying embers of the fire in the hearth, and a slightly older woman was sitting at a wooden table hunched over a glass. She glanced up as we entered. 'Another waif, Fee? Really?'

Fee was still smiling. 'This is the one I was telling you about. From the tartan shop.' She looked at me. 'It's Mairi, right?'

I nodded.

Fee pointed at the seated woman. 'That's Flora,' she said. 'And the grumpy one by the fire is Jane.'

Jane sighed loudly with obvious exasperation. 'For fuck's sake, Fee, I'm not grumpy. I'm not a teenager having a tantrum.' She tossed down the iron poker and glared. 'I've got every right to be pissed off. We should *all* be pissed off.'

I stared at her. Fee pulled a face. 'Don't take it personally,

Mairi,' she said. 'It's not about you. Jane is upset that there was another execution at George Square today.'

I flinched involuntarily.

Jane raised her voice. 'You know what she said? You know what that woman said before they hung her?'

'Let's not get into it now,' Fee murmured.

'Why not?' Jane demanded, putting her hands on her hips. 'We have to do something about it! They're still taking fucking babies, Fee! She said they're killing them and—'

I couldn't stop myself. My stomach lurched and I ran to the kitchen sink by the small window. A beat later vomit spewed out of my mouth, splattering its ceramic sides. Even after my stomach was empty, I continued to retch over and over again.

'Now look what you've done,' I heard Flora say.

'It wasn't my fault,' Jane snapped. 'Just because she's got a weak constitution...'

'Wheesht, the pair of you,' Fee said. She held out a clean towel and rubbed my back. 'There now. You're okay.'

I gripped the edges of the sink, breathing hard, then took the towel and wiped the clammy sweat from my face. I turned on the tap and gulped down some water, clearing the taste from my mouth and the vomit from the sink. Only then, when I felt calm again, did I turn and send a look of apology towards Fee.

'Were you there?' Jane asked. 'Were you at George Square too?'

I looked down.

'You're right,' Flora said. 'She doesn't talk at all, does she?'

'I don't think so.' Fee reached forward and tilted up my head. 'Do you speak, Mairi?'

I shook my head.

Jane sniffed. 'Then how can you be sure?'

Fee tapped her nose. 'Do me a favour,' she said to me gently. 'Will you hum?'

I frowned at her. Hum?

'Or whistle. Anything like that.'

I gazed at her in confusion.

'Humour me,' Fee said.

Coming here was a huge mistake. I looked away, but then I hummed a single low-pitched note. Whatever.

Fee, Jane and Flora exchanged glances. 'Crikey,' Flora breathed.

Fee smiled with deep satisfaction. 'See?'

THE FOUR OF us were seated at the kitchen table. Fee offered me some food – a vegetable stew that looked delicious – but after the events of the day, and with the hollowness in my chest, I didn't feel remotely hungry. I doubted I could have kept anything down. I accepted a mug of tea, however, and sat hunched over it while I waited for an explanation.

'What do you know about magic, Mairi?' Fee asked.

An image of a stern-faced Mage flashed into my mind, followed by Isla's face as they placed the noose round her neck. I grimaced. Pain. Fear. All-encompassing power. That's what I knew.

'You think only the Mages can wield magic, right?'

I nodded.

'And that to be a Mage you have to be male?'

Well, yeah, that went without saying. But what had happened with Nicholas earlier today had planted enough seeds of doubt in my mind to make me come here.

Jane muttered something under her breath and stared hard at me. I shifted uncomfortably under her gaze.

'The truth is,' Fee continued, 'that certain women can use magic just as much as men can. The only reason that all the Mages are male is because they seek out female children who show signs of power and eliminate them before their magic becomes too obvious.'

My mouth felt suddenly dry. Eliminate them? So what Isla had said was true?

'Aye, they kill them,' Flora said. 'Or so we believe.'

I stared at her.

Fee leaned forward across the table, her expression sombre. 'Inevitably some slip through the net. It's to be expected. But usually those of us who escape can only boast of minor powers. We're not strong enough to be noticed by the Mages.'

Us?

Fee smiled slightly. '*Belzac.*'

The fire in the hearth roared, changing from a small flickering glow to a temporary inferno. I jerked, spilling the tea in the process. Jane laughed, but there was no humour in the sound.

My mouth formed the word, *Why?*

'You mean,' Fee said, 'that if women can use magic as well as men, why do the Mages hunt them down and stop them?'

I nodded. Surely more Mages would be a good thing. Something might be able to be done about the Afflicted, not to mention that more magic would allow for better living conditions for everyone.

Fee's face darkened. 'We think they're afraid that women with magic will steal their power.'

My eyes widened. That was possible?

'When a woman with magic has intimate relations with a man with magic, the woman is imbued with some of his powers.'

I must have looked confused because Jane leaned in towards me. 'If a Mage fucks you, he doesn't just deposit his sperm. He deposits some of his power in you, too.'

I blinked.

'Unfortunately for us, the Mages are circumspect when it

comes to choosing partners,' Flora said. 'Otherwise, we might be able to make more of that particular fact.'

Disgust washed through me and didn't go unnoticed.

'The Mages possess absolute power over us,' Jane said. 'They kill us when it suits them. They take the best of everything. They tell us that without them we'd have no protection against the Afflicted or the monsters from other realms, but they use daemons to enhance their power and we cannot leave our own homes after nightfall. Wouldn't you use every tool at your disposal to bring them down if you could?'

I thought about it. Before today I would have said no; there were moral lines that I wouldn't have crossed. Now things were different.

Fee got to her feet. 'People are beginning to see the truth. We have a growing resistance network of both men and women. More and more people are tired of being subjugated by the Mages. We're trying to affect real change.' She met my eyes. 'The reason I was at your shop is because I knew the Mages would be there sooner or later. I was trying to eavesdrop and see what titbits I could learn from their chatter. I didn't expect to find someone like you there as well. I'm sorry if I shouted at you in the street. I was … taken aback. And a little afraid.'

She hadn't shouted at me, not any more than I was used to.

'The thing is, hen, we need to find out as much as we can about the Mages. There's still so much we don't know about them. Knowledge is power, and we must know our enemy inside and out before we strike. And believe me, Mairi, sooner or later, we *will* strike.' Fee's hands curled round the back of the kitchen chair. 'You can join us. You can help us and be part of something real. *You* have the power to affect change.'

Something indefinable stirred inside me; there wasn't a name for what I felt. It was resolution, mixed with hope, mixed with the desire for revenge and a whole lot of other things. I wanted to help them, I wanted to be a part of this, though I didn't know what I could do or what part I could play. I raised my chin and gazed at her, the question in my eyes.

Fee nodded her understanding. 'Magic is tied to language,' she said. 'Some words are stronger than others and can only be mastered by powerful practitioners. I can wield eleven of them. Flora can manage eight.'

'Nine,' Flora interrupted. 'I've been practising hard on the latest one.'

Fee inclined her head. 'Nine, then. Jane is the strongest of all and can use sixteen.'

I folded my arms. I couldn't speak, therefore, I wouldn't be able to use magic. My vision of attacking the Mages and bringing them to their knees vanished.

My thoughts must have been written all over my face. 'Babies can't speak, either,' Fee said gently. 'But if they have strong magic, someone with an ear can identify their power through their sound alone. You don't have words, Mairi, but you most definitely have magic. Screeds of it, even with your muteness. It's a wonder you have survived this long.'

Flora looked my way. 'Do you know who your parents were?'

I shook my head; I had no memory of anything prior to St Mags.

'It's likely that your mother was also strong like you,' she said. 'Magic usually runs in families – not always, but it tends to be the case. Perhaps your mother used her magic to silence you to keep you safe.'

Fee seemed to agree. 'It seems the most likely explanation.' She walked round the table and put her hands on my shoulders before lowering her mouth to my ear. 'Join us, Mairi. Join us and help us bring the Mages to their knees once and for all.'

CHAPTER TEN

IT WAS A LONG NIGHT. ALTHOUGH I WAS EXHAUSTED, HEAVY WITH fatigue that had settled in every nook and cranny of my body, sleep seemed impossible. Fee set me up in the back room on a makeshift bed that was both warm and comfortable, but I could have been in the most luxurious four-poster feather bed and I still wouldn't have slept.

Too much had happened for my mind to quiet. I kept seeing flashes of Isla's face, and turning over the revelations I'd heard from Fee and the others. Like any sensible person, I'd avoided the Mages when I could and maintained a healthy fear of them. Yes, I was aware that they sometimes abused their power, and I knew there was an element of corruption to all that they did, but it was the same as recognising that each morning the sun would rise. The Mages were an absolute; there was nothing I could do about them. I had to live my life like everyone else, hoping to stay beneath their notice and eke out a living without questioning their strictures too closely. The thought that there were people wanting to usurp them and that I could be part of those people – let alone the idea that I could wield real magic myself – was almost too much to consider.

When I finally gave up on sleep at around four in the morning, I sat in the kitchen and stared out of the darkened windows. I knew what I had to do, even if I didn't have a clue how I'd do it. I'd already abandoned becoming an apothecary and I'd walked out on Belle and Twister; rebellion was all that remained.

There was a fire in my belly that had been stoked into a roaring inferno during the long dark hours of the night. I'd make those bastards pay for what they'd done to Isla and those baby girls, not to mention the rest of us. I'd show the entire city what those fucking Mages were really like, and I'd make them pay – regardless of the consequences.

An hour or so before dawn, the rest of the house began to stir. I listened to the sounds of life above my head, the soft murmur of voices, the creaking floorboards and the opening of doors.

Unsurprisingly, it was Fee who appeared first in the kitchen. She smiled at me, put the kettle on to boil and joined me at the window. 'Have any Afflicted been out there this night?' she asked.

I shook my head. I hadn't seen or heard a thing.

'We think the Mages created them, you know.' Her mouth flattened into a grim line. 'Fear is an excellent method for keeping your populace in line.'

I stared at her and she patted my arm. 'Have you decided, Mairi?' she asked.

I straightened my shoulders, and it was more than enough to answer her question. A ghost of a smile crossed her face, although I noted something else behind her eyes: faint regret, perhaps.

'Good,' she said. 'You're doing the right thing. I'll send word to the Gowk as soon as it's light. They'll see what can be done to unlock both your tongue and your magic.'

The Gowk? I raised an eyebrow, but Jane appeared before

Fee could explain and launched into a long description of a strange dream she'd had. Then Flora walked in, brushing her long dark hair and muttering about all the work she had to do that day.

I found a spot in the corner and watched them, noting that Jane's voice was different when she addressed Fee, suggesting she was desperate for Fee's approval. Fee spoke to both women in exactly the same manner as she had spoken to me; she clearly didn't have favourites.

I saw how Flora looked inextricably sad when she thought nobody was looking and rubbed her thumb absently across a tiny birthmark on her wrist. Above all, I saw how all three of them kept glancing expectantly in my direction. Fee had said that my humming revealed that I possessed magic by the bucketload. I wondered if they'd throw me out if it didn't manifest itself sufficiently.

As it was Sunday, both Fee and Jane had the day off. Flora, who was a housemaid at one of the big hotels, still had to work. Jane left with her to run a few errands. 'The things we do to look normal and unthreatening to the rest of the world,' Flora told me with a rueful smile. She gave me a meaningful look. 'Good luck today.'

'If she can't speak,' Jane said on her way out of the door, 'she's all but useless to us.'

My eyes narrowed. She'd said it loudly enough to ensure I would hear.

'Pay her no mind,' Fee told me. 'Her bark is much worse than her bite. Jane doesn't find change easy, and having you here is a massive change for us all. It's been only the three of us for more than two years now. You are welcome here, Mairi. We all need to adjust, but you are very much wanted.'

I wasn't entirely convinced, but I would wait and see what the day brought before I made any more rash decisions.

IT WAS strange having nothing to do. Although Belle and Twister's tartan shop was closed on Sundays, I usually had work to complete – I'd catch up on cleaning and prepare a few meals for later in the week, then sit down to study.

Here there was none of that. I didn't have an established place in Fee's household and she waved me away whenever I tried to help her. I spent most of the morning envisaging ways to destroy the Mages, pretending to ignore the ache in my chest from my grief, and the unanswered questions I still had about so many things.

It occurred to me that I ought to communicate to Fee what had happened with Nicholas on both the occasions that I'd met him. I couldn't understand why the daemon had helped me – and for reasons I couldn't articulate, I wanted to keep what I knew of him to myself. At that point, I had no reason to trust anyone; that included Fee, Jane, Flora and even Nicholas himself.

By mid-morning, despite my best efforts, I was itching for action. I hadn't come here to sit around; I wanted to know what I might be capable of and work on a plan to attack the Mages head on. I didn't want to sit and stare out of a window feeling sorry for myself.

In truth, my desire to *do* something meant I'd quite likely have scooped up my bag and headed out of the door by lunchtime. I'd have stalked up to the City Chambers and tried knocking on their door with a knife concealed in my breeches if there hadn't been a visitor at Fee's door just before eleven.

The Gowk had arrived.

I supposed I'd been expecting a woman. Despite the name, I'd also assumed that, as someone with power of their own, the Gowk would be tall, lithe and Amazonian. I certainly wasn't expecting a hunched-over old man with wizened features. His right hand was curled and claw-like, covered in a web of old scars, and his mouth drooped to one side as if an invisible thread were tugging his lips downwards. He blinked at me owlishly, then let out a cackling laugh that echoed round Fee's kitchen. 'You're Tartan Twister's lass, right?'

Not any more. I shrugged and tried to offer a smile of greeting; it was more of a spasm than a smile, but it was the best I could do.

The Gowk didn't appear fazed. 'He'd probably have a heart attack if he knew what's been under his roof. You've left there?'

I nodded.

'And are you still in touch with him and his wife?'

I shook my head.

The Gowk gave a satisfied jerk of his head. 'Good. There's worse than Twister and Belle about, but you cannae trust them. Their interests will always be self-serving.' He fixed me with a sharp, beady-eyed gaze. 'The question is, can *you* be trusted or not.'

'She's mute,' Fee interjected. 'She's hardly going to be blabbing all our secrets.'

'Uh-huh. Can she read and write, though?'

I folded my arms. I didn't speak, but that didn't mean I was illiterate – and I didn't appreciate being spoken about as if I weren't there.

The Gowk gazed at me. Without warning, his claw hand snapped out and he pinched me hard on the arm. I let out a sharp cry of pain and surprise.

'Well,' he said. 'Well, well, well. I guess that answers that question. She's not in the Mages' pocket. The Mages would never permit a female with that amount of latent magic to exist.'

I glared at him, annoyed that he'd managed to come at me like that. How could he tell whether I had magic in me or not? He was male; if he could recognise magic in me, then why wasn't I already with the Mages? He wasn't the only one in this room who had trust issues.

Fee reached into a drawer, took out a notebook and pen and handed them to me. I scribbled down my question and gave it to him.

The Gowk took the notepad and read what I'd written. His lip curled, held up his deformed hand and thrust it in my face. 'I wasn't born like this, lass. The Mages did this to me. It's a miracle I got away from them. If they knew where I was, you can be sure they'd come after me. Man or woman, magically inclined or not, if you dinna agree with what they do or how they act, they'll try and end you as quickly as they'll drown a baby.'

I couldn't help recoiling. For a moment the Gowk's face softened, then he dropped his hand. I took back the notebook and wrote down another question.

'Why am I called the Gowk?' he asked. 'Because that's what I am. Gowk is an old word for fool.' His withered lip curled. 'That's what they called me. I could have been one of them, with all the power and riches that come with being a Mage. I have enough magic potential to be one of their number, but I chose a different path. Don't get me wrong, lass, I'm a grizzly bastard – but even I have limits.'

There was a bitter edge to his words. It couldn't have been easy to walk away from the Mages, especially when the alternative was hiding out for the rest of your life. I had the feeling there was a lot more the Gowk wasn't saying.

My brow furrowed and I wrote down two more words: *How long?*

'How long since I turned my back on the Mages?' he asked. 'How long since they tortured me and tried to kill me?'

I nodded.

'Thirty-two years.' He tilted his head up proudly. 'Thirty-two years, and they've not caught up with me yet.' He wiggled his hand at me. 'So you'd better not be the one to break my streak, lassie.'

He shouldn't be concerned about me; he should be concerned about the fact that he'd had more than three decades to do something about the Mages and he'd achieved nothing. He had Fee and Flora and Jane, and no doubt there were many others. So why had I never heard of their resistance movement before?

Fee must have noted my scepticism because she touched my hand gently. 'We do what we can, Mairi. Although our numbers our growing, the Mages still have the upper hand. They have the history and the power and most of the magic. But we're working on it. We've saved a lot of people from them.'

They hadn't saved Isla. I bit the inside of my cheek hard enough to draw blood. As the unpleasant metallic tang filled my mouth, I gave a small nod. This ragtag group was better than nothing. For now.

CHAPTER ELEVEN

WE USED THE BASEMENT.

'It's unlikely that any Mages will wander down this street,' Fee said. 'They tend to avoid this area altogether. The wee shops here don't sell anything that they'd be interested in, and most of the people here are poor, law-abiding and beneath their notice. I live on Sauchiehall Lane for a reason.'

She smiled. 'But we can't be too careful. Staying underground will help mask any stray magic. We estimate that less than one percent of the population can wield magic, though obviously it would be higher if those fuckers didn't murder half of us because of it. There's a strong likelihood, however, that there are more people out there who can sense magic when it's being thrown about nearby. We can't be too sure.'

Whatever. Although both Fee and the Gowk seemed convinced that I was filled with magic that was merely waiting to be drawn out, I still doubted it. I didn't speak – and magic required words.

Still, at least the basement was suitably atmospheric. It was dark, damp and smelled of mould; it was all-but perfect.

The Gowk lit several large candles and placed them at

strategic points around the room, creating a pocket of light in the centre. He dragged over a barrel, took a coin out of his pocket and placed it flat on the barrel's top. 'We'll start small, shall we?' he asked. He motioned towards the coin. 'All I want you to do is levitate the penny.'

I crossed my arms. Sure, no problem. Raise an inanimate object into the air and defy the laws of physics. Piece of cake.

The Gowk smiled humourlessly. 'Just try, without any guidance to begin with. Let's see what you can do without any help.'

I already knew what I could do: nothing. Zero. Not a damned thing. I sighed, then I turned my eyes to the coin and focused on it. *Rise*, I commanded silently. *Up you come. Into the air. Up. Up. Up.*

Nothing happened. What a shocker.

Neither the Gowk nor Fee looked surprised. He glanced at her and raised an eyebrow. 'What's the word, Fiona?'

'*Folis*,' she said softly.

I stared at the coin. It still hadn't moved.

'You see, lass,' the Gowk said, 'even if you possess command of magic words, they don't work unless you place intent behind them. I could say *"folis"* in a hundred different ways and with a hundred different accents, but nothing will happen unless I push the correct intent behind the word.' He moved closer to the barrel. '*Folis. Folis.*' He raised his voice and boomed, '*Folis!*'

The coin didn't budge.

The Gowk took several steps back until he was outside the circle of candlelight and almost concealed by the darkness. In a barely audible whisper, he said the word again, '*Folis.*'

This time I felt it; I felt the actual power behind the quiet word. I looked at the coin and watched in wonder as it rose into the air, seemingly of its own accord, and hung about a metre above the barrel like it was waiting for instructions.

The Gowk exhaled and the coin dropped back down with a thud. 'Your turn,' he said with quiet satisfaction. 'If you can't say the word then think it. And when you think it, think it with meaning.'

I swallowed. My mouth suddenly felt dry and my palms were clammy. I couldn't do this – could I?

I looked at the coin. It was a small thing, tiny. It weighed next to nothing. I focused on it and then on the word. *Folis.* I pushed more strength into the thought. *Folis.* Then I inhaled deeply. *FOLIS.*

It didn't move.

My shoulders sagged. For the briefest moment, I'd thought I could make it work. I'd believed in myself. I should have trusted my gut; it didn't matter how much magic lurked within me, if I couldn't speak I couldn't wield it.

I didn't know whether the Gowk was disappointed or not because his face remained shrouded in darkness. As I started to turn away to hide my feelings, Fee spoke. 'This time,' she said, 'hum.'

I flicked a look at her. A hum wasn't a word; there was no meaning behind a single note.

'Go on,' she urged.

I sighed and looked back at the coin, thought the word and emitted a small hum. I didn't expect anything to happen – and at first nothing did.

I was pulling a face to communicate to Fee and the Gowk that this was a waste of time when, without warning, goose-bumps appeared on my skin. I didn't feel cold – in fact, the sensation was pleasant.

As I reached up to rub my arms, the little penny jerked abruptly. Instead of rising gently up into the air as it had when the Gowk was in control, it shot up like an arrow until it was three metres high and almost skimming the rafters. It hung there for several seconds before it started to spin, slowly at first and then faster and faster. Next, it zipped to the right with such force that it smacked into the far wall and sent a cloud of brick dust in its wake.

For a moment, nobody moved. It was Fee who finally walked over to the wall to inspect it. 'It's completely embedded,' she murmured. 'Several inches deep.'

I stared stupidly as the Gowk joined her. 'Hmm,' he said neutrally. 'That suggests a considerable lack of control on the lass's part.'

Fee whacked him on the arm and rolled her eyes.

'Alright,' he conceded grudgingly. 'Fair dos. She has power.'

She hit him again.

'A lot of power,' he added.

They both turned to gaze at me. All I could do was gaze back.

'How long will it take to bring her up to her full potential?'

The Gowk sucked on his bottom lip as he considered Fee's question. 'Eighteen months, I reckon. With the magic that lass has inside her, she could master the entire language. There's no telling what could happen after that.'

Eighteen months? *Eighteen fucking months?*

'Obviously,' he continued, 'we'll have to be very careful. We can't afford to let the Mages hear any rumours that she exists. Not all the Mages are bastards, and I can think of one or two we might be able to trust, but it's still too risky. I have a friend on a farm outside the city. We'll take her there and train her properly, then we can hit them where it hurts.' He started to tick off his fingers. 'We could interrupt their supply chains.'

Or I could go to the City Chambers and kill the Ascendant.

'We could ramp up our efforts to spy on them and thwart their future plans.'

Or I could go to the City Chambers and kill the Ascendant and as many other Mages as possible.

'We could use her to find ways to diminish their power.'

Or I could fucking go to the City Chambers and kill the fucking Ascendant, along with every other fucking Mage that had ever existed.

'The possibilities are endless,' Fee agreed, She looked at me. 'Can you be ready to leave this afternoon? Do you have any loose ends that need tying up?'

I ground my teeth in frustration. I didn't want to leave for eighteen months to be trained. In normal times, I was perfectly patient – I was used to waiting – but these weren't normal times, not any more and not for me. I wanted more than Fee or the Gowk were proposing. If I really possessed the potential to wield magic, I had to strike as hard and fast as possible.

I grabbed the notepad and pen once more. *Why wait? Let's attack them now. Teach me the words I need to destroy them, and I'll go there today.*

The Gowk read what I'd written and gave me a long, patronising look. 'You can't just click your fingers and get rid of the Mages. If it were that easy, they'd have gone long before now. There are several hundred of them in this city alone.' He pointed his clawed finger at me. 'You might have more magic inside you than anyone we've seen for a long time, but you'll never match that many Mages, let alone the Ascendant himself. It's simply not possible. We must attack them sideways and in small increments. Anything else means death.'

I didn't fear death. Not after Isla.

Fee tried to be kinder. 'I understand you want to hurt them now.'

She didn't understand anything.

'But you can't go from knowing how to levitate a single object to wielding the sort of the power that can bring about regime change in a single day. There are levels involved in using magic – you can't skip the more basic words and go straight to the most powerful ones. Nobody can do that.

'Think of it like exercise. You can't learn to walk one day and run a marathon the next. You have to build up your strength and knowledge, Mairi. We don't know what your limits are yet. Even the most experienced Mages sometimes fail.' She wagged her finger at me. 'Right now, your emotions are so strong that they're impossible to ignore, but magic and emotion don't go well together. Too much emotion, and you'll find you can't use any magic at all.'

She offered me a smile and patted my hand. 'The only way we damage the Mages and limit their power is by being smarter than they are. We need to learn our own limitations and strengths so we can attack them in a way that will truly hurt.'

I looked from her to the Gowk and back again. Their hearts were in the right place, and they'd given me a glimpse of what I might be capable of at great risk to themselves. But we weren't on the same page – not by a long shot.

I took the notepad one final time. *I need some time to think about this.*

The Gowk opened his mouth to argue but Fee placed her hand on his arm. 'That's not a problem, Mairi. You do what you need to. We'll be here when you're ready.'

I ALREADY KNEW that the floorboards upstairs creaked at the faintest pressure, and I didn't want Fee to think I was snooping around her home, even though that's exactly what I was doing. But I'd learned a single magic word and I reckoned that if I could levitate a damned penny, I could also levitate myself.

I left Fee talking to the Gowk in the kitchen, having gestured that I was planning to take a nap. Neither of them looked surprised; in fact, the Gowk said that magic was an exhausting business and it would take time to build up my stamina. He didn't need to know that I was feeling more, rather than less, energised as the day went on. I simply smiled and walked away, closing the kitchen door behind me.

I stopped at the foot of the stairs, waiting to see if either Fee or the Gowk would follow me. When it was clear that neither of them would, I drew in a deep breath. I looked down at my feet. You can do this, Mairi, I told myself. As long as I didn't end up embedded in any walls like the penny had, everything would be fine.

Making as little noise as possible, I hummed the same quiet note I'd used in the basement. *Folis.* This time, the effect was instant: my body jerked as magic overtook gravity. My stomach rose into my mouth and I had to clamp both hands over my mouth because I was certain I was about to vomit.

Instead of gently floating vertically, I spun until I was horizontal. My head banged against several of the lower steps, then I was raised higher until I hit the ceiling with – fortunately – little more than a quiet thud.

I swallowed my nausea. It occurred to me belatedly that while I had learned how to levitate an item, I had no idea how to stop it. It was too late now to worry about that.

I tilted my body and gazed down at the floor. Using breast-stroke motions, I lowered myself until I was halfway between the floor and the ceiling. There. That ought to work.

Using an odd combination of water-less swimming and the nearby banister, I pushed myself through the air up to the first floor of the house. There was a tiny bathroom to my left, and two other doors. I made a beeline for the nearest one and pointed my hands towards it. I only managed to move a few inches forward but I was able to grab the door handle and use it as a lever to propel myself into the room. I certainly didn't feel like I was flying; there was far too much effort involved and no sense of grace or weightlessness. But it was enough to move me silently towards my goal. Right now, that was the best I could hope for.

Fortunately, I'd chosen the right door. Inside the room were twin beds, indicating that this was where Flora and Jane slept. Last night, although Jane and Fee had been dressed in durable work clothes, Flora had been wearing a pretty dress. I was gambling on the theory that she'd have more than one dress.

I fumbled through the air, pulling myself along by way of the bed frames, until I reached the heavy oak dresser. I ignored the beads of sweat that popped out on my forehead and the damp sensation under my arms as I continued to expend magical effort and energy. Then I opened the dresser.

I rummaged past the trousers and shirts and reached for the three dresses. Two were fairly utilitarian, albeit stitched with care and made out of fabric that I knew was good value for money. The third dress was a different beast altogether: the upper half was corseted and had sheer sleeves, and the draped skirt was made out of some sort of satiny material. The pale-green colour definitely wasn't to my taste, and the dress was both inappropriate for winter weather and too small for me, but it was perfect for my needs. I sent the absent Flora a silent apology for taking it, snatched it up and returned the way that I'd come.

It was far harder going downstairs than it had been floating up. I spun round and round on several occasions, and each time it took more effort to set myself straight. By the time I reached the ground floor again, my heart was thumping painfully against my ribcage and I was gasping for breath. Little black dots were dancing in front of my eyes. No matter how much I blinked to clear them, they got worse.

I focused on the door to the back room. If I could get inside, I could cope with whatever came next and find a way to bring myself back down to solid ground. Then the front door opened.

My stomach dropped. Feeling sick with guilt, I turned my head to see who was there. Jane. Oh shite.

She stared at me, her face white. I didn't blame her for being shocked; after all, I was suspended in mid-air, clutching a stolen dress and probably looking green around the gills.

'You mad eejit,' Jane whispered. 'What are you doing?'

Even if I'd had the voice to explain, I doubt I could have. I half-closed my eyes, expecting her to raise her voice and call for Fee, but instead she darted forward, grabbed me by the elbow and hauled me into the back room.

'Fucking *folis*,' she muttered. 'You need to release yourself or you'll end up with a bloody aneurysm.'

I stared at her, wide-eyed. I didn't know how to release myself.

'Your mind is hanging onto the word,' she said. 'You have to let it go, but that's not an easy thing to learn.' She grimaced. 'Picture a padlock in your mind's eye. It's locked shut right now but you have to open it up. Quickly.'

I did as she said. Nothing happened.

'Shite.' Jane's eyes dropped to my hands. I followed her gaze and saw that the veins along the back of my hands were bulging and purple. I jerked with fear – I wasn't afraid of dying, but I didn't want to go like this. I could feel the pressure building in my head, and my body felt like it was on the verge of exploding in a mass of blood and bone and goodness knew what else.

'Okay, okay. The padlock didn't work so you need to try something else. Imagine something that means release to you, something that symbolises freedom and escape. You have to bridge the gap between your mind and your magic and break the two apart.'

I was struggling to focus and her words were growing indistinct. I took a shuddering breath. I couldn't cope with this.

'For fuck's sake, Mairi. Think of something!' Jane hissed.

Something about the exasperation in her voice made me

snap and my whole body tightened. I gritted my teeth as the tension threatened to overcome me – and then a bird popped into my head. It was a beautiful thing with pristine white feathers and long outstretched wings. Its dark eyes glittered. Suddenly it flapped its wings and flew away, out of the darkness in my mind. I exhaled once – and my body crashed onto the hard floor.

Fee's voice called out. 'Mairi? Are you okay?'

Jane replied for me. 'It's only me! I tripped on the rug. Don't worry.' She crouched down beside me and peered into my face. 'I think you owe me an explanation,' she said quietly.

DIFFICULT AS IT was to convey the truth, I had no choice but to try and communicate it to Jane. Isla would have understood because we'd had years to perfect our own sign language, but it was much harder with Jane. With no pen and paper to hand, it took a great deal of miming and twisted facial expressions to get her to understand. It was lucky that she'd already guessed half of it on her own.

'If I've understood you correctly, I can tell you that it won't work. We've tried similar things before and never got close.'

I tightened my mouth into a thin line.

'All that will happen is you'll end up getting yourself killed,' she said. 'Or worse. You've seen what they did to the Gowk, right? The only saving grace is that they can't get you to talk, no matter what they do to you, so we won't have to worry about you giving the rest of us up.'

In which case, she had nothing to lose by letting me go. I gave her a pointed look.

Jane folded her arms across her chest and sighed. 'Fee and the Gowk talk a good game, but we're not even a vague annoyance to the Mages. We've achieved nothing against them. Fee keeps saying she's intel gathering, but how much do we need to know? We should be acting, not dithering.' She grimaced. 'Of course, the last time anything was planned against those bastards, they found out before anything happened and put a stop to it.' She stared at me. 'That time, twenty-two people were executed in one go. They called it the Day of Bloody Reckoning.'

I shivered involuntarily. I remembered that day. I hadn't known why all those people were summarily killed, and I'd avoided George Square like the plague when it was happening. 'Move against the Mages at your peril' had been the city's mantra ever since.

'Why now?' she asked. 'I get that you might not have known before that you had magic, but why move against the Mages now? You could have fought them before, with or without any power.'

I hadn't communicated anything about Isla to them because I didn't know how to. For want of anything else, I wrapped both hands round my throat in a squeezing motion and shrugged.

Jane frowned at me for a long, uncomfortable moment. 'It must suck being you,' she said, not unkindly. 'But, hey. What are we fighting for, if not the freedom to make our own bad decisions?' She glanced at the closed door. 'If Fee and the Gowk catch up with you, don't tell them I helped you.' She nodded at the dress in my arms. 'And don't wear that. It's too obvious. I've got something far better.'

CHAPTER TWELVE

LESS THAN THIRTY MINUTES LATER, I WAS TROTTING BACK ALONG Sauchiehall Lane. I wasn't wearing the clingy, inappropriate satin dress but a short jacket that skimmed my waist, tight trousers and a tight blouse that was a size too small. I had to admit it was better; I didn't look like I was trying too hard, but neither did I appear soft in the head by wearing a party dress to wander around the streets in the middle of winter.

I'd written a note that was now tucked into my pocket. Although Jane had repeatedly told me this was a fool's errand, I was confident I was doing the right thing.

The woman who'd led me to Fee's house yesterday stared at me as I passed her. There was a wariness in her expression, and she didn't acknowledge me. Her eyes drifted to the bag slung over my shoulder. *Yes*, I sent silently, *I'm leaving*. Even if my hastily cobbled together plan didn't work out, I didn't think I'd return.

That didn't mean I had a plan B but I had to forge my own path, despite what Fee had done for me. Hopefully, it would be a path of pure destruction for anyone who happened to be a

Mage. Yes, I might indeed be an eejit but I was an eejit with a purpose. There were worse things.

I reached the end of the street and turned right, heading back towards the city centre. I was grateful that I didn't have to go as far as George Square because I didn't think I had it in me yet to go past it. I couldn't help wondering what they had done with Isla's body. The thought made me feel nauseous all over again – but it also hardened my resolve.

I stopped when I finally reached the City Chambers. The building felt even more oppressive and intimidating. I gazed at the line of ever-present ravens and they gazed back. You don't scare me, I thought.

I straightened my shoulders and walked up the steps. I didn't have an appointment this time, and I wasn't carrying a heavy load of expensive tartan. I'd simply have to cross my fingers that I could gain admittance and this would work.

Holding my head up high, I raised my fist to knock on the door. This time, the doors didn't open by themselves; I wasn't expected, and ordinary citizens were not permitted to stroll into the City Chambers when they pleased. After all, I thought snarkily, if they did wander in when they wished, anything might happen.

I reached for the heavy iron handle and twisted it. The door didn't budge although I felt the ravens' eyes grow sharper and more malevolent.

I pursed my lips. Fair enough. I turned round, ignoring the wide-eyed stares from passers-by, and searched for another way in. As I skirted round the western side of the building, my shoulders relaxed when I spotted a narrow, nondescript door.

My progress didn't go unnoticed. As soon as my fingers touched the cold metal doorknob, there was a loud caw. I ignored it and rattled the knob. A raven was hovering less than a foot above my head.

I glanced up at the bird and offered it a small nod of greeting. It opened its beak and cawed loudly again. A moment later, another raven joined it. Then another.

Not yet defeated – and not completely intimidated – I continued walking round the building. After the next corner, I located a small unobtrusive entrance that probably led to the staff quarters or back rooms.

As I reached for the door handle, one of the ravens swooped and used its sharp beak to peck at my outstretched hand. It didn't draw blood but its meaning was clear.

I stepped back from the door and held up my hands in apology. It couldn't be a coincidence that this was the only entrance where the birds had intervened. This door had to be unlocked.

I swivelled left, as if I were about to walk away, then snapped back, grabbed the door handle and turned it. The ravens screeched, sounding their terrible alarm.

The birds knew their business, and they understood where I was most vulnerable. The largest one swung round and tried to attack my eyes with its beak. I managed to get inside and slam the door after me in the nick of time. I heard a frustrated shriek, but it didn't matter what the raven thought of me. I was in.

'What the actual fuck do you think you're doing?'

My stomach dropped to the soles of my feet. Shite. I turned, half expecting to be blasted with a wave of incapacitating magic, but it wasn't a Mage glaring at me with shocked, icy rage: it was the stern, pinched-face woman whom I'd met with Belle and Twister. Ailsa, that was what the Mage had called her.

'Thanks to those ravens, the Mages will know you're here. They'll be on their way right now. The best thing you can do – the *only* thing you can do – is run away as fast as you possibly can.'

I met her grey-eyed gaze head on. I wasn't running, and it was important she realised that.

'They will kill you without a second thought. You can't waltz in here like this.'

I shrugged.

Ailsa shook her head and stared at me. 'You're the lass that was with that couple, aren't you? The tartan folks.'

Finally. I bobbed my head and reached for my pocket. Unfortunately, Ailsa seemed to think I was about to bring out a weapon because she snatched up a nearby broom and waved it threateningly at me. 'Try anything,' she said, 'and—'

She didn't get the chance to finish her sentence. Two Mages, both in swirling cloaks and with thunderous faces, appeared from a door to her left. I recognised the first one as the Mage who'd nearly caught me the night I'd gone to St Mags.

I hid my expression and dropped the piece of paper I'd taken out of my pocket before sinking to my knees and lowering my head in a show of complete submission. From this point, I could rely on little more than luck.

'Ailsa,' barked the nearest Mage. 'What's going on?'

The housekeeper didn't say anything. Her face pale as a sheet, she glanced in my direction.

The second Mage raised his hands. '*Kall moy.*'

His magic worked instantly and all the air rushed out of my lungs. My fingers scrabbled at my throat, and I gurgled and choked as I tried to breathe. Shite. *Shite.*

The Mage stalked over and bent down, looking at me curiously. As my vision started to blur around the edges, he picked up my note and unfolded it. My lungs burned as he passed it to his companion. This was what drowning felt like, I thought dimly.

A third Mage appeared. 'What's the problem?'

I didn't look up; I had far bigger problems.

Ailsa finally found her voice. 'I think she made a mistake – or perhaps she's soft in the head. She walked in here, but I don't think she means any harm, my Lord. In fact, she—'

'I know her.'

I fell forward onto my hands and knees, barely clinging onto

consciousness. There was nothing I could do to save myself –
not a damned thing.

'Release her.'

'With all due respect—'

'Release her.'

I gasped. The overwhelming feeling of constriction vanished
from my chest. Spluttering and with tears pricking my eyes, I
looked up. It was Noah, the young Mage who'd flirted with me
back in the tartan shop.

'*To whom it may concern,*' the first Mage read aloud from my
note, '*my name is Mairi Wallace and until recently I worked at a
small tartan shop nearby. Unfortunately, the shop can no longer
sustain my employment and I am searching for an alternative position. I can think of no greater honour than serving the great Mages of
this city. I can cook, clean, sew, and am willing to undertake any work
you so desire.*' He rolled his eyes. 'What do you think we are?
Some kind of employment charity? Unbelievable!'

Noah frowned. 'Enough, James. That's the shop we visited. I
believe we took a consignment of tartan from them?' He raised
his neat eyebrows at Ailsa. 'Is that right?'

'Yes, my Lord.'

'Have they been paid yet?'

She coughed. 'Uh, no sir.'

Noah nodded. 'I see.' He strolled to my side and helped me
up, his hand wrapping round my waist to support me. He
offered a kind smile. 'You lost your job?' he asked.

I sniffed slightly and cast my eyes downwards.

'I'm sorry to hear that,' he said. It sounded like he meant it.

'Hear what?' James said. 'I didn't hear anything.'

'Mairi is mute,' Noah said softly.

The other Mage, whose name I didn't know, suddenly
looked interested. 'Mute, you say? Does she have a tongue?
Open your mouth, girl.'

I did as he ordered and he peered at it. 'She looks fine. It must be a psychological issue. I wonder if...'

Noah interrupted him. 'No, Ross. She's not for you.'

I tried to keep the curiosity from my face. Noah looked to be the youngest of the three by quite some margin, but he appeared to possess the most authority. He looked me up and down and I saw approval in his eyes. Jane had been right to make me wear these clothes; the dress would have overplayed my hand.

'We do need some more help,' he mused. 'We've had a vacancy since old Ma McIntyre passed. And we know that Mairi here will keep her mouth shut. We'll have no fears on that score.'

'What if she's not really mute? What if it's some ploy?' James asked. He was continuing to eye me as if I were a deformed cockroach.

Ailsa piped up. 'Begging your pardon, my Lord, but she was here when the tartan was delivered and she didn't say anything then.'

'Nicholas confirmed it,' Noah added.

I breathed out. And the daemon couldn't lie to the Mages. He'd already told me as much.

'Mute or not,' Ross sneered, 'we can't offer employment to every waif and stray who needs it, especially when they sneak uninvited into our very home.'

'I'm guessing, Ross, that desperate times call for desperate measures,' Noah said. 'This one is clearly no threat to us.' He smiled at me again. 'Did you lose your home along with your job, Mairi?'

I nodded.

'We can't leave her out there on the streets with the Afflicted,' he said. 'Can we, Ross?'

'Of course we can. She's not our concern.'

'Every citizen of this city is our concern,' Noah chided.

James sent him a sharp look laden with meaning that I couldn't understand, then sighed audibly. 'Noah is right – and we do need the extra help. The shelves in my office are an inch thick with dust. As long as nobody discovers that she sneaked in here and we gave her a job, I suppose she can stay. On a trial basis, anyway.'

'There now,' Noah said. 'It's settled.' He turned to Ailsa. 'You'll see that she knows her duties.'

The housekeeper curtsied. 'Yes, my Lord.'

Noah rubbed his palms together. 'Excellent.' He grinned at me. 'Welcome to the family, Mairi.'

'We should check with your uncle before we allow her to stay,' Ross said.

The tone of Noah's voice altered significantly. 'The last thing my uncle wants is to be bothered about the recruitment of a servant girl. Besides, I think it's time the three of us went back to work, don't you?'

A dark cloud crossed Ross's face but he didn't argue. Noah nodded decisively and left, his heels clipping on the stone flags as he walked off with the other two Mages in his wake. I stared after them. I'd done it. I'd actually gone and done it.

Ailsa moved next to me and lowered her head towards mine. 'You've fucked things up for yourself now, lassie,' she muttered. 'If you'd known what was good for you, you'd have stayed out there with the Afflicted.' She shook her head in dismay then jerked her finger at me, indicating that I should follow her.

CHAPTER THIRTEEN

ALTHOUGH I'D CROSSED THE THRESHOLD OF THE CITY CHAMBERS with Belle and Twister, I'd not seen much of the interior of the building before now. I doubted many people had. I trotted after Ailsa, trying to ignore the deep ache that persisted in my chest after the Mage's attack, and paying as much attention as possible to my surroundings. It didn't help that Alisa moved at a tremendous pace, as if I'd interrupted her in the middle of a race and she desperately needed to make up ground.

I craned my neck from side to side as we marched down a narrow corridor, turned left, turned right and then turned left again.

'The Mages are not easy masters,' Ailsa snapped over her shoulder, clearly still enraged at how easily I'd gained admittance. 'And it doesn't matter how busy you are, if you see a Mage coming in the opposite direction you move to the side and wait for them to pass. They always have right of way, no matter how high or low ranked they are.'

I thought of the begrudging deference that the other Mages had shown Noah. Other than the Ascendant, I hadn't been aware that there were Mage rankings. It didn't matter to me; as far as I was concerned, they were all culpable.

Ailsa turned a corner and paused at the foot of a curving staircase. 'Most of the time, you will use these back passages and stairways. The Mages don't enjoy having the likes of us underfoot, and it's better to keep out of their sight wherever possible. Unless your work takes to you to a particular room or area where it cannot be avoided, you should stay out of their way.'

She glanced at me. 'They're capricious,' she said, 'and if any of them take against you...' She shook her head. 'It won't matter that the Ascendant's nephew has taken a shine to you if you get on the wrong side of one of the others.'

A chill shudder rippled through my body. Ah, so that was why Noah was afforded such respect, despite his youth: he was directly related to the Ascendant. Nepotism in all its corrupt glory – even here.

Ailsa continued to talk as she ascended the stairs. I scampered after her, still struggling to keep up. 'You'll start work at five in the morning. Most of the Mages come for breakfast between nine and eleven, so that should give you enough time to clean everything down before they appear. While the Mages are taking their meals, whether breakfast, lunch or supper, you will clean and tidy their rooms and offices. Once they have finished eating, you will clear away the dining room. You will also be expected to run errands as requested, although it is unlikely anyone will ask you to do anything important until you have gained their trust.' She sniffed. 'And that might never happen.'

Neither should it. The Mages should never trust me because I was here to destroy them all.

'Most of the Mages have individual offices on the first floor, and private quarters on the second and third floors. You will be responsible for all of the east wing. Your own quarters will be located there.'

Okay – but which wing belonged to the Ascendant? Could he be in the east wing? Could I really be that lucky? A sudden vision of my fingernails clawing out his eyes before I stabbed him in the heart over and over and over again flashed into my mind.

'The east-wing Mages,' Ailsa said, all-but answering my unspoken question, 'are the newest and lowest ranked. You might think that would make them easier to deal with, but often the opposite is true.' Her voice took on a grim edge. 'They feel they have more to prove.'

Shite. I wouldn't be cleaning up after the Ascendant then. But that was only a minor setback; now I was here, I could bide my time and act only when I could be certain of success. I hadn't been able to muster any patience before, but I could find some now. If I were smart, I'd have the opportunity to avenge Isla properly and learn what magic I could from the Mages in the process. *If* I was smart, I repeated sternly to myself.

'The best thing you can do,' Ailsa continued as she reached the first-floor landing, 'is to make sure that you always—' She suddenly stopped talking.

I frowned and hurried up to join her on the top step. I realised instantly why she had gone quiet. Oh.

The landing was less like a small functional area for marking out the space between flights of stairs and more like a cavern filled with light and art and possibilities. And not only did it hold vast paintings, several sculptures, two chaise longues and a towering window, it also contained a shirtless daemon.

Nicholas was suspended in mid-air, but not in the wobbly, spinning way that I had been in Fee's house. He was hanging in the air like an angel might. His eyes were closed and his arms were outstretched. Tiny blue flames danced along his bare arms.

I stared at his sculpted body. Anatomically, it was all but identical to that of a human's – but no human male I'd ever seen possessed such unblemished skin and such well-defined muscles. Every bare inch of him glistened. At first, I thought it was sweat from the effort of maintaining his position, then I realised that it was his skin. It possessed a silver sheen and glimmered in sharp contrast to the dull metal of the cuffs around his wrists and neck.

Unlike his face, his torso was unmarked by tattoos, although I glimpsed two curling black marks reaching over both his shoulder blades, suggesting that there were intricate tattoos on his back. My eyes travelled downwards and noted the inky dark hair that disappeared beneath the waist of his loose-fitting breeches.

He'd look good in a kilt, I thought. Very good. Then I shivered and glanced up to see that he'd opened his eyes and was watching me.

'Begging your pardon, sir,' Ailsa muttered. She dropped into a shallow curtsey and nudged me to do the same. I managed a tiny dip before she grabbed my elbow and hauled me to the left.

We didn't get very far. Nicholas lowered himself to the ground. With what looked like lazy ease, but had to be incredible speed, he planted himself in front of us and barred our way. He stared at me. 'What are you doing here?'

I swallowed. My mouth felt painfully dry.

Nicholas turned to Ailsa. 'Well?' he demanded.

'She's the new servant. She's going to take Ma McIntyre's place.'

A dangerous glint lit his green eyes. 'I see.' He folded his arms. 'It's about time somebody replaced her – she's been gone for two months.'

'Yes, sir.' Ailsa's lips tightened. 'We need to move on. I have to give her a tour of the east wing and settle her in before I get back to my duties.'

Nicholas looked amused as he stepped back to give us space. 'Far be it for me to get in the way of your good work, Ailsa.'

She gave him a curt nod. 'Thank you, sir.' Gripping my

elbow even tighter than before, she dragged me away. I heard Nicholas's soft laugh as we headed down the corridor away from him.

'If you listen to nothing else I say,' Ailsa muttered, 'then listen to this. Stay away from him. He's very, very bad news.'

AILSA SWEPT me around the remainder of the east wing. There was a lot to take in, and I wasn't convinced that I'd remember any of it – it was likely that I'd get lost every time I left my bedchamber on the very top floor.

Although my room was sparse, it was no worse than I'd been used to at Belle and Twister's. There was a narrow bed with a reasonably comfortable mattress, and a washbasin. All in all, it was more than I could have hoped for.

Ailsa thrust a pile of clean uniforms into my arms and told me sharply to get changed into something more appropriate. She gave a knowing sniff at the tight clothes I'd borrowed from Jane, then left me alone.

I sat on the edge of the bed and rubbed my eyes. Everything had happened so quickly; although it was exactly what I'd hoped and planned for, it still seemed incredible that I'd made it here. If it hadn't been for Noah, I might not have done.

I undid the buttons on my blouse and gazed down at my chest. There wasn't a mark or blemish on my skin, but I could still feel the pain in my lungs from what the Mage, Ross, had done to me. All I could manage was a bit of wobbly levitation. The Gowk had been correct on one count at least: I had a lot to learn before I could take on the Mages, let alone kill the Ascendant. But I was in the right place to do it.

I thought about Ross's words before his magic had attacked me. *Kall moy.* I mouthed them, savouring their feel, then reached into my small bag and took out my notebook and pen. I scratched the words down, along with their meaning – at least as I understood it – and searched for somewhere to hide the book. Eventually I prised up a floorboard and wedged it underneath. That would have to do. It wouldn't stand up to close examination, but it would pass any cursory checks.

I changed into the servants' uniform of shapeless grey breeches and a cream shirt. The material was a bit scratchy but it was serviceable. I left the room once I'd done what I could to make myself presentable, hoping to find my way back downstairs to the dining room where Ailsa had told me to meet her.

What I wasn't expecting was a man lounging against the wall outside and closely examining a cut on his hand. He looked to be about my age, with a messy mop of ginger hair and the faint shadow of a beard across his jaw. From his clothes he was a servant like me, although I could only guess what his duties might entail.

He snapped to attention when he saw me, then offered an easy grin. 'Hey. Mairi, right? Ailsa told me to wait for you. She thought you might not find your way back to the ground floor, so I told her I'd show you. It takes a while to learn your way around this place, and it's not like you'll be able to ask anyone for directions. Ailsa said you don't talk. What's that like? I'm not sure I could manage to go without speaking. I'm always getting into trouble for yapping too much. Don't let a Mage called Ross go near you – he'll find out what makes your tongue quiet and force the rest of us be like that, too. That one likes experimentation, and not usually in a good way.'

I thought about the way Noah had spoken to Ross after he'd examined my mouth and shuddered. Oh. Then I realised that the ginger-haired man was still talking. In fact, he hadn't stopped.

'It won't take you long to learn which Mages to avoid,' he said. 'Some of them are alright and some of them are bastards.' He shrugged with casual ambivalence. 'It's the way of the world.'

I stared at him. I hadn't thought it was possible to speak quite so much without pausing for breath.

He stared back at me, then laughed. 'I'm sorry! I didn't tell you my name. I'm Billy.' He shoved his hand out and I shook it warily. 'Billy the Blawhard, that's what my ma used to call me.' He winked and I felt the corners of my mouth tug upwards in an involuntary smile. 'There!' he chortled, 'I knew you had it in you! It's really good to meet you, Mairi. Really good.'

I nodded to indicate that I felt the same. Billy beamed, clearly understanding me. I pointed at the wound on his hand and raised an eyebrow.

'Cut myself on a pair of shears when I was pruning some of the plants in the garden.'

I was startled. There was a garden?

'It's fine,' he dismissed. 'It's only a wee cut. It's a bit sore, but it'll heal in no time.'

I wasn't so sure about that – it looked to me like it was getting infected – but there wasn't much I could do about it right now. Billy was already striding ahead, indicating that I should follow. With little choice, I did as he wanted. I guessed my settling-in period was already over and it was time to get to work.

CHAPTER FOURTEEN

—

THE NEXT FEW HOURS WERE A FRENETIC WHIRLWIND OF ACTIVITY. We had to prep the grand dining room for dinner by setting elaborate table placings before ensuring that every corner was free of dust and smears. Once that was done, we brought platters and tureens of steaming food up from the kitchen.

I goggled at the food on offer. There were piles of green vegetables, the likes of which I'd never seen before and would never have believed would grow at this time of year. Elegant tureens were filled with golden roasted potatoes dotted with gem-like salt flakes. There were jugs of glossy gravy and pots of glistening apple sauce and – the *pièce de résistance* – three spit-roasted suckling pigs.

I could count on one hand the number of times I'd eaten real pork, so it was hard to tear my eyes away from the meat as we placed it in the centre of the long dining table. I reckoned there was more than enough to serve three times as many Mages. I was salivating, even though I cursed myself repeatedly for being affected so deeply by something as simple as food.

'You'll get used to it,' one of the other female servants told me with a knowing glance. 'The Mages always eat well. Usually, we're allowed to have the leftovers. One of the perks of the job.'

I supposed the magical bastards had to do something to ensure the loyalty of their servants, but I wouldn't allow a single beat of my heart to be swayed by something as pathetic as scraps from the Mages' dining table. Even so, I wished that I didn't feel like drooling.

Ailsa, who had barely taken her eyes from me, frowned when she saw the girl chatting. She clapped her hands. 'Get a move on, the lot of you! Where's the wine? It should be on the table by now!'

We scurried to do her bidding. Only when she was completely satisfied with the table did she nod at one of the older servants. He bowed and strode towards the gong beside the door. I watched, fascinated, as he picked up a wooden stick and hit the circular piece of metal three times. The sound reverberated around the room, then the dining-room doors opened and the Mages began to pour in.

Whether I'd planned for this or not, I felt rigid with terror at the thought of being in the same room as so many Mages. There was nowhere to hide.

I shrank against the wall in a vain attempt to make myself invisible, but Ailsa spotted me and stalked over. 'You do remember what I told you about your duties? When the Mages are eating, you're to clean their rooms. Most of them have already been done today by the rest of us, but it won't do any harm for you to check them over and understand the standards we expect. Work your way through the study rooms on the first floor. You'll find all you need in the cupboard by the stairs. And don't touch anything or disturb any piles of paper or books – just take out the rubbish, remove any plates or cups, wipe down any spills and sweep the floor. Got that?'

I nodded shakily.

She gave me a little nudge. 'Well, go on then.'

I turned and scuttled out of the room as fast as my legs would carry me. It didn't take long to find the cleaning cupboard and haul out what I needed. Looking at the long corridor and the many doors that stretched in front of me, I couldn't imagine how I could clean all those rooms during the space of a single meal – especially as this was also the perfect opportunity to have a good snoop around and see what secrets I could unearth. There was no one to complain to, however, so I squared my shoulders. I had no time to waste.

I strode into the first room, tripping over my feet in my haste. The small space was exactly what I'd been expecting. There were piles of books everywhere – virtually a king's ransom of knowledge – and a heavy oak desk covered with papers. Shelves lined the walls laden with items ranging from glass bottles and dried-out branches to a staring, empty-eyed human skull.

I stared at the skull, wondering which poor soul it had once belonged to. Then I shook myself. Move, Mairi. This wasn't a sightseeing trip; I had work to do.

I emptied the wastepaper basket of its collection of snotty tissues and picked up the balled-up paper from the floor. Glancing over my shoulder to check the hallway behind me was clear, I moved to the desk with my dusting cloth.

The largest pile of papers was covered with long lists of ingredients, several of which I recognised from my apothecary studies. Belladonna, water hemlock, nightshade – in the right quantities they were all poisons. A trickle of fear edged down my spine, and I leaned in closer to try and decipher the scribbles next to each plant. Whichever Mage used this study had worse handwriting than Twister.

As I squinted, something outside flitted against the window and I drew back abruptly. Shite. There was a raven out there, perched on the windowsill and glaring at me through the glass. I swallowed hard and pretended to dust the papers whilst avoiding its hard, beady eyes. What did a damned bird know about cleaning? I was merely doing what I'd been told.

I headed for the next room. It was virtually identical in terms of layout, but the desk was clear except for several stained cups. I scooped them all up and placed them outside the door to take back to the kitchen, then popped my head back inside. A book on one of the shelves had caught my eye, something with gilt lettering about *Magicks for the Modern Mage* that I wanted to skim through.

I wasn't going to get the chance today. The raven had hopped to the window of this room and was continuing to watch me. I ignored the tightening in my belly. It was only my first day; it made sense that I would be watched. The best thing I could do was to act normally and cross my fingers that I'd earn more freedom to look around soon. I needed to play the long game.

I rushed through the next rooms, picking up rubbish, sweeping floors and doing what I could to clear the few empty shelves and desks of any lingering dust. The raven followed me from window to window and, after a while, I managed to forget almost completely that it was there. Almost.

Whilst I didn't waste time or raise any further feathered suspicions by sneaking a look at anything I wasn't supposed to see, I did file away several mental notes. I tried to learn what I could about the occupant of each study. The Mage in the fifth study was a complete slob; the eighth one didn't appear to be doing any work beyond completing crosswords; the ninth had vials of what looked like blood neatly arrayed on his desk.

I couldn't draw any conclusions from what I saw – not yet – and I didn't learn anything that was immediately useful, but I was building up a picture of what the Mages were up to and how they operated. It was fuzzy and indistinct but there was vital information to be found here if I was given enough time to search for it. I felt the first stirrings of hope.

There was a closed door at the far end of the hallway. I was into a rhythm now and didn't think anything of it as I twisted the doorknob and marched inside with my broom.

It was darker than the other rooms and it took my eyes some time to adjust to the dim light. A heavy, oppressive smell tickled my nostrils and I was certain I detected the faint scent of something rotting. I noted the thick, heavy curtains against one wall and strode towards them; some light would definitely help.

I was reaching for them, ready to yank them apart, when a disgruntled voice rumbled from the far corner, 'Who the fuck are you, and what in the name of all that is holy do you think you're doing?'

I froze. There was a creak from behind me and then footsteps approached. I swallowed hard and turned.

Thanks to the lack of light, at first it was hard to make out the features of the man standing in front of me. What hit me was the rancid odour of his skin. I blinked and focused until I could see a pair of narrowed eyes gazing at me furiously from beneath bushy, unkempt eyebrows. I hadn't thought that eyebrows could be unkempt, but there was no other word to describe the tangle of hair that confronted me.

My gaze drifted down and registered a straggly beard and some sort of stained dressing gown. He looked more like one of the Afflicted than a Mage. Shite. Maybe he *was* Afflicted. Maybe...

The man folded his arms across his chest and glared. 'I asked you a question.' He loomed towards me. 'Be sure to taste your words before you spit them out, mind. Your very life depends on it.'

All I could do was stare at him. He started to tap his foot impatiently. When I still didn't speak, he sighed loudly and slowly unfolded his arms with such a deliberate movement that I was sure he was about to whack me into oblivion for my lack of deference. Then he spun away to the door and wrestled it open.

'Ailsa!' he bellowed down the hallway. The walls vibrated with the power of his voice. He muttered to himself. *'Inzel ya,'* then yelled again, 'Ailsa!'

I felt the magic in his shouted summons. The air throbbed with it. I licked my lips; I had no idea what was going to happen...

Ailsa appeared abruptly from the staircase at the far end of the hallway. 'My Lord!' she gasped. She picked up her skirts and ran towards us. 'My apologies!'

'Who is this ... creature?' the Mage enquired icily.

'This is Mairi, sir,' she said. 'She's new. She's here to clean your room and—'

'I don't need my room cleaned!' he shouted, spittle flying from his lips. 'If I needed my room cleaned, I would tell you. We have been through this time and time again. She didn't even knock! And she's clearly either soft in the heid, or some kind of ned who's here to cause trouble, because when I spoke to her she didn't say a word. All she did was stare at me like *I* was the intruder.' He thumped his chest. 'Me!' He raised his voice again. 'This is my room, Ailsa! Mine!'

Ailsa drew in a deep breath before pulling out a small, folded handkerchief and dabbing at her face to remove the saliva that the Mage had generously bestowed on her.

I had no idea what to do so I stayed where I was, hoping that Ailsa would offer an explanation and extricate me.

'For pity's sake!' she snapped.

I was so startled by her tone that I took an involuntary step backwards. Every other time Ailsa had spoken to the Mages her attitude had been completely subservient, but she was talking to this man in the same way she spoke to me.

'I've been ordered to the Ascendant's rooms, and your magical summons will make me late.'

The scruffy Mage waved a hand airily. 'Ascendant shmascendent.'

My mouth dropped open.

'I knew it was too much to hope that you were hurrying down that corridor just for me,' he continued, He waggled a bony finger in her face. 'I have considerable magic, you know. I could turn you into a frog.'

'Why, Sir Angus?' Ailsa enquired. 'Because I think that you're a slovenly idiot who should stop living in such grubby squalor? Because I dared to arrange for your study to be cleaned?'

My gaze travelled from Angus the Mage to Ailsa and back again. I didn't know what to think or how to act. Admittedly, my mental reference book, *How to Deal With Angry Mages Who Execute People They Don't Like*, was not brimming with useful information, but talking back to a Mage like he was little more than an unruly teenager was definitely not in there.

'Who is she? Where has she come from? Why have I never seen her before?'

Ailsa heaved a tremendous sigh. 'The Ascendant,' she began, 'is—' Angus cleared his throat deliberately and she sighed again. 'Her name is Mairi. Lord Noah—'

There was a snort.

Ailsa gave him a pointed look. 'Lord Noah offered her a position here.'

There was another snort. 'He wants to get into her knickers.'

I started. Ailsa simply shrugged. 'You haven't seen her before because this is her first day.' She tilted her head to one side. 'There. I've answered all your questions. Now I must go.'

'She is not to clean my rooms. Not my bedroom. Not my bathroom. And certainly not my study.'

'Aye.' Alisa nodded, then she peered round Angus to glance at me. 'Mairi, you are to clean all of Sir Angus's rooms.' She paused. 'Every day.'

The Mage roared. 'No! She will not.'

'Wheesht,' Ailsa said. She was already walking away. 'You'll like her. She's mute.'

'I wish you were mute!' he yelled after her.

Ailsa kept walking.

Angus turned and looked at me. 'Do you have a tongue?' he demanded. 'A physical one?'

I managed a half nod.

'Show me.'

I opened my mouth. He glanced at it for a moment and sniffed. 'You're not mute.' The corners of his lips twitched as if he were about to grin. 'Not naturally, anyway.' He reached past me, unhooked a black robe from the back of the study door and shrugged it on. 'Don't touch any of my papers. Or my books. Or my samples. Got that?'

I nodded quickly.

'Good.' He straightened his back and marched down the corridor towards the staircase. 'Fuckety-bye, darling.'

I watched him until he disappeared from sight, then I picked up my jaw off the floor and re-entered Mage Angus's study so I could clean it before the magicked loon decided to return.

CHAPTER FIFTEEN

I WAS EXHAUSTED BY THE TIME I WAS DONE. THE RAVEN THAT HAD been following me had vanished after I entered Angus's room, but I was too tired to contemplate rummaging around for magic secrets and too wary of getting caught, especially since several of the Mages had begun to trail back to their study rooms. Instead, I scooped up the rubbish I'd collected and went back downstairs.

Fortunately, I spotted Billy. He offered me an easy smile and nodded in understanding when I gestured helplessly down at the bags in my arms. He showed me where to leave them, then led me towards the kitchen to grab a plate of the Mages' leftovers.

As I shovelled the food into my mouth, I was aware that this was probably the best meal I'd eaten in years. I gnawed the meat off a pork rib and declined a second helping, telling myself that I must describe the food to Isla next time I saw her. Then I abruptly remembered that I wouldn't see her ever again, and the bone dropped to my plate with a clatter.

Less than a day in, and I was already letting myself be seduced by the trappings of my supposedly privileged position.

My insides turned ice cold and I had to fight again to suppress rising nausea.

'You alright, there?' Billy asked, concerned. 'You look all peely-wally.'

I tried to smile to indicate that I was fine, but I couldn't quite meet his eyes. He offered me a sympathetic pat on the shoulder. 'It's a lot to take in,' he said. 'I've been here almost two years, and I still feel it. I came here from a wee village near the mountains where life couldn't be more different.'

Glad of the distraction, I turned to him and gestured for him to continue. I'd not met many folk from out of the city before; urban migration was generally frowned upon unless there was a specific need to fill within the cities. But I knew it was just as dangerous, if not more so, to live in the countryside; the Afflicted didn't confine themselves to densely populated areas.

'I worked on a farm,' he told me. 'I was a right teuchter.' He grinned, using the lowland word to describe a rural highlander. 'I like working alongside the animals, but I also have an affinity with crops.' He held up his hands and wiggled his fingers. 'Green-fingered, see? These babies are why I got the job here tending the Mages' garden.'

I couldn't see any green, but I could definitely see the inflamed red around the wound on his right hand. It looked worse than it had done a few hours ago. I pointed at it and frowned.

Billy brushed away my concern. 'Dinna fash yerself. It's only a wee cut.'

A wee cut that could lead to sepsis in a heartbeat. I frowned harder but this time he didn't notice. 'Come on,' he said. 'I'll show you back to your room if you like. Unless you think you can find it yourself?'

Fat chance of that. I nodded gratefully and allowed him to lead me away from the warm kitchen. He chattered non-stop, pointing out various quirks of the building and explaining where all the important rooms were.

I was surprised to find myself grateful for his company. It wasn't exactly a two-way street, and I doubted he gained much from my silent presence, but he helped me. While I certainly didn't feel at home, he did encourage me to relax slightly.

I vowed not to act too friendly in his presence. Sooner or later, whether I was successful or not, my true motives for being here would be discovered. It would be better for the likes of Billy if he were not associated with me more than he needed to be.

Either way, I'd have to do something about the cut on his hand. It didn't appear that anyone else would help him – and it would give me something else to focus on beyond my unslaked desire for fiery revenge.

I WAS DISORIENTATED when I woke up as the first few foggy moments between sleeping and waking clouded my mind. When I remembered where I was, and what I was doing, I sat bolt upright. I was here. In the City Chambers. I'd made it into the lion's den.

I slipped out from underneath the covers, shivering as the cool air hit my skin. It was pitch dark and I didn't possess a candle. Somewhere, I thought, there were magical words that would illuminate the darkest corners but, even if I knew them, thinking such words and wielding such obvious magic was not a good idea. My path to success lay in keeping my infantile abilities to myself. Any whisper that I possessed the skill to use magic and I'd end up on the same scaffold as Isla. I'd got this far; I wasn't going to slip up on something as silly as creating a night-light.

Wrapping my arms round myself, I padded over to the

narrow window and peered out. It was a cloudless night and the moon was high in the sky. I nibbled my bottom lip. Although I'd slept like the dead, the unfamiliar bed and surroundings had made me wake early. It was likely only about three in the morning, and Ailsa had told me that my duties didn't begin until closer to five. That allowed me more than enough time to find what I needed – and if I were to come across any Mages at this hour, I had a genuine excuse. I didn't know whether it would cover me or not, but I couldn't simply lie back and doze until it was time to get up.

Billy had kindly provided me with a greying flannel, a cheap toothbrush and toothpaste. I grabbed them and headed to the tiny shared bathroom down the corridor. I wet the cloth and washed my body as best as I could before brushing my teeth and putting on my uniform, then I slipped out to the stairs and tried to get my bearings. I had to find the garden; vast building or not, there were only so many places it could be.

The nooks and crannies of the servants' quarters were dark and the corridors were unlit, but by the time I reached the first floor there was more evidence of life. A few large candles were still burning in their sconces and I could hear the faint murmur of voices and the clink of china. Some of the kitchen staff were already up and preparing for the day ahead by baking bread and the like. Despite my big meal the previous night, my stomach gurgled. I glared down at it as if a dirty look could quell my physical urges.

I knew the garden wasn't by the kitchens because I'd have noticed it last night. The main entrance was to my right, and the kitchens and the back entrance through which I'd inveigled my way in yesterday were beyond there. It made sense that the gardens were somewhere to my left.

I walked quietly down to the ground floor and located the first likely looking door then crossed my fingers. A little superstition wouldn't hurt.

The hallway I found myself in was wide, with rich ornate wallpaper and numerous paintings, most of which appeared to be of stern Mages from times gone by. I avoided their fixed eyes and kept moving. There was no point trying any of the doors to my right – I already knew they faced the street. The garden could only lie in the opposite direction.

I followed the hallway, checking a few doors. None of them were locked. When I peered into each one and saw the books and papers and shadowy bottles, I had to batten down the urge to investigate further. I made a mental note of the rooms and what they contained, but I didn't allow myself to get distracted. Not this night. They would wait for another time.

My footsteps echoed down the hallway, sounding painfully loud. I resisted the temptation to tiptoe; if someone did notice me, it would be better if I didn't appear to be skulking around. Obviously, I wouldn't be able to talk my way out of my situation if I were caught; the best I could hope for was that a confident façade would make anyone I bumped into think I was supposed to be there. With that thought in mind, I ploughed ahead.

I turned round another corner and felt an odd waft of cool air, followed by a light, earthy scent. I pulled back my shoulders: the garden. It had to be – nothing else in this godforsaken place could possibly smell that natural. I moved more quickly, ignoring the increased sound my feet made. It was up ahead, I was sure of it.

I marched faster, spinning first left and then right, and that was when I saw it.

I had spent a lot of my free time over the years getting to know the city parks. I knew what plants could be found where at any particular time of year, and I'd occasionally managed to cultivate a few of my own in particular spots where they wouldn't be disturbed. I wasn't green fingered in the way that Billy was, and my attempts were often hit and miss, but I did my best and I'd had some success.

A few times, I'd managed to gain entrance to some richer folks' gardens and pilfer the odd herb from a greenhouse. I'd always believed that anyone who could boast of a glass house in which they grew plants without fear of the elements was beyond lucky. That was before I saw the Mages' garden. I'd had no idea such abundance was possible. It was like nothing I could ever have imagined.

The garden wasn't outside at the rear of the building as I'd expected. It was inside, in a large space that suggested several rooms had been knocked together to create it. The walls were made of glass, and there was a warm, glowing light coming from the far side. I gaped, barely able to believe my eyes. Everywhere I looked there were plants – tall ones, stocky ones, some which were flowering and some which displayed such varying shades of verdant green that they took my breath away.

I could hear a quiet hum from beyond the glass. At first, I couldn't work out what it was then, from the corner of my eye, I saw something move. I realised that humming had to be from insects. Hundreds, maybe thousands, of insects.

'It's quite something, isn't it?'

I jumped at least three feet in the air. Noah, who had seemingly appeared out of nowhere, was standing by my shoulder. He wasn't gazing at the glass-contained garden. He was gazing at me. Without thinking, I took a step backwards and moved away from him.

He smiled softly. 'It's alright, Mairi. You don't have to be afraid of me.'

That was easy for him to say. I blinked and did my best to appear both completely innocent and utterly terrified. The latter certainly wasn't hard to achieve.

'Let me guess,' he said in the same gentle tone. 'You couldn't sleep. Right?'

I nodded slowly.

'I'm not surprised. All this must be a world away from what

you're used to. It's bound to be disturbing, at least to begin with, but you'll get accustomed to the chambers and our silly Mages' ways before too long.' His eyes turned serious. 'And you don't have to be afraid of anything. I'll look after you.' His hand reached for mine, his warm fingers entwining with my own. 'Would you like to enter the garden?'

Daft question.

Noah chuckled at my expression. 'Of course you would.' He tugged my hand. 'Come on. I'll show you round.'

He led me along the glass wall and paused at the far end, then he muttered something under his breath, a few magic words that I strained to hear but, vexingly, didn't catch. A moment later, the glass panel in front of us swung open.

'The garden is forbidden to anyone who is not a Mage or who does not have express permission to enter it from one of the Mages,' Noah told me. 'You would not be able to enter it without me.'

I wouldn't be able to enter it? Or I *shouldn't* enter it? It was more than a semantic difference, and the answer could be important.

Noah understood more of my thoughts than I'd given him credit for. 'Don't try,' he warned. 'You'll be found out. Worse than that, your entrance could cause serious problems. This is a very delicate ecosystem. There's a lot of magic in play here, creating the balance needed to sustain all sorts of life. We need this garden for a lot of the magic we use – the plants help with research and they generate ideas. More importantly, they provide us with the tools we need to protect the city. Maybe one day one of the plants will give us what we need to cure the Afflicted. Some of these specimens are unbelievably rare, and we can't afford to lose any of them. One wrong step, or one wrong touch from someone who doesn't know what they're doing, and goodness knows what might happen.' His fingers tightened round mine.

I did the only thing I could and met his gaze head on, my eyes as sombre as his. He loosened his grip, although he still didn't release me. Suddenly he flashed me a grin. 'Good lass,' he said approvingly. 'Come on. If you're with me and you don't touch anything unless I say so, you'll be fine.'

We stepped across the threshold. The difference in the air was immediate: the atmosphere beyond the glass walls was cold and dry, but inside the heat and humidity were startling.

It wasn't only the air that stunned me. The smell was almost overwhelming. A myriad of scents filled the area, heady and exhilarating and unfamiliar all at the same time. I inhaled deeply.

Then I paused. There was something lingering beyond the green smell of the plants, something bitter and strange. I frowned as I tried to grasp it and hang onto it but, before I could, Noah tugged my hand again and led me down a narrow, slabbed path deeper into the gigantic glass house.

A huge red butterfly flapped across the path, its enormous crimson wings stirring the air around us. It was followed by a large bee striped more brightly than any that I'd ever seen outside during the summer months.

'Watch out for those,' Noah warned darkly. 'Their stings are venomous. The last gardener, the one before Billy, nearly died after he was stung. If one of those attacks you, you'll feel like you've been skelped by an army.'

I wasn't surprised; that was no ordinary bee and that had been no ordinary butterfly. No wonder the entire garden looked so impressive: every corner and every leaf hummed with magic. I could feel the power rippling across my skin even when I was standing still.

Noah knelt and pointed to an aloe plant, its thick succulent leaves curling upwards as if attempting to draw more magic from the air. 'Aloe vera,' he told me. 'It's excellent for all sorts of skin care, and can be used as a treatment for stomach ulcers.'

What? I'd never heard that before. I flicked Noah a look from under my eyelashes. Did he know more about the plant's properties than I did, or was he merely making up stories?

'And this,' he murmured, gesturing towards what was unmistakably nightshade, 'is monkshood. It's incredibly poisonous so I wouldn't touch it, if I were you.'

I suppressed a smile. Yes, it was poisonous, but no, it wasn't monkshood. I relaxed slightly. For some reason, it was comforting to know that a highly placed Mage such as Noah could make basic errors with such absolute confidence. If he made mistakes so could the other Mages. And where there were mistakes, there was opportunity.

He led me deeper into the garden, continuing to point out plants and herbs, some of which he got right and some of which were clearly wrong. I was pretty certain that he invented names on at least a few occasions. He was trying to impress me and, strangely, I liked him the more for it. It made him seem more human. Perhaps, I thought grudgingly, not all Mages were bad – though I was growing less sure about the garden.

I didn't know whether it was the humidity or the magic, but the longer we spent inside the glass house the more uncomfortable I felt. My skin was itching and there was an unpleasant prickle between my shoulder blades. The acrid scent I'd noticed earlier was growing stronger and beginning to make me feel slightly nauseous and faint.

I'd spotted several plants that I wanted to take samples from to help Billy but, when Noah's back was turned and I had the opportunity to nab a few leaves, something in me resisted. The garden was beautiful, beyond beautiful, and the very fact of its existence was a marvel. Yet something about it felt wrong. It was as if there were a dark, insidious rot lurking somewhere inside that I'd yet to see.

I was almost glad when there was a sudden, sharp knock on

the glass exterior and a shadowed figure on the other side beckoned us.

Noah cursed under his breath. 'Duty calls,' he muttered. 'Even at this hour.' He straightened his back, his expression smoothing from warm and friendly to a business-like mask. 'Come on. We'd better go.'

There wasn't one person waiting for us beyond the garden but two. Despite the glower I received from the cloaked Mage, and the glance of curiosity that Nicholas shot me, the relief I felt at leaving the oppressive glass house was profound. It was only when Noah closed the panel and shut off the garden that I realised how the atmosphere inside had been clawing at me. Being away from it was like tasting freedom for the first time.

'The Ascendant is waiting for your report,' the Mage said to Noah.

There was a faint hint of disapproval in his tone and I wondered if Noah would react to it. Instead, he simply adjusted his cuffs and smiled easily. 'I'm on my way there now.'

The Mage sniffed. 'Good.'

Noah looked at me. 'It was a pleasure spending time with you, Mairi. I hope to do it again soon.'

It occurred to me belatedly that he was still holding my hand. When he finally released it and moved away to do his uncle's bidding, I felt a strange sense of loss. 'Perhaps I'll see you later,' he said. He turned to Nicholas. 'Show her back to her room,' he ordered.

The daemon bowed. 'Of course, my Lord. Although I suspect that she's wanted in the kitchens by now.'

'Well, take her to the kitchens then!' Noah snapped. He rolled his eyes as if Nicholas were being deliberately obtuse, then stalked off with the other Mage on his heels.

Nicholas pulled himself up straight and watched Noah's departure with a mocking smile. He offered me his arm and smiled even more broadly when I recoiled. 'What?' he asked.

'You don't find my prospects as attractive as those of the Ascendant's nephew? You ought to be careful, little Mairi. All that glisters is not gold.' He paused, his tone growing silky and dangerous. 'I can imagine why you are wandering around the City Chambers at this hour, but I don't suppose good Noah deigned to tell you what *his* reasons were.'

No, he hadn't – but then I hadn't asked. I rubbed my arms and started to walk away. I still didn't have what I needed for Billy, and I was keen to get away from the garden. I could find the kitchens on my own.

'You felt it, didn't you?' Nicholas called after me. 'You felt the rotting core at the heart of that place.'

I halted.

'What you sensed,' he said, so quietly I wasn't sure he'd spoken, 'was death. Despite its appearance, the Mages' garden is not a place to be enjoyed. It's a place to be feared.'

There was a nasty ring of truth to his words. I shuddered and continued walking. As Nicholas caught up with me, I moved faster. 'I have to escort you to the kitchens,' he said.

I could find them on my own. All I had to do was follow my nose.

'Neither of us have a choice in the matter,' he added cheerfully. He clinked his wrists together and held up the metallic cuffs. 'I've been given a direct order. I cannot physically refuse.' He reached for me then dropped his hand as he seemed to think better of it. 'I belong to them, but I am not them.' His eyes flashed. 'But that doesn't mean that you can trust me, little Mairi.'

I stared at him, but he didn't say another word.

CHAPTER SIXTEEN

IN THE END, I FOUND ENOUGH IN THE KITCHEN SUPPLIES TO SERVE my needs. The resulting concoction wouldn't be perfect, but it was certainly better than nothing.

The head cook eyed me curiously when I pilfered a few cloves of garlic, and he raised an eyebrow when I took a pinch of ground turmeric from the spices set aside for later that day, but he didn't say anything.

I picked up a small ceramic bowl and a fork and took them to the servants' table at the back of the room. While I chewed on a slice of bread, I mashed up the garlic vigorously to encourage the natural oils to seep forth, then I mixed it with the turmeric, humming as I did so.

Two women, whom I recognised from last night's dinner service as other general servants, came and sat beside me. They watched my actions with a frown. 'Whit ye doing?' the older, blonde one asked.

I shrugged.

'That's the lass that doesnae speak,' her companion said. She smiled at me. 'I'm Trish. That's Lottie.' She leaned in towards me and lowered her voice. 'The Gowk wants to speak to you. He'll be at the bandstand in Kelvingrove Park from two till four this afternoon. You'll have a break, so you can get out and see him.' Then she pulled back abruptly.

I froze. What the actual fuck?

Lottie had clearly heard the exchange but didn't comment on it. Instead, she lifted up her cup of weak tea and slurped it noisily. I looked at the pair of them, my mouth dry. How did they know? *What* did they know?

Neither of them elaborated. Instead, they launched into a detailed and embarrassingly loud discussion about whether Ailsa was stepping out with some guy called Keith McBright who worked in a posh hotel nearby. I couldn't imagine that Ailsa had time for romance, and it wasn't any of my business even if she did.

No matter how much I pleaded silently for Trish and Lottie to say more about the Gowk, neither of them did. They ate quickly and departed, leaving me bereft of answers or explanations and slightly shaky as a result.

I finished the dregs of my weak tea and saw Billy wander in. He looked paler than yesterday and he was stifling a yawn. The heavy bags under his eyes indicated that he hadn't slept well.

I flattened my mouth into a grim line and put Trish, Lottie and the Gowk out of my mind. It was as well that I'd made the poultice because Billy definitely needed it. I grabbed my little bowl, sprang up and marched over to him.

'Morning, Mairi.' He smiled at me. 'How did you sleep? First night and all that? You look well rested.'

That was more than I could say for him. I nodded briskly to show that I couldn't be better, then reached out and took his right hand. He winced. I raised my eyebrows to suggest a question. Fortunately, he understood.

'Ach, it hurts alright. It was only a wee nick, so it shouldn't be so painful.' He pulled back his hand. 'It'll heal in a day or two.'

Not without help it wouldn't. I reached again for his hand

and examined the wound carefully. It was definitely infected; the skin around the cut was more swollen and redder, and green pus was forming in the centre. I couldn't help wondering if the wrongness I'd sensed at the heart of the garden – and to which Nicholas had alluded – had as much to do with the wound as the shears. I tugged Billy towards one of the free sinks.

'I've washed it already,' he protested. 'It's fine. Besides, Ailsa has come in. You need to go and start setting up for the Mages' breakfast.'

I angled myself away, ducking slightly behind Billy so that Ailsa wouldn't notice me, then carefully held Billy's hand under the tap and cleaned it as best as I could. He drew in a sharp breath when the cold water hit the wound, but he didn't try and stop me.

He pulled a face when I showed him my yellow-tinged garlic poultice. 'That reeks!'

I ignored his protest, used my index finger to scoop out a small amount and pressed it gently against the cut. Billy hissed. I patted his arm reassuringly and repeated my action, adding more paste to the wound. Once I was satisfied, I motioned to him.

He peered at my splayed fingers. 'Five hours?' he guessed.

I nodded, then rubbed my hands.

'And then I wash it off?'

I nodded again and mimed adding more of the garlic mixture as I handed him the little bowl. There was enough there to last for two days. After that, either the infection would have cleared or he'd be in bed with a dangerous fever.

Billy scratched his head. 'Uh, thanks?'

I grinned at him. *You're welcome*, I projected back.

'Mairi!' Ailsa bellowed from the other side of the kitchen. I jumped. 'You need to get your arse into gear!'

I looked round and realised that it wasn't only Ailsa who was staring at me; most of the other servants milling around the kitchen were doing the same. I did my best to look embarrassed and meek and ignore the speculative looks and pursed lips. Then I scuttled away to do Ailsa's bidding.

THE REST of the morning passed quickly. It was much the same work as the night before. Together with several other servants, I had to set up the dining room for the Mages' breakfast and then, when they emerged from their bedrooms, clean the rooms at high speed so that they would be spick and span when they returned.

The sleeping quarters weren't as interesting as the study rooms. There was more to do, so I only spent a few precious moments looking for anything that might be of use. I found a few books relating to magic on the bedside tables. I glanced through them quickly before I did anything foolish like open the curtains and invite close examination by any watchful ravens. None of them made any sense to me; most of the words were gibberish to my untrained eyes.

I filed away a few phrases with the notion of trying them out as soon as I got the chance. I couldn't be sure what the results would be, but I hadn't come here simply to pick up after the Mages and empty their rubbish bins.

Whenever a heaviness descended on my shoulders, I allowed Isla's freckled face to drift into my mind. I won't forget, I promised her. I'm here now and I will find a way to avenge you. I could already see how the monotony of feeding the Mages then clearing up after them could lull me away from my purpose but I wouldn't let that happen. I'd learn from the Mages and take everything I could – and then I'd do my utmost to destroy them all. Even soft-eyed Noah. He was one of them, and I couldn't allow myself to forget that.

Ailsa found me after the lunch dishes had been cleared away. 'It's almost two,' she said. 'You can have a break. Take a nap, get some air...' she waved a hand. 'It's up to you. It's the only free time you'll get, so use it wisely.' She raised her eyebrows. 'You might find yourself regretting the way you walked in here yesterday, but don't go thinking you can change your mind or run away. This is one of those jobs you don't walk away from.' She offered me a long look laden with warning and suspicion. She was far warier about my presence than the Mages; that meant she was far smarter.

I was tempted to forget Trish's whispered message and retire to my room to try out some of the words and phrases I'd gleaned from my travels around the east wing. The Gowk wasn't my keeper – and neither was Fee, for that matter. But it might be useful to have contacts on the outside. I might need them more than they needed me.

I slipped out of the same door at the back of the City Chambers through which I'd gained illegal entrance only the day before. There were three ravens perched outside, watching with beady eyes. The black-feathered trio gazed at me malevolently, but thankfully they didn't try to peck out my eyes again, and they didn't bother to follow me. Now I'd been granted servant status, I was probably not worth their attention. But somehow, I didn't think they'd forget that I'd managed to sneak past them, and I reckoned they were the sort of creatures who held grudges.

I moved quickly through the streets. Kelvingrove Park wasn't far away. It was a logical place for a shadowy secret meeting – it was a park, after all, and people wandered through it and lingered inside it all the time. Neither the Gowk nor I would look out of place.

Rounding the corner, I side-stepped a man in a hurry and almost smacked into a familiar woman. Ma McAskill did a double take and her face broke into a wreath of smiles when she realised who I was. 'Mairi! Lass! I heard what those tartan bampots did to you.' She reached out and drew me into a massive hug, nearly squeezing the life out of me with her enthusiasm. 'The wee shites. I never liked that Belle, you ken, although I thought mair of Twister.' She clicked her tongue. 'You deserve better than those two.'

Over her shoulder, I saw the Gowk cross the road towards the park. His hands were in his pockets and he was whistling. Nothing to see here folks, he projected. Just a man out for some fresh air.

Ma McAskill released me and stepped back, still beaming from ear to ear. 'What are you up to, then? Have you found a new job?'

I nodded, trying to appear as if I were paying attention to her whilst keeping an eye on the Gowk.

'Och, that's good,' she said. 'Where...?' Her voice trailed off as she clocked my drab uniform and her smile vanished. 'Oh.' She moved back a foot. 'You're working for the Mages.' She retreated some more. 'Well, that's good you got a job.' She obviously couldn't wait to get away; suddenly I was no longer someone who could be trusted. I could hardly blame her for thinking that.

Unwilling to approach the Gowk directly, I waved off a relieved Ma McAskill before walking slowly in the opposite direction, round the other side of the park rather than towards him. I wouldn't speak to him until I was absolutely sure it was safe.

I scanned the skies for any spying ravens as I kept him in view. Nothing seemed out of the ordinary. Two women were heading into the park after him, wheeling prams and chatting gaily. A group of children was playing tag on the grass nearby, screaming and shouting as if this were a braw summer's day instead of mid-winter.

I waited and watched. The Gowk hadn't been followed, and I

was as confident as I could be that it was safe. I supposed I ought to go and find out what he had to say, but I certainly wouldn't stay if he bawled me out for not doing what he wanted. I'd give him a chance to say his piece, but what happened after that would depend on his words and intentions.

I padded up to the bandstand and sat on the bench next to him, albeit leaving a considerable gap between us to suggest we were two strangers who were merely resting in the same place. I felt a sudden thrill of clandestine pleasure and quickly quashed it. This wasn't about fun. This was all business.

The Gowk coughed once but didn't glance at me. 'You're a bloody eejit, lass,' he murmured. 'You're going to get yourself killed.' He reached into his coat pocket and pulled out a newspaper, then laid it deliberately between us on the bench.

When no more words were forthcoming, I reached for the paper and realised he'd tucked something inside it. A notepad and pen. I inhaled deeply and scratched out a quick response: *Can't wait 18 months. Will learn what magic I can from them, lull them into thinking I'm not a threat, and then strike them all down.*

I replaced the notepad inside the newspaper and returned it to its original spot. After a moment or two, the Gowk picked it up and read what I'd written. He sighed heavily.

'I was afraid you were going to say something like that. It won't work. We've tried it before. This is my fault, and Fee's. We put ideas in your head. You might have the potential for magic, lassie, but that's a different thing to using it properly. Without training, you'll never be able to wield the sort of magical words you need to damage the Mages. I mean, what are you planning? Are you going to murder the Ascendant in his sleep?'

Something like that.

'Have you even crossed paths with the Ascendant?'

I'd barely done a day at the City Chambers. There was time enough for that.

The Gowk kept going. 'I showed you what they did to me.

They'll do worse to you when they catch you.' His tone grew grimmer. 'And mark my words, they *will* catch you. You can't do this. You don't have the power and you won't have the training.'

I counted to ten in my head. When the burst of fury I felt inside didn't subside, I turned my head slightly towards him. *Kall Moy.* Then I hummed.

The Gowk gasped. His hands scrabbled at his throat and his face turned puce. That was probably what I'd looked like yesterday, I thought, but at least the Gowk wasn't crawling around on his hands and knees like I had done.

He croaked and wheezed as a young couple emerged giggling from behind a clump of bushes nearby. They glanced at him curiously. Almost immediately, I pictured the bird in my mind breaking free and flying up into the sky. The Gowk choked as he was released, spluttering and coughing until his colour returned to normal. The couple walked on until they were out of sight.

'Fuck me, lass,' he managed. 'When did you learn that?'

I managed to gesture enough to convey an answer.

'Yesterday?'

I nodded.

'Fuck me,' he repeated. He lifted his clawed, misshapen hand and pushed his sweat-soaked hair back from his forehead. 'I realised you were strong and quick to learn, but that's something else.'

For the first time, he looked at me directly. 'I didn't think you were up to this, not just because of your lack of learned magic but because I didn't think you had it in you. But you're more ruthless than I gave you credit for.' He paused before adding quietly, 'Good for you.' He looked ahead again. 'You'll still likely get caught. You'll still likely die. And soon.'

We all die. I shrugged. This time the Gowk smiled. 'Fair enough.' He hesitated. 'What's your plan?'

I considered how to answer. I drew my index finger slowly across my throat.

The Gowk hissed. 'The Ascendant?'

Sure.

'Other Mages?'

Probably.

He hissed again, this time drawing out the sound so it was more sibilant. 'It's harder than you might think to take a human life. Bear in mind that, no matter how much you hate the Mages and how culpable they are for the state of this country, not all of them are truly evil. Some got sucked into that way of life and didn't realise their mistake until it was too late. I was almost the same. You could end up murdering someone in cold blood who could still do some good. And until you're faced with the situation, you won't know if you have it in you to kill.'

I'd almost killed *him* a scant minute ago, but I understood what he was saying. I wasn't expecting it to be easy, and I was aware that not all the Mages were tyrants. Noah was alright, and he was the Ascendant's nephew. But that didn't matter; their bloody regime had to be stopped and I knew of no other way to achieve that.

Unfortunately, I was fairly certain that the Ascendant could easily defend himself against a magical attack like the one I'd just performed. I couldn't make a move until I was guaranteed results.

The Gowk massaged his crippled hand and sighed. 'Let's say you achieve some success – let's say you get into a position where you can kill the Ascendant and get away with it. Maybe some other Mages end up dead, too. What do you think happens then?'

His tone was gentle but insistent. 'There are other Ascendants, other cities, other Mages. He'll be replaced by someone else, maybe by someone worse. And a lot of people will argue that the Mages are a necessary evil because without them we'd be over-run by the Afflicted. We'd end up cut off from the rest of the country. And even if the Afflicted didn't become an unmanageable problem, we'd likely end up starving to death.'

My eyes sparked with anger. If he was suggesting that we should let the damned Mages get away with whatever they wanted to, including public murder then—

'Relax,' he muttered. 'I'm not saying we should leave things as they are. I've been trying to move against the fuckers for years, remember? I've been at this shite since before you were born, lassie. What I'm trying to say is that we don't need the Mages to disappear, we need them to become more accountable.'

I snorted aloud. And who exactly would hold the Mages to account?

The Gowk understood my unspoken question. 'The people,' he said simply. 'The people of this city already fear the Mages, they already despise them, but they won't move against them because they're afraid. But there's always a tipping point where fear is no longer enough, and where rage takes over and goads people into action.' He sent me a sidelong look. 'I don't know exactly what brought you to Fee's door, but I'm guessing it was something along those lines.'

I didn't look at him. I didn't have to.

He nodded, pleased with himself. 'Find proof,' he said. 'Find incontrovertible proof of the worst atrocities the Mages have committed.'

I mimed a noose around my neck; if executions weren't proof enough, then what the fuck was?

The Gowk understood. 'They spin enough tales to justify those deaths. A few words and accusations, and people are scared enough to give them the benefit of the doubt. And they don't conceal the executions. What we need is the stuff they hide, that nobody is aware of, and that the Mages know they can't broadcast. If we can present that to the good people of this city, I believe they will demand a change. One person alone can spark a revolution – but one person alone cannot see it through.'

I imagined myself stabbing the Ascendant through the heart over and over again, my face a vicious mask of hatred. Then I imagined the whole of Glasgow standing up against the conclave of Mages and demanding more. Demanding better. What was more important? Revenge or re-birth?

I sighed and my shoulders dropped.

The Gowk smacked his lips together in satisfaction. 'Fee was right. You've got intelligence, as well as power. I'll work on things from this end, drum up some support and get our people ready for whatever's to come. Do you have any thoughts on what you might uncover?'

Murdered babies. Yeah. I had some thoughts. I sniffed.

'I thought you might,' he said. 'Let's meet here every thirty days and you can keep me updated with what you find. If you need to get hold of me quickly or you have anything urgent to communicate, Trish will help. You can trust her.'

I wasn't willing to trust anyone completely but I nodded anyway.

'I've left you a wee note in the back of the paper,' he continued. 'Use it as best as you can. I'll see what else I can get for next time to help you.' He rose to his feet. 'Don't get caught in the meantime,' he warned.

He walked off in the same direction as the couple had done. I watched him go, wondering if I'd made a deal with the devil or if this could be the start of a brave new world. Only time would tell.

I waited a moment or two then reached for the newspaper. There was a sheet of paper tucked in towards the back. I pulled it out and pressed my lips together when I saw what was written there: it was a list of about twenty phrases. *Bish var.* For temporary strength. *Altus ish moy.* Cast light. *Indah sal.* Create a breeze. I couldn't stop myself from smiling.

The Gowk had come prepared with these words. I'd likely never know whether giving them to me had been dependent on how our meeting went, or whether he'd always planned to pass them over, but I felt a brief rush of gratitude. Even though he had disagreed with my rash decision to go to the City Chambers and get a job, he was still prepared to do all he could to help.

I wasn't stupid; I knew it could be as dangerous for him as it was for me. I mouthed each phrase over and over several times, then glanced round. Nobody was nearby. I could do this.

I focused on a small, half-dead shrub by the stone steps leading up to the bandstand. Its leaves were brown and curling, and it didn't look as if it would survive the winter. *Chelta.* I hummed a single note as I thought the word. Grow.

The leaves seemed to stir, but that might have been the light wind. Nothing else happened. I stared at the bush for several moments. Okay. I couldn't be successful every time. It simply meant I'd have to practise and try as often as I could.

I raised my chin and gazed over the rooftops until my eyes landed on the barely visible spire of the City Chambers. I'm coming for you, I promised. You'll all get what you deserve. And so will we.

CHAPTER SEVENTEEN

SEVERAL DAYS PASSED. I KEPT MY HEAD DOWN AND DID AS I WAS told, snatching any spare moment to practise the phrases. Some I found easy, but others remained tantalisingly out of reach. I could feel the magic brush across my skin when I tried them, but little happened beyond that.

I was careful not to attempt any magic when I was inside the walls of the City Chambers. I was mindful of what I'd been told about how using magic could be sensed. I saved my practice sessions for those occasions when I could leave the building and get well out of reach of any of the Mages.

Despite the phrases I'd been given by the Gowk and the ones I picked up during the course of my job, my progress was painstakingly slow. However, I knew that mastering magic was my means of overtaking the Mages, so I didn't consider giving up or taking a day off. I had to prove to myself that I'd taken the right course of action by coming here; I couldn't afford to be lazy, not for a moment.

Billy's cut healed nicely. Although I overheard several sardonic comments about how strongly he reeked of garlic, I also noted more than one approving glance in my direction.

Maybe I should have felt pleased that my healing work had been noted, but I didn't want the attention; the less I was noticed, the better.

Unfortunately, it wasn't only the other servants who made a point of noticing me.

I bumped into Noah many times over the course of each day, so often that I started to think he was deliberately engineering situations where he could see me. Despite his relative youth, his status as the Ascendant's nephew meant that he didn't reside in the east wing with the other Mages who were of similar age and experience, and yet he often appeared there, smiling at me crookedly and approaching with idle chatter. On each occasion he took my hand – and each time, I felt a warmth and comfort spread through me. I should have hated him in the way I hated all the other Mages, but somehow he was different.

I also saw Nicholas regularly. More than once, I came across him when he was bare chested and performing his odd, meditative routine. Each time he would open his eyes and offer me a lazy grin. Although he'd done little more than help me, I felt uneasy around him. Every time he looked at me, I had the sensation that he could see into my soul. It was unnerving and a little scary.

The ravens continued to keep out of my way, though I often glimpsed them – especially when I was on my own and taking the opportunity to do some snooping. They reminded me that I was always being watched and couldn't afford to drop my guard. Not that I was likely to do that.

I was constantly on the lookout for opportunities to learn more about the Mages' weaknesses, and to come up with ways to win against them. Frustratingly, I still hadn't set eyes on the Ascendant. He was like a malevolent ghost hanging over the City Chambers; his presence was always felt but he was never seen. It was starting to feel like he was an existential threat rather than a physical one.

I didn't even see him during the night, when I continued to wake early and slip out to wander the quiet halls and get to know my temporary home. I learned which passageways to bypass so that I avoided any Mages who were also up at that hour. I didn't see Noah that early again.

I felt more confident each time I went out. Now I had a better understanding of where the rooms were, not just from my night-snooping but from my cleaning work.

I learned more about what each Mage did with their time. Ross focused on the physical body; I often came across jars of amputated body parts floating in watery solutions in his study. New ones appeared every couple of days, making me wonder if he deliberately sought out people so he could hack off an arm, a finger or an ear. It wouldn't have surprised me, although I uncovered no real evidence about where the body parts came from.

Arthur, a pimply young Mage who'd transferred from Aberdeen, studied poisons. If I hadn't known so much about plants and which leaves to avoid touching, I was certain I'd have near killed myself when I was cleaning his study. To be honest, I was astonished that he hadn't already killed himself.

I resisted the temptation to nab some of his more potent herbs and drop them into a vat of soup so I could kill all the Mages in one swift go. Large-scale poisoning was indiscriminate, however; the cooks might taste the soup before they sent it out and also end up dying. The Mages might sense the poison before the soup touched their tongues and execute anyone who'd gone near it. Besides, poison seemed like a coward's way out. When I destroyed the Mages, I wanted them to know that I was responsible. I wanted them to see what their actions had done.

There was a group of older Mages who remained in the east wing despite their advancing age and who worked together deciphering ancient texts. Their studies were filled to the ceiling with old tomes and dusty papers. As far as I could tell, they'd uncovered the secrets of ancient sewers, and located some dubious missing 'treasure' that seemed to consist of bent silver coins and broken pottery. They'd been translating what they thought were old magic spells but looked more like bad poetry.

A team of younger Mages was working to produce a new whisky that allowed the imbiber to avoid hangovers. Their research seemed to involve little more than tasting lots of whisky samples and occasionally chucking in a few herbs to see if anything happened.

Not all the Mages' work was without merit. Michael, a prematurely bald Mage, was experimenting with magic that could increase the yield of certain crops. Lewis, a chatty Mage who always asked me questions and seemed to forget I was mute, was working on a new water-filtration system powered by magic. Patrick, who blushed every time he saw me, appeared to be seeking a way to develop artificial light that would keep the Afflicted at bay for longer. But I knew that any positive effects from their magic would rarely filter down to the normal folk of the city; most of what the Mages did benefited their own lives, rather than anyone else's.

What I didn't discover was evidence of what they did with baby girls who displayed signs of magic.

The Mages' duties didn't merely consist of their own pet projects. Groups of them wandered out during the day, supposedly to keep the peace and ensure the populace acted like the obedient, respectful citizens they were supposed to be.

A different group of Mages patrolled the streets through the night, just like Ross had been doing when I'd nearly bumped into him and first met Nicholas. I learned what time those Mages returned so I knew when to hide to avoid being discovered wandering around the City Chambers. I didn't know what they were up to while they were out, but I assumed it was something to do with the Afflicted.

When it was clear that not a single night had passed without several of them venturing out in timed patrols, my curiosity got the better of me. I wanted to know what they were up to – and why. Maybe the proof I needed to stir the city into action would come from their night activities. I didn't believe they were strolling around in darkness to protect the general public; that wasn't the Mages' way.

Rather than letting myself sleep and wake in the wee hours to sneak around the building unhindered, on Friday night I stayed awake. I knew I'd suffer for it the following day, but I hoped it would be worth it.

I stayed in my small, draughty room, my body twitching with anticipation, until I heard the distant bells indicate it was midnight. The first night patrol would be returning and the second group of Mages would be venturing out; unbeknownst to them, I was planning to accompany them. This was the deepest, darkest part of the night; not only would it be easier for me to remain undetected, but it was also likely to be when the most action would occur.

It had been an easy matter to visit the laundry room earlier in the day and 'borrow' a black Mage's cloak. The colour would conceal me in a way that my usual uniform would not. I wasn't sure what the penalty was for dressing like a Mage, but I doubted it would matter compared to spying on them in the middle of the night.

I wrapped myself in the dark fabric and pulled up the hood to cover my hair, then I tiptoed down the servants' staircase to the entrance hall and waited for the right moment. I hid in a dark cranny where I knew I wouldn't be seen.

Less than five minutes after I'd arrived, the heavy front door creaked open and three Mages came in. I recognised two of them; the third looked familiar, but I knew he didn't stay in the east wing.

As they shrugged off their cloaks and gloves, they were

approached by three more Mages who were preparing to head out. The Mages who had just entered nodded formally to their replacements before disappearing deeper into the Chambers. Not a particularly chatty bunch, then. It didn't matter; they weren't the ones I would be following. I focused instead on the three who were preparing to head out.

My eyes narrowed on Ross. His face had a peculiarly blood-less look, even more so than usual, and I fancied I could smell the rot of his personality. I had no doubt that I'd end up hung, drawn and quartered for his own delectation if he spotted me. All the more reason to find out exactly what he was up to.

He was accompanied by a more senior Mage. I thought he was called Fred but I knew nothing about him. I realised with a jerk that the third Mage was crotchety old Angus – the only magic master that Ailsa would talk back to.

He looked less impressive now than when he had confronted me in his study. 'Well?' he enquired loudly. 'Are we leaving or aren't we?' He couldn't have sounded less enthusiastic if he'd tried.

'Are you in a hurry, old man?' Ross asked. 'Keen to get up close and personal with the Afflicted? Maybe you have your eye on one or two, and you're planning to grab them and lay down in the middle of George Square for a little—'

'*Tez chi.*' Angus folded his arms and glared. I stared in fasci-nation from my shadowy corner as Ross's mouth snapped shut, clearly sealed by magic. This was the first time I'd seen friction between any of the Mages, and I was all for it.

Ross went wild. He lunged at Angus with his hands outstretched, forming a fist and throwing it towards Angus's head. For an older man, Angus was nifty on his feet. He side-stepped the punch easily and, while he didn't laugh out loud, there was a mocking smile on his face. Naturally, that only riled Ross even more and he threw himself at Angus again.

The third Mage, Fred, stood back and watched without

getting involved. He didn't appear surprised. Perhaps this sort of thing was a regular occurrence and I'd been unlucky not to witness it before now.

A deep voice interrupted. 'Enough.'

It wasn't a loud shout or a bellowed screech, but the voice was imbued with power. I felt the potential magic in that single word shiver against my skin. I drew further back, suddenly afraid even though I was certain that I couldn't be seen.

Angus and Ross stepped back and moved away from each other. Ross put his hands up in submission, while Angus seemed to roll his eyes. Three more figures appeared from the hallway, and I knew instantly who had given the command to halt. It was the Ascendant.

During Isla's execution, he had appeared larger than life on the scaffold, but up close he was shorter than I'd realised. He had heavy-set shoulders, slightly bowed legs and a distinctive walk. His stomach was trim, despite his build, and there was a suggestion of muscle beneath his purple outfit.

On the surface he looked like an ordinary man; apart from his clothes and overly waxed moustache, he could have been a farmhand or a dye worker. But I knew he was anything but ordinary. The magic and power that emanated from him were so strong that even the smallest child could have recognised the Ascendant for what he was.

'You are Glasgow Mages. You should act better than unruly common folk.'

I had the feeling that if Ross could speak, he'd have pointed his finger at Angus and whined that the other Mage started it. He certainly had the expression of a sulky teenager.

'Release him, Angus,' the Ascendant ordered.

Angus shrugged as if he didn't care one way or the other but did as he was told. He flicked his wrist and removed the spell.

'Your Highness,' Ross began, his cheeks red. 'He is—'

The Ascendant shook his head firmly. 'I don't want to hear

it. You shouldn't be so weak as to let another Mage get the better of you like that. It's like dealing with children.'

'Sir Angus often lets his temper get the better of him, does he not?' observed Noah from behind the Ascendant.

I'd been so focused on the Ascendant's power that I'd not registered that Noah was one of the trailing figures. The other one was Nicholas. My heartbeat suddenly sounded very loud, thumping in my ears as if it were trying to give me away. I'd certainly chosen an interesting night to follow the Mages. Something important was going on.

The Ascendant barely acknowledged Noah's words. He sniffed imperiously. 'This is not an ordinary patrol, as the three of you well know,' he said. 'There are important matters at stake. I will not have petty squabbles preventing your mission from being achieved.'

Mission? Despite my fear of being discovered, I leaned forward, keen to hear more. This sounded more and more interesting. Then I saw Nicholas's head turn towards my hiding spot and his bright green eyes narrow. He could see me. He knew I was there even though I was invisible to the others' eyes.

I didn't move a muscle, certain that he would give me away. He gazed at me unblinkingly for what felt like the longest few seconds of my life, then he looked away and cleared his throat. 'Shall we get on with it?' he drawled, sounding bored.

'Yes, yes.' The Ascendant waved an irritated hand. 'You all know what we're looking for – a young specimen, as healthy as possible. Sex is unimportant. What is vital is that they are unharmed and unmarked during capture.'

My mouth was dry. Capture?

'Work in pairs. Ross with Fred. Angus with Nicholas.'

My eyes widened. Nicholas was going out as well? I grimaced. He wouldn't take well to me trailing him.

Ross snorted. 'I guess you need an enslaved bodyguard, old man.'

The Ascendant turned to the young Mage with such an icy look of disapproval that Ross blanched and stepped back. I almost applauded with satisfaction.

'It's been almost three weeks since we lost the last one,' the Ascendant snapped. 'We need a replacement and nobody has managed to bring one in. Even Noah failed. I am counting on you four to do better.'

'We'll have what you need before dawn,' Ross said. Fred nodded eagerly, but I noticed that Angus's lip curled slightly in distaste. Nicholas gave nothing away.

'Do not disappoint me,' the Ascendant told them. 'Good hunting.' He held out his hand, allowing it to hover in mid-air. All three Mages stepped forward and, one by one, bent to kiss the heavy ring that adorned his middle finger. Either Nicholas wasn't considered good enough, or it simply wasn't expected of him.

The four of them trooped towards the open door and vanished into the night.

'Do you think they'll do it?' Noah asked his uncle once they'd gone.

'They'd better,' the Ascendant growled. 'My patience is growing thin. Let's hope they have more success than you did.' He muttered a few words at the main door and it swung shut with a dull thud. 'Come on,' he said. 'We'll wait upstairs.'

CHAPTER EIGHTEEN

I WAITED FOR SEVERAL MOMENTS LONGER THAN I NEEDED TO. Seeing the Ascendant had startled me. Although I knew it would be harder to catch up to the patrolling Mages once I made it outside, I wanted to be sure that both he and Noah were out of the way before I set off.

It seemed more important than ever that I found out what they were up to. There was only one thing that made any sense, based on what I'd overheard, but I couldn't confirm my suspicions until I saw the Mages trying to capture one of the Afflicted. What in the name of all that was holy would they do with one? Could this be related to the missing baby? I shuddered at the thought.

Although the Ascendant had used magic to close the main door, it wasn't locked. I breathed a silent sigh of relief as I slipped outside. I was sure that all the ravens would be sleeping at this hour, their heads tucked under their wings and their eyes firmly closed. All the same, I took a moment to glance upwards and check that I wasn't being watched.

The air was cool and crisp, and the stars above my head twinkled. It was almost pleasant; it was a shame that fear of the

Afflicted meant few people enjoyed the night. I reminded myself sternly to stay alert; it was not long ago that I'd come close to brushing up against them.

I twisted my head left and right, trying to ascertain which direction the Mages had taken. Given the choice, I'd follow Ross and Fred rather than Nicholas and Angus. The daemon knew I'd been watching from the shadows, and he would be aware if I tried to follow him. I'd prefer not to have to try and silently explain myself to him again. I pulled back my shoulders. Left, I decided for no good reason.

I pulled my purloined cloak tight around my shoulders and set off at a fast pace, keeping to the balls of my feet to avoid my heels making a noise as they struck the cobbles. I shouldn't have worried about being overheard, however; I hadn't gone far when voices carried over to me.

'Mages like Angus should have been out to pasture long ago,' Ross said. 'He might have been powerful once, but he's losing his grip. And,' he added with a confident flourish, 'I don't believe he's completely loyal to the Ascendant.'

'Aye, Ross,' Fred said.

'I should have been sent out long before now. I'll catch one of those fuckers and haul him back. I'm more than strong enough to do it.'

'Aye, Ross.'

'Make sure you don't get in my way. I don't want to be tripping over you when the time comes.'

'Aye, Ross.' There was a pause. 'I mean, no, Ross.'

I suppressed a smile and jogged to the next corner, peering round until I could see their backs. They were heading west and walking purposefully; it was clear they knew where they were going.

I stayed where I was, keeping them in sight until the road curved and they disappeared out of sight, then I nipped out. Hugging the shadows at the side of the street, I followed. If I kept a decent distance between us, they'd remain ignorant of my presence.

We walked for a couple of miles. Once, Fred turned his head and I pressed flat against a wall to avoid being seen, but that was the only close call. It wasn't long before we were heading downstream along the bank of the Clyde.

Ross had finally lapsed into silence, which was probably more of a blessing for Fred than it was for me. Now I could hear the water lapping as it rippled in the breeze, and the odd scratch or skirl from whichever nocturnal creatures had dared to come out. It was rather peaceful – until a loud, guttural scream ripped through the air,

Before that point, Ross and Fred had been moving steadily but slowly. As soon as they heard the screech, they started to sprint. So that was it: they were definitely trying to capture an Afflicted.

I hung back for a few seconds, then ran after them. One of the Mages must have cast some sort of magic because they moved with preternaturally fast speed. No matter how much effort I put into keeping pace with them, they pulled ahead.

I strained my eyes to keep track of their direction. That was easy enough when they maintained a straight route, but when they veered off to the right into a tangle of narrow streets away from the river bank, I was too far behind to see which road they'd taken. I gritted my teeth and opted for the first right turn instead of the second.

Another sky-shattering scream sounded, this time from somewhere behind me. I must have gone the wrong way. I hissed and spun round to change direction, but I moved too quickly and slipped on a near-invisible patch of ice. My feet flew out from under me and I fell onto my back. Shite.

I was lucky not to hurt myself. The fall had been so unexpected that I'd not had time to tense my muscles, so I landed without serious injury. All the same, my limbs were stiff when I heaved myself back up to my feet.

I was barely upright when I heard another Afflicted shriek, this time even further away. I cursed myself to hell and beyond. This was an important night. I'd never heard a whisper before that the Mages were capturing the Afflicted. If their intentions were to keep them off the streets, surely they would proclaim their efforts loudly and proudly to the rest of the city? From the secretive way they were acting, and from what the Ascendant had intimated, there was far more to what they were doing than maintaining public safety. By falling behind, I could no longer see what they were up to. They didn't know I was here and they'd still managed to beat me. So much for me.

I rubbed the base of my spine and limped away. I wouldn't be able to catch up to the two Mages now, even if I knew where they'd gone. The best thing would be to hoof it back to the City Chambers and wait to see what, if anything, Ross and Fred brought back with them. It was as good a plan as any.

Mildly irritated with myself, I turned away from the direction of the Afflicted's scream and made my way back towards City Chambers. My mind kept turning. Perhaps the Mages were working on ways to return the Afflicted to a normal state of being, and they were keeping quiet until they achieved success and could present it as a fait accompli. It sounded too good to be true, given what I already knew of the Mages. But Noah was involved, together with the Ascendant, and he'd always appeared polite, professional and – well, good. I wasn't naïve enough to think that all Mages were automatically evil; the world was far more complicated than that.

A cold wind appeared out of nowhere, skittering the dried leaves caught between the pavement and the road. I pulled the black cloak closer round me and shivered. Now that the adrenalin had drained from my body, I was feeling the cold.

I tilted my head. I was close to Kelvingrove Park, where I'd met the Gowk last week. I could cut across and shave a few minutes off my journey. Crossing the road, I glanced left and right. I saw nothing more than a few stray bits of litter being blown this way and that.

Once in the park, I ducked under the low-lying branches of a sick-looking tree and jogged towards the opposite side. My unexpected presence startled a dozing bird and it squawked unexpectedly. I twisted to look behind me, suddenly afraid that a raven had spotted me.

The bird had already vanished into the night air, but the tension didn't leave me. Something was there, over by the band-stand – something that hadn't been there eight days earlier.

I altered my course and made a beeline for it. As I drew closer, I realised what it was and my fear transformed into astonishment. The shrub: the tiny shrub that I'd tried to push magic into had grown. It wasn't dead looking any longer; it was an enormous bush that almost blocked the side of the band-stand. Thick, glossy leaves gleamed in the dull moonlight. I stared at it and tentatively reached out to touch it.

That was when somebody grabbed me roughly from behind.

I squeaked but reacted quickly enough to pull away and spin round, my palms raised in pathetic defence. I suppose that part of me hoped it was Nicholas, waiting with a sardonic smirk and a lazy scolding, but deep down I knew that it wasn't. When I gazed into the wild eyes of the Afflicted woman standing in front of me, I was certain that my life was over.

She was covered in a layer of grime, and her once-blonde hair was matted. Old wounds and scars were visible across her bare arms and legs –the cold obviously didn't affect the Afflicted.

I backed up one step, then two. That was when she attacked again – and this time she shrieked as she did so. She was alerting the others to her prey, I thought dully, as I dived to the side to avoid her clawed hands and kicking feet.

I tumbled to the ground and rolled away from her, then scrambled up and tried to sprint away. Her foot caught me at the base of my spine and connected with the slight bruise that was forming from my earlier fall. I went sprawling down again.

I was done for. All I could think was that I'd failed Isla; I'd tried to avenge her and it had come to naught. I'd achieved nothing.

The Afflicted woman, down on all fours as she loomed over me, pinned me down. Her breath reeked of something dead and fishy. A cloud of noxious air nearly choked me as her jaws widened to tear open my throat.

Bish var. Temporary strength. It was one of the phrases the Gowk had gifted to me almost in this very spot. I brought it to the forefront of my mind and hummed a single note. Panic reverberated in the sound, then I felt the magic stir briefly deep in my bones and a surge of instant, blessed relief.

But the moment was too short and the flare died down as quickly as it had arrived. It wasn't enough; I couldn't summon the power I needed to escape. Fee had told me that magic and emotion didn't mix. I supposed this was cold, hard proof of that.

The woman snarled as if she were aware of my attempt, but that made her loosen her grip on my arms slightly. I took full advantage, ripping myself free and rolling away yet again. I tried to calm myself. *Bish var. Bish var. BISH VAR.* I hummed with growing desperation each time, each sound becoming more and more high pitched despite my best efforts to remain level headed.

The magic choked and spluttered inside me but it didn't do what I needed it to. My powers weren't strong enough yet to overcome my deeper emotions. It was a bitter truth to learn.

The Afflicted woman landed on top of me and I rose up – maybe I could throw her off without magic. Her arms clung to me and wrapped round my throat, squeezing hard. I started to wheeze. My fingers tingled as the magic I'd called up tried to

HELEN HARPER

force its way through once more, but it still wasn't enough. I didn't have it in me.

The woman's head bent towards mine and I felt something wet on my cheek. Her tongue. She was tasting me. She smacked her lips in obvious anticipation and I closed my eyes.

There was a loud scream from further away. At first, I thought it was more of the Afflicted coming to join the woman for this unexpected and potentially tasty meal. But the woman jerked and pulled back. Across the city, I heard answering shrieks and calls that were undoubtedly from other Afflicted souls.

She let me go. One second her nails were digging into my throat and her weight was on my back, the next second she was gone. I remained where I was, the fight drained out of me. I kept expecting her to launch herself at me again, but she'd gone. The woman had answered the call of her comrades and departed into the bleak, cold night as suddenly as she'd arrived.

CHAPTER NINETEEN

NOBODY KNEW HOW THE DISEASE TURNED NORMAL HUMANS INTO the wild Afflicted. Some said it was through bites; some suggested it was miasma, transferred through the air. Others proclaimed that it was a punishment wrought on those who were not pure of heart and deed. Whatever, I could not be sure that I had not been infected.

I limped back to the City Chambers. Instead of waiting to see what had happened with Ross, Fred, Nicholas and Angus, I heaved myself up to my room.

Rather than going to bed, I scrubbed myself from head to toe, leaving no inch of skin unscoured. I was red raw by the time I was done, and I didn't know if it would have any effect. The best I could hope for, if I were on the verge of becoming Afflicted, was that I'd infect all the damned Mages at the same time and bring the City Chambers crumbling into pockmarked destruction.

Physically I felt fine; emotionally, I remained in turmoil. It wasn't difficult to decipher what had happened: I'd escaped not through my skills or ability, but sheer luck.

It galled me that I probably had the Mages to thank. I reckoned they'd captured – or nearly captured – one of the Afflicted. The female who'd attacked me had heard their cries and left her prospective meal to go and help.

I replayed the events in my head. The distant scream that had made her bolt had sounded different to the other shrieks and calls. It was a scream for help – and that told me several different things. The Afflicted weren't mindless; they didn't hunt in groups simply for ease or improved opportunity, they looked after each other and were a community. They still possessed feelings. Despite the attack, my attitude towards them had changed in ways that I couldn't quite express.

That didn't impact on what had happened that night, however. I had called upon magic and I'd been left wanting. In the heat of the moment, my panic and fear over-rode any power inside me. Regardless of what I'd achieved up till now, I wasn't as strong as I needed to be – and that had to change.

I dragged myself through my duties that day as my tired mind considered the possibilities. How could I improve? Practice was key, but that was easier said than done when I only had an hour or two a day when I could extricate myself from the City Chambers and go somewhere to work on the magical words and phrases I already possessed. Maybe the Gowk was right: eighteen months hidden away out of the city, where I could learn and grow and meet my full potential, might have been a better option. But I was here and no longer had any choice but to seek out a faster track.

I was still mulling over the problem as I mopped the east-wing staircase. It was a thankless task. On more than one occasion, a Mage stomped up with dirty boots and ruined all my efforts so I had to start again before Ailsa bawled me out for being neglectful.

'There you are,' a familiar voice drawled as I scrubbed at a particularly stubborn stain. 'Did you enjoy yourself last night?'

I didn't bother looking up at Nicholas. No, I hadn't enjoyed myself at all.

He came up the stairs to join me. Unlike the passing Mages who trod heavily on my carefully scrubbed tiles, Nicholas took care with his feet and left no mark. 'Have a care, Mairi,' he warned in a low voice. 'Your mute tongue and pretty face will only carry you so far. If the Ascendant had seen you lurking in the shadows last night, I doubt anything could have saved you.'

I didn't need the daemon to point out how dangerous my actions were but I bit out a nod as I continued to clean the grimy stain.

'It's not merely night-time investigations that could see you hanging, you know,' he continued. 'The only reason nobody noticed the magic clinging to that garden boy was because the stench of garlic was so strong. Healing his wound was commendable, but if any of these fools had spent more than a few seconds in Billy's company they'd have noticed what you'd done. It would have been traced back to you in seconds.'

Magic? It was a simple poultice. I paused in my scrubbing. I hummed, I realised: whenever I made a healing concoction, I hummed. I had been using magic without realising it.

I blinked rapidly. Oh. It was so frustrating that I'd conjured up healing magic without knowing, but couldn't defend myself with magic when I was desperate for it.

'You didn't know?' Nicholas tutted. 'You're more of a risk to your own soul than—'

'I hope you're not bothering the serving staff, Nicholas,' Noah interrupted. 'Mairi has duties to attend to, and it looks to me as if you're getting in her way.' He walked down the stairs until he was standing on the step above me. 'Is he bothering you, Mairi?'

Yes. I shook my head to say no.

Noah snorted mildly. 'You're too kind to say otherwise.' He jerked his head at Nicholas. 'Leave the poor lass alone.'

I didn't see Nicholas's reaction. Noah reached out and, as his hand brushed my shoulder, I felt the same surge of warmth and comfort that I'd had when he'd touched me before.

I looked up and met his eyes. He really was very good looking. His chestnut-brown hair was soft and silky, and a single artful curl fell across his forehead. When he smiled, as he was doing now, a dimple appeared in his cheek. He managed to exude boyish charm and alluring masculinity at the same time.

I felt myself swaying towards him. I knew that Noah had noticed because his eyes crinkled at the corners and the faintest colour rose on his unblemished cheeks.

Another Mage started up the staircase from below us and Noah's head snapped towards him. 'What the fuck are you doing, man?' he snapped. 'Pay attention! Those steps have just been cleaned and you're messing them up with your dirty great big feet!'

The Mage, a thin, narrow-faced fellow who put me in mind of a weasel, looked terrified. 'Apologies, Lord Noah. I was not paying attention.' He bent down and used the cuff of his long-sleeved robe to rub at the marks he had made.

Noah sighed heavily and clicked his tongue. 'You're only making it worse.' He glanced at me in a way that was meant to convey shared exasperation. 'Don't worry, Mairi,' he said. 'I'll fix this.' He raised his hands and, in a deep voice, intoned, '*Belz vee.*'

My skin prickled with the magic and the dirty marks disappeared in an instant. In fact, the entire staircase was now gleaming with pristine perfection. Ailsa would be pleased – but I had to wonder why the Mages employed people like me to clean when two words could have had the entire place sparkling.

'That's better,' Noah said, satisfied. He waved at the pale Mage. 'Go on with you. Be on your way.' The Mage scuttled off.

Noah smiled again at me. He shuffled his feet slightly and looked vaguely abashed. 'I wanted to ask you something,' he said. 'But I don't wish to put you in an awkward position. I want you to know that you can refuse and nothing bad will happen to you.' He took my hand in his. 'The Grand Central Hotel has a wonderful restaurant, and I have it on good authority that they've had a consignment of fresh venison. Eating alone is no fun – would you like to dine with me there tomorrow evening?'

Of all the things I'd been expecting him to say, this was not one of them. He'd be dining with a mute. How much fun could that be? But I'd never been to a real restaurant before, not that I could remember. And Noah liked to talk. A couple of hours in his company and I might learn all sorts of things.

I swallowed and nodded. *Yes. Yes, I would love to dine with you,* I projected.

Noah beamed. 'You have no idea how happy that makes me.' He lifted my hand to his lips and pressed his lips against my skin. There was a sudden searing heat, and something flared deep in the pit of my belly. 'I'll count every minute between now and then,' he promised. 'It will be exquisitely pleasurable agony.' Then he straightened up and left, pausing at the foot of the staircase to send me a long backward glance laden with meaning.

I remained where I was for several moments. If I weren't already mute, I reckoned I'd just have been struck dumb.

I DIDN'T SEE Noah for the rest of the day, although often I caught myself searching for him. The other Mages seemed to be giving me a wide berth, with the notable exception of Angus who was in a fouler mood than usual. He yelled at me for disturbing the spiders in his room and for letting in 'dratted light and fucking fresh air' when I opened the curtains and hauled up the sash window. Midnight ventures must not suit his temperament.

He stomped around, glaring at me whenever I seemed to do

something unacceptable such as breathing. And when a raven tapped at the window with its beak, he marched over with a heavy book in his hand and threw it at the glass. I finished as quickly as I could, keen to get out of his way.

In contrast, Ailsa seemed to be in extraordinarily high spirits. Every time I saw her, she was smiling; I even caught her whistling to herself. I wasn't the only one who noticed the difference. Once the Mages' evening meal had been served and cleared away, and I'd sat down with the other servants to a plate of leftovers, Trish and Lottie also commented on her behaviour.

'They must have finally shagged,' Lottie said, a knowing glint in her eye. 'Her and that Keith fellow. It's the only explanation.'

'Was she in her room here last night?' Trish asked. 'Or did she go to his place?'

Lottie wrinkled her nose. 'He didn't come here. Can you imagine? Whispering sweet nothings while a hundred Mages slept nearby? She wouldn't dare. Maybe it was an afternoon quickie. Whatever it was, it must have been good. That's one helluva lingering orgasm she's enjoying. Pure belter – at least for Ailsa.'

Trish snickered. 'Good for her. You ken, I heard that when she first came here, she had a thing with Ascendant.'

Lottie's eyes went as wide as saucers. 'You never told me that!'

'It was when he was young, and long before he became the Ascendant. Lots of the Mages like to dip their wick.' She nudged me. 'Am I right, Mairi? Or am I right?'

'Mairi's not been here long enough,' Lottie said, with a wink. 'Give her time.'

I waggled my eyebrows, trying to join in the banter. Both women laughed good-humouredly and the conversation moved on to other things. But when I'd finished my duties and headed up to my room, I was still thinking about it. Maybe there *was* a way to fast track my magic after all.

CHAPTER TWENTY

DESPITE MY LACK OF SLEEP THE PREVIOUS NIGHT, I WOKE AROUND three in the morning as usual. I lay where I was, staring up at the cracked ceiling. What I was planning was morally wrong, I knew that.

I thought back to Fee's warm kitchen, and what Flora and Jane had told me. Having sex with a Mage meant that some of their magic was passed on if the recipient of their amorous actions was magical themselves. I was magical – but I needed more of it. I needed to be able to call upon what power I had in times of stress and panic. I was prepared to murder – but was I prepared to yield my body?

I came to a decision and slipped out of bed. If he said no, I'd back away immediately. It would be a joint decision. That was a lie, but I tried not to dwell on it. At the end of the day, it was for the greater good.

I wrapped a blanket round my body and headed out into the silent corridors. I made little sound as I passed from floor to floor; I knew where I was going and I was confident of my bearings. As I walked, I tried to play out the various scenarios in my head but in the end I gave up. What would happen would happen. In the great chessboard of life, I was nothing more than a pawn. But perhaps this night, I would be able to double up.

I was half-expecting to see a few other people wandering about, especially given the action from the night before, but not even any Mages were around. I had no idea if they had managed to capture one of the Afflicted last night, or where a prisoner might have been taken, although presumably it was somewhere deep inside the City Chambers. It was tempting to try and find out, but it would be a risky manoeuvre right now. It was too soon after the event.

Given my lack of success in seeking out the missing baby, the evidence the Gowk was looking for surely lay with the Mages' motives for taking one of the Afflicted off the streets. Until I knew more about what was really happening, it would be an eejit move to make any pre-emptive plans. Power first, proof later.

It was with this thought in mind that I raised my fist and knocked on the wooden door. I used my fingers to comb through my hair, pinched my cheeks for some colour, and waited for my knock to be answered.

The door swung open and he was there, bare chested, gazing down at me without an inch of surprise. Against his bare skin, the metal cuffs around his wrists and arms gleamed. 'Well, well, well,' Nicholas murmured. 'What do we have here?'

I shifted my weight. I supposed I could try licking my lips suggestively or tossing back my hair; maybe I should be fluttering my eyelashes. I did none of those things, however; I simply looked into Nicholas's emerald-green eyes.

He stepped back and let me into his room. It was a lot sparser than I'd expected. The Mages' bedrooms were filled with ornate bedding, elaborate paintings, and all sorts of complicated ornaments, but Nicholas had only had what appeared to be a wooden box with some clean clothes inside it.

My umbrella – the one he'd taken the first night we met – lay neatly on the floor next to it.

'Welcome to my palace.'

I swivelled round, taking it in, then allowed my blanket to drop to the floor in a puddle of fabric. I looked at him again.

'Are you sure you want to do this?' he asked roughly. He knew exactly why I was there. I didn't take my eyes from him.

'Once it's done,' he said, 'it can't be undone.'

Aye. I was more than aware of that. I stayed where I was.

Something dark and indefinable flashed across his face. 'I told you before that you cannot trust me. That still stands. I am dangerous to you.'

Everyone was dangerous to me. Besides, I wasn't here to trust him.

Nicholas sighed. 'You have to make the first move,' he told me. 'This has to be completely your decision.'

That wasn't true – it was his decision as well. It took two to make a party like this. But clearly Nicholas had already made up his mind – and with considerably less torment than I had.

I drew in a deep breath and stepped towards him. This was proving to be both harder and easier than I'd expected. With trembling fingers, I loosened the buttons on my shapeless nightgown and it joined the blanket on the floor. A muscle clenched in Nicholas's jaw, but that was the only visible sign that he had reacted to my naked body. Fine, then; I guessed he was going to make me work for it.

The thought flitted into my head that at any moment he would burst out laughing and throw me, stark naked, out of his room. I swallowed and hoped that wouldn't be the case, then took another step and placed my hands on his chest.

Nicholas's breath quickened and I felt his chest rise and fall with increasing speed beneath my fingertips. I moved my hands slightly. Now I could feel his heartbeat thrumming against my touch. I trailed my fingers down to the waistband of his loose trousers and fumbled with the button as I pushed myself on my tiptoes and allowed my lips to brush, feather light, against his. He remained frozen, like a statue.

I pulled back slightly and gazed into his face with a question in my eyes. Nicholas stared at me before quirking an eyebrow in response. Okay then. Okay.

I finally managed to undo the button on his trousers. As they began to slide down his hips, I lifted my head towards his again. This time I didn't brush my mouth against his, I grabbed the back of his head and pulled him towards me, kissing him hard. For the first three or four seconds he remained immobile, then he gave a deep groan and reached for me, opening his mouth to let me in.

I had planned this out logically and rationally, but all reason fled when I tasted Nicholas's tongue against mine and felt his arms around my body. He pushed me back until my spine was pressed against the cold stone wall but I barely felt it. All I could feel was him. The heat of his body pushed away all other sensations.

I hooked one leg around his as his mouth left mine. I immediately felt bereft, but I needn't have worried because he started to trail a line of hot, searing kisses down my skin. His mouth moved across my jawline, down my neck, nibbled at the base of my throat and then descended to my breasts. I moaned when he took one nipple gently in his teeth and the tip of his tongue circled it.

In response, I moved my hands to his hips and caressed his skin before questing inwards and down until my fingers found his stiff, hard length.

Nicholas groaned again. 'Mairi,' he whispered, almost in pain. 'It's been a long time for me since...' He didn't finish his sentence – he didn't need to. I understood his meaning and, in truth, I felt the same.

As much as I wanted to take my time and explore his body,

the desire building inside me was overpowering. I half-nodded and moved against him, raising myself up until I could feel the tip of his swollen cock. He thrust upwards and it was my turn to groan.

His body filled me. I clutched at him, realising that his skin was now as slick with sweat as mine. My breath was coming in short, sharp gasps. Every time Nicholas thrust into me, I felt the heavy build-up of ragged want and desperate need. I pressed against him, as if somehow his body could absorb mine whole.

As Nicholas moved his hips his emerald eyes met mine, then he closed his eyelids and slammed into me one last time. I couldn't stop myself. I threw my head back and let out a cry as my body shuddered with the ecstasy of release.

We stayed where we were, our bodies fused. My heartbeat was still drumming faster than normal as Nicholas's breath grew more even and steady. 'I'm sorry,' he whispered in my ear. 'That was faster than it should have been.'

It was perfect.

I felt Nicholas jerk and his head turn to mine. He was staring at me. 'Mairi,' he murmured, 'I have to say, I didn't expect that.'

I frowned. He didn't expect the sex? Or was he referring to something else?

Why me? Why not Lord Noah? His words had a mocking edge to them.

My frown deepened – and then I realised that he'd not spoken aloud. My mouth dropped open and I pushed him away.

Intimacy has its own rewards, Mairi, but perhaps not the ones you were expecting.

This time I was sure his lips hadn't moved. I reached for my forehead, touching it like a deranged numpty before brushing my fingers against my temples.

What is going on? I projected, wondering if he truly could hear me.

A slow smile grew on Nicholas's face. *We're linked now, you and I. Quite possibly forever.*

No. This isn't happening.

The look of satisfaction in his eyes deepened. *I can assure you that it is.*

Ignoring the fact that I was still naked, I crossed my arms over my chest and glared at him. *Oh yeah? Then what number am I thinking of?*

Twenty-eight. Nicholas winked.

My chest tightened and I stumbled backwards. Oh God. Oh no. What had I done? If he could hear my thoughts, then he'd know everything. Nothing would be secret any more. All my plans...

'Hush.' This time he spoke aloud. 'You can guard against that. It's not difficult. Right now, you're projecting every thought and every emotion, but you can hide them from me. You don't need to communicate everything.' His voice darkened. 'Neither should you.'

My eyes darted from side to side, searching for an escape route. *How?* I demanded. *HOW?*

Nicholas winced. *There's no need to yell.* He reached for my hand but I moved further away from him.

I was too exposed, too vulnerable. I snatched up my night-dress and hastily pulled it over my head. When I looked at him again, his expression was shuttered.

'Picture a wall in your head,' he said in his normal voice. 'Use it to barricade your thoughts from me and control what you let out.' Despite his emotionless face, his voice was gentle.

I immediately did as he said. *What number am I thinking of now?* I questioned.

I heard no response and Nicholas's face didn't alter.

You're a slimy daemon.

He didn't react.

That was better sex than I could have ever imagined.

Nothing.

Then, finally, *I'm going to kill the Ascendant.*

Nicholas didn't so much as blink. He could have been acting – at that point, anything seemed likely – but I felt like I could trust him. For some reason, I didn't believe I was in any danger from him and I didn't think he could now hear my thoughts.

I allowed myself to relax a fraction and sat down on the edge of his pallet. This time I allowed him to hear me. *This is unbelievable.*

The corners of his mouth crooked up. *You're telling me, sweetheart.*

I shook my head in amazement. Even with Isla, gestures, miming and our own sign language had got us only so far. I'd never held a proper conversation with anyone, not that I could remember.

I lifted my head and met Nicholas's steady gaze. *I hate the sound of someone next to me eating an apple. The chomping and the slurping and the crunch when they bite into it – I can't explain it, but it turns my stomach.*

Nicholas laughed aloud.

When I was eight years old, I had a doll. I don't know where she came from. She must have been a donation to the orphanage that somehow made its way to me instead of someone else. I called her Trixibelle, but nobody ever knew her name apart from me.

Nicholas watched me. *What happened to her?*

One of the boys from the orphanage stole her. He threw her into the river.

I'm sorry.

I grinned suddenly. *It's okay. I got my revenge when I put buckthorn extract in his porridge. He had the shits for three days.*

He didn't laugh this time, but he did smile. *Your parents?*

I don't know. I have no memory of them. I paused. *Yours?*

Alive and well, he answered. *Or so I hope. I've been with the Mages a long time.* His expression hardened.

I wanted to ask him more about how he'd ended up here, but Nicholas didn't give me the chance. He returned to his original question, and this time there was an edge to it. *So, why me?* he asked. *Why not our illustrious Lord Noah? He would not have turned you away if you'd knocked on his door. You'd have had as much chance of leeching his magic from the act of sex as you would mine.*

My eyes flew to his and I paled. Nicholas laughed humourlessly.

I am many things, Mairi, and I have many faults. I am not, however, stupid. He flashed me a look of cold amusement. *It's not true, though.* *The rumour that a magical woman will steal a magical man's magic during acts of lovemaking has persisted for years, not only amongst the populace but amongst the Mages as well. I can assure you that it's not a thing.* He gestured towards me. *See for yourself. In that at least, you are unchanged.*

I swallowed, embarrassed at having been caught out. I looked down at the floor, and I also searched inside myself. He was right: the well of magic that I'd felt since that morning at Fee's house was the same as it had always been. My shoulders sagged. I was disappointed – but not as disappointed as I should have been.

You didn't say anything, I communicated, with a semi-accusatory edge.

I felt, rather than saw, his smile. *I have no objections to being used for sex. Not by you, anyway.*

I started slightly and Nicholas chuckled.

Noah has been on a mission to possess you since he met you in that tartan shop, he continued. *He's been using his magic to seduce you. Not just for sex – he wants you to fall in love with him. Lord Noah enjoys being adored. You are far from his first target.*

I thought about what Nicholas had just said. That Noah had been flirting was obvious; I knew exactly what he wanted and why he'd invited me for dinner at a posh hotel so far out of my league that it was utterly ridiculous. But I hadn't appreciated that Noah was using magic to persuade me to his side. Now it made sense: the strange sensations when he touched me; the warmth when his skin brushed against mine, and the sense of loss when he moved away.

Noah had been turning my own body against me to get what he wanted. I felt a ripple of anger, followed suddenly by guilt. It wasn't all that different to my motives for coming here to Nicholas. Noah's true reasons were simply baser than mine.

Nicholas quirked an eyebrow. *What happened between us was a result of free will on both our parts. Don't feel bad about it. I don't.*

I stared at him. He'd read my thoughts again when I'd believed I was guarding them.

He shook his head. *I don't need to read your mind to know what you're thinking, Mairi. It's written all over your face.* He leaned back, a smug expression lighting his tattooed features. *And, truth be told, I also know why you came to me instead of our esteemed Lord Noah – despite his best efforts. I only wanted to hear you say it out loud.* He waved an amused hand. *So to speak.*

My brow creased and I sent him a suspicious look.

I used no magical persuasion. I didn't flirt. But you still wanted me instead of him. You told yourself you were coming here for magic. You were really coming for me. His eyes danced. *And you still want me now.*

I knew you were arrogant, I shot back. *I hadn't realised that your ego was mountain sized.*

Nicholas laughed again. With two long strides, he was by my side. He brushed away a loose curl from the side of my face and, despite my better intentions, I shivered. He dipped his head and I felt his hot breath against my cheek. My mouth was suddenly dry. 'Aye,' he murmured aloud. 'You want me.'

Unfortunately, he was right. I bit my lip and moved in for another kiss. What the hell.

Nicholas, however, pulled back with a regretful sigh. 'The second time will be slower than the first and, once we start, we won't be able to stop. But it won't be long until everyone else rouses, and it won't go well for either of us if you're found here. You should go now.'

He cupped my face, his next words smoky with promise. 'There will be more nights, Mairi. I can promise you that.' He hesitated for a fraction of a second. 'And I can help you with your quest against the Mages. Maybe you have it in you to free both of us.' He looked into my eyes. 'I told you already. I am not them, regardless of any appearance to the contrary.'

The Gowk's words returned to my head: one person can spark a revolution, but one person alone cannot see it through. Maybe an enslaved daemon was the answer to all our hopes.

Thank you, Nicholas. I stood up and walked to the door.

My name isn't Nicholas, he told me. *That's the name the Mages gave me. My real name is Laoch.*

I paused. *Laoch.* I nodded once. *It's nice to meet you.*

And then I left his room to return to my own.

CHAPTER TWENTY-ONE

I SPENT MUCH OF THE ENSUING DAY IN A DAZE. EVEN IF I'D
wanted to forget what had happened between Nicholas – no,
Laoch – and me, my body wouldn't let me. I ached in all the
right places, and the memory of our conversation echoed in my
head over and over again.

It had been a real conversation. I'd communicated in actual
sentences, whether they'd been voiced aloud or not. When I
caught a few spare moments, I tried to speak to him again,
sending out curious questions to see if he could hear me. He
never responded and I felt nothing but an empty silence.
Perhaps we had to be face to face for the telepathy to work. I
discovered that I liked that idea; it made me feel as if I could be
normal for once in my life.

In contrast to my mood, Ailsa's good humour from the
previous day had vanished. She scowled at me frequently, and I
was at the cutting edge of her tongue more than once. I had no
idea of the reason for her antagonism until it was time for my
afternoon break, and she declared loudly that I was allowed off
for the remainder of the day so I could go gallivanting with the
Mages.

With Laoch filling my mind, I'd forgotten about my dinner with Noah. The thought of it turned my stomach, but I nodded and turned to the door to go to my room and make myself look as presentable as I could.

Ailsa followed me into the corridor and grabbed my elbow. 'I hope you know what you're doing, lassie,' she hissed at me. 'He'll break your heart in the end. Have a care and guard yourself.'

For a strange moment I thought she meant Laoch, then I realised she was referring to Noah. Even with his seductive magic, and the way he used it to manipulate my emotions, I knew it would never be true.

Despite – or perhaps because of – his magical influence, Noah still seemed better than the other Mages. I'd seen no evidence that he possessed the same edge of brutality as his uncle and I found it hard to imagine him standing on a scaffold ordering an execution. But, regardless of what he did or didn't do, I wouldn't ever be his. He was a Mage and he'd proved he was devious. However, I could still use him for my own ends in the same way he was trying to use me for his.

I nodded at Ailsa to acknowledge her warning and scuttled off.

I'd assumed that I would wear the clothes I had arrived in. The outfit that Jane had given me wasn't particularly high quality, but it was the nicest thing I'd ever owned and the only alternative was my servants' uniform.

When I walked into my room and saw the dress lying on my bed awaiting my return, I knew I shouldn't have been so naïve. Noah was a highly placed Mage whose uncle was the Ascendant; he wouldn't want to be seen in public with someone who was wearing anything less than high fashion.

I was more shocked to note that the dress was made from a generous swatch of Belle and Twister's tartan. I recognised it immediately. It was turquoise blue with a criss-cross tartan in burnt orange and deep green. I felt nauseous that their business had been brought to the brink of bankruptcy so the Mages could show off on a few vaguely romantic dates.

Despite my feelings, I knew what was expected of me so I put the damned thing on. It looked good, even if it did expose a touch too much skin and was cut in a style that was eerily reminiscent of the garment I'd been forced to wear for the Mages when they'd come to the shop. I swept my red curls into a manageable – and hopefully pretty – hairstyle and headed out to find Noah. It was galling that I had to walk through the City Chambers like this; lots of people would see me, and all of them would make assumptions, but there wasn't much I could do about that.

I passed Billy, who whistled and applauded. Trish and Lottie cheered, despite dark looks of warning in their eyes. Ailsa scowled. Several of the other servants, whom I felt I'd been getting to know, turned their backs in disapproval.

It wasn't the weight of the other servants' censure that I felt pressing down on me, it was the look in Laoch's eyes as he turned into the main hallway and saw me waiting for Noah. His disapproval and disappointment were palpable, and there was more than a hint of fury in the glance he sent me.

You're still going out with him. It wasn't a question.

It would look suspicious if I cancelled at the last minute. Besides, you know the real reason I'm doing this.

Laoch turned away. *Will you sleep with him like you did with me? How far are you prepared to go with this, Mairi? I know almost as much about what goes on here as he does. I can tell you anything you need to know.*

A Mage passed, his cloak swishing as he strode by. I pretended to adjust my cuffs so he'd believe I was absorbed in my appearance and not my silent chat with Laoch. *Where are they holding the Afflicted prisoner who was captured the other night?*

There was a moment of silence, then Laoch's voice in my

head said stiffly, *I can't tell you that. I've been explicitly forbidden to speak of him. Once my orders have been voiced, I cannot physically gainsay them.*

So the Mages had captured one of the Afflicted. I raised my eyebrows slightly, as if to tell Laoch that he'd made my point for me. *What can you tell me about female babies who are stolen away in the middle of the night?* I asked.

Across the hallway, he turned back in my direction. *How do you know about that?*

How do you? I questioned. *Have you been involved in their...* I hesitated. I wasn't willing to use the word murder. Not yet. *...disappearances?*

'Mairi!' Noah appeared, his arms spread expansively wide and his warm brown eyes sparkling. 'I knew you'd look too bonnie for words in that dress and I was right.' He planted a kiss on my cheek. I felt the familiar tingle where he touched me and couldn't suppress my smile. I knew what he was up to. 'You're beautiful.'

I curtsied to indicate my thanks. Over Noah's shoulder, I saw Laoch's face darken before he whirled away and disappeared into the library.

'We're going to have a wonderful evening,' Noah told me. 'Just you wait and see.'

I allowed an image of Laoch's naked body to fill my mind, and my cheeks turned pink as a result. It did the trick: Noah beamed happily and held out his arm. I took it.

I have to do this, I sent to Laoch. *I have to find concrete evidence that proves what evil the Mages are up to.*

If he heard me, he didn't respond. Less than a minute later, Noah and I walked out of the City Chambers.

'I DON'T WANT to alarm you,' Noah said, as we swept through the entrance of the Grand Hotel, 'but we will be leaving the restaurant here after dark has fallen. It will only be by a couple of hours. We all know that the Afflicted are dangerous and that they roam the streets at night, but it's only a short distance to the City Chambers and you'll be safe with me. I'm powerful enough to fight off an army of the Afflicted.'

I doubted that very much, but I also doubted that we'd be in any danger. From what I'd already learned from my two night-time expeditions, the Afflicted didn't come this close to the city centre even in the dead of night.

I affected the wide-eyed expression that I knew Noah expected and he chuckled. 'I suppose you've never been out after the sun has fallen, have you? That's wise when you don't have a Mage by your side. Things will be different from now on, Mairi. You'll see.'

Noah clearly thought this was already a done deal. I smiled prettily and dipped my head. At least I wasn't expected to give voice to an answer.

The maître d' appeared and we were ushered through to our table. I didn't bother to conceal my amazement. Several hotels were maintained throughout the city for the few businessmen or rich families who could afford to travel, as well as the Mages from other cities who appeared from time to time. The Grand Central Hotel certainly lived up to its name: opulent splendour dripped from every corner.

I stared openly round the room and took my time examining the other guests. There were two Mages that I didn't recognise, seated together and silently supping bowls of green soup. In the far corner there was a family with two straight-backed children in clothes finer than I'd ever seen before. There were three couples clearly from wealthy backgrounds and, to my surprise, Angus, the surly Mage whom Ailsa had bantered with. He was sitting on his own, and he was the only diner who didn't glance up at me with blatant, judgmental curiosity.

'It's quite some place, right?' Noah asked softly. He looked momentarily abashed. 'I hope you don't feel too awkward. I suppose I wanted to bring you here to show off. You deserve more than a job as a servant, Mairi.' He waved a hand. 'You deserve this.'

While I certainly wasn't going to argue with him, I wondered what he thought I'd done to merit such a statement. Why did I, in particular, deserve this sort of venue or a different job?

If Noah had been planning to explain, he didn't get the chance. A waiter appeared out of nowhere with two pristine napkins. He placed one in my lap and the other in Noah's, as if we were far too special to manage such a mundane task ourselves. Then he handed Noah a menu and, with a soft murmur, took a step back.

I waited, watching Noah's eyes scan the words. Perhaps I would also have my food cut up into little pieces for me and be spoon fed. It wouldn't have surprised me.

'The lady and I,' Noah said, with a flash of a smile in my direction, 'will have the salmon to start. Then I will have the sirloin and she will take the venison stew.'

Would I like salmon and venison? I'd never eaten either, so I had no way of knowing.

'Very good, sir.' The waiter removed the menu and departed smoothly.

Noah leaned across the linen-covered table and rested his chin on his hands. 'So, Mairi,' he drawled, 'how are you finding working for us Mages?'

There were only so many answers I was capable of giving. I managed a small shrug and a smile and then, because I felt that he wanted more detail, mimed a yawn.

Noah chuckled. 'Yes, I imagine it's very tiring. Your hard

work has been noticed. My uncle, the Ascendant, was commenting on what a great addition you are to the team.'

The Ascendant had never noticed me. I smiled, but my discomfort was growing. Maintaining 'small talk' like this was difficult; I wasn't used to being the focus of another person's attention. Only Isla – and Laoch – had spent this much time chatting just to me. I knew that white lies and social niceties were part and parcel of conversation, but everything felt disjointed because I couldn't offer them back.

I licked my lips and thought about how to do better. I pointed towards Noah, fluttered my hands and tried to indicate that I'd been impressed with the way he'd used magic to clean the staircase for me the previous day.

He grimaced slightly and squinted at my hands. Eventually he raised his shoulders in a defeated shrug. 'I'm sorry,' he said. 'I don't know what you mean.' He pulled a face. 'I should have brought a notebook so you could write down what you want to say. That was remiss of me.'

As Noah reached for my hands and squeezed them, his lips moved and he whispered something under his breath. I realised that he was gradually increasing his magical pressure on me; now that I was more aware of what he was doing, it was obvious and I chided myself for not noticing before.

Goosebumps shivered along the length of my bare arms as I felt his seductive magic ripple over my skin. Fortunately, he didn't appear to notice. 'I'll find a way to help you,' he said. 'I've already found several books in the library that detail various healing spells. There will be a way to make you talk, Mairi, I'm sure of it.' His eyes were shining. 'Imagine what you would say if you could speak.'

Uh-huh. I withdrew my hands and clasped them together to indicate a hopeful plea. This was what I needed; anything Noah said about his work could be useful. I gestured with a question in my eyes.

'Yes.' He nodded vigorously. 'I believe I can do it. It's what we Mages do. I know it doesn't always seem that way on the other side, but all our actions are intended to help the people of this city. We keep the water running and the food growing, and we are working on ways to heal the Afflicted and prevent anyone else from catching their terrible disease. It's such an honour to be part of that work. The Mages keep our city and our country safe, but we can do more. We can help people like you.'

From the side of our table, somebody cleared their throat. I started, surprised. I'd been so focused on Noah's fervent words that I'd not noticed a couple approaching and neither had he. He blinked in surprise and rose to his feet to greet them. 'Good evening.'

'My Lord Noah.' The man bowed. 'I do hope we are not interrupting. I wanted to come over and say hello. It's been some time since we spoke.'

I couldn't tell whether Noah was pleased or dismayed by the man's appearance, but he clapped him on the shoulder, smiled and gave every impression that he was thrilled. 'Alistair Browning, right?'

The man nodded and pointed to the quiet woman by his side. 'This is my wife, Margaret. We won't keep you. I merely wanted to thank you for your intervention at my factory last month. Your aid was invaluable.'

My ears perked up. This sounded interesting.

'All in a day's work,' Noah smiled.

Margaret curtsied. 'From what I heard,' she said, 'it was far more than that. The information you got from that Farris fellow was more than enough to put a stop to those fools who were trying to cause trouble.'

'We can't have the good work that you do stopped because of a few disgruntled bampots,' Noah agreed. He shot me a satisfied look. 'I was only just telling my companion here that our job as

Mages is to keep the city safe and prosperous. What happened at your factory is an example of that.'

'It was well done.' Alistair Browning bowed again. 'Thank you so much.' He took hold of his wife's wrist and the pair of them backed away to their own table.

I tilted my head at Noah, hoping he would elaborate on what had occurred with Browning. And who was Farris? The waiter took that moment to arrive with the first course, however, and the moment was gone.

I tried not to let my frustration show. Baby steps, I told myself. Every single scrap of information could be useful.

CHAPTER TWENTY-TWO

THE REST OF THE EVENING PASSED WITHOUT INCIDENT. NOAH maintained a steady stream of chatter, but for the vast part it was inconsequential. No matter how hard I tried to read between the lines and draw conclusions, there was nothing substantial that I could take to the Gowk.

Even the food wasn't as spectacular as I'd been expecting. The dishes were certainly good to look at, and the ingredients included many things I'd never tasted before, but they didn't delight my tastebuds. And the venison was surprisingly tough.

Part of me had hoped for some action on the journey back to the City Chambers. If one or more of the Afflicted emerged from a dark side street and attempted an attack, I could learn a lot from how Noah warded them off. However, nothing untoward happened – although two ravens, who were out after their bedtime, followed us. From the way he kept glancing up at them, I suspected that Noah was as unsettled by their appearance as I was.

When we went through the main doors of the City Chambers, he didn't suggest that I joined him for a nightcap in his room but hastily made his excuses. 'I'm afraid that duty calls,

Mairi. I'd hoped we could continue this with a stroll in the garden, but my uncle needs me and I am bound to answer his summons.'

He leaned forward, a cloud of his wine-scented breath hitting my face. 'May I?' he asked carefully. 'Before I take my leave?'

Despite his gentle question, I knew I couldn't decline because I needed Noah on my side. Damning myself for it, I nodded. He smiled and put his arm round my waist before lowering his head to kiss me.

It wasn't a long kiss and it wasn't deep, but Noah's mouth was skilful. A detached part of my mind noted that he knew what he was doing, but he was too distracted to throw any magic into the act – either that or he was noble enough not to use magic when it came to something intimate like a kiss. Regardless of the reason, I was relieved that he didn't try to spell me because it made me appreciate that, despite his proficiency, the kiss didn't stir me.

'Adieu, sweet Mairi,' he murmured. 'I will seek you out tomorrow.' He smiled at me and departed, taking the stairs two at a time before turning right towards the west wing of the building.

I had to bite back the temptation to trail after him and find out what was going on. I knew I'd be noticed in an instant. I curled my hands into fists, feeling the dull pain as my finger-nails cut into my palms.

Well, it looks like you had a fun evening.

I wasn't remotely surprised to hear Laoch's voice pop into my head – somehow, I'd expected it. I glanced round, aware that he had to be nearby. My eyes fell on the shadowy corner where I'd hidden and watched the Ascendant and the other Mages as they'd prepared to head out to catch an Afflicted prisoner. I drew back my shoulders and joined him there in the gloom.

You're jealous. A strange, unlikable thrill went through me at the thought.

Laoch took a moment before answering. *Yes,* he responded finally. *I suppose I am. Foolish as it may be, given that I know you used me and I know you are using that boy as well.* He reached out and, with a silken touch, brushed my cheek. *But,* he added, *I also know you still want me more than him.*

I do. I had no reason not to be honest with him. *But I can't fling away the reason I came here because of a tattooed daemon who's as much of a slave as I am.*

I would not ask you to.

The question all but asked itself. *Then why are you here now?*

His cold laughter echoed in my head, although I didn't know if he was amused at me, himself or the situation. *To remind you of my presence, I suppose. And to give you a gift.*

I raised my eyebrows, surprised. *A gift?*

The realm I come from is not dissimilar to this one. Naturally, we are more civilised, but a lot of our ways are the same. We possess the same magic but our knowledge of it is stronger.

I hesitated then asked, *Then how did you come to be enslaved to the Mages?*

Laoch's answer was curt. *That is a tale for another time. Suffice to say that I have more power than the Mages know. They cannot force me to tell them of what they are unaware.*

I became very still. *But you'll tell me?*

To tell you is to trust you. And I am not yet convinced I can do that.

I sucked in a breath. *You can trust me. Even if we had not shared last night, I know enough to believe you feel the same way about the Mages as I do. I won't betray you to them.* I motioned towards my mouth. *And I am mute.*

There are plenty of ways to communicate other than by speaking. Laoch shook his head. *It's not merely trust that you won't betray me. You still cannot trust me, Mairi. You can never trust me.*

His words were so fervent that I half-expected he would prove his point by sounding the alarm to inform the Mages about what I'd been up to. Instead he relaxed slightly before continuing. *I can't afford knowledge such as this to end up in the wrong hands. But I grow tired of this place and I need an escape.* He clinked his wrist bands together. *Enslavement is ... draining.*

I registered the deep-seated pain in his words and reminded myself that it was not only me or my city that was under the Mages' magical thumbs. I desperately wanted to learn from Laoch, but it had to be his choice. That was freedom: being able to choose for yourself, whether your decisions and actions led to the right or the wrong consequences.

I bit the inside of my cheek and waited. I couldn't force him to do this, and I would no longer try to persuade him. It had to be on him.

He gazed at me for a long moment while I held my breath. From behind me, I heard Mages bustling around. Judging from the snatched conversation that drifted over, it wasn't just Noah who had been summoned to the Ascendant. Something was happening, something big. I wished I knew what.

The black streaks of Laoch's tattoos shifted, altering subtly in a manner I'd not seen before. He knelt and picked up a small box from near his feet. *You'll need this.*

As I held out my hand to take it, there was a sudden strange scratching sound from within. I pulled back sharply and hissed.

Shhh, he cautioned. *It's fine. Dinna fash yourself.*

His use of slang was clearly intended to relax me. It didn't. *What the fuck is in that?*

Laoch held the box out again. *Take it and see.* He offered a brief, amused glance. *Although it might bite.*

I snorted, thinking it was a joke. I remained fearful but I took the box, flipped open the lid and gazed inside. A tiny pink nose sniffed up at me. Oh. Indeed it might bite. *A mouse?*

Laoch smiled. *I selected this one specially.*

I looked up at him. *I don't understand.*

You'll tire quickly. The smaller the beast, the harder it becomes to maintain, and any injury sustained will be matched to your human form.

I blinked at him. *Whititty-what?*

The risks are great.

I scratched my head. *Uh, Laoch...*

His green eyes suddenly crinkled. *It's been a long time since I heard another person use that name. It's surprising how much difference it makes.*

Good. I nodded. *Can we get back to the mouse?* Its sharp teeth appeared to be making a beeline for my finger. I hastily closed the box lid before it drew blood.

The Mages control the ravens. They use them to retrieve messages, and they can see things through their eyes if they concentrate hard enough. They are clever birds and capable of a great deal, but my magic can do a lot more than control a bird.

I was beginning to feel very dubious about this. *You can control mice?*

Oh no – I can become *a mouse. Or a cat. Or a fly. There's no limit.* His mouth flattened. *Or at least there wasn't until the Mages gave me my slave cuffs. With these on, I cannot manage the transformation.*

My brow creased. *I don't understand.*

It's easier to experience than to explain.

There was a loud call from somewhere beyond the hallway. 'Nicholas! Where the fuck are you?' We both stiffened. I recognised that voice and my lip curled. It was Ross. 'Nicholas! *Ish var*! Come here now!'

Laoch's face contorted. There had been a thrum of magic to Ross's bellow; he was commanding Laoch who was compelled to obey. *The words you need are* belsh za tum. *Use them carefully, Mairi. I must go.* He grimaced in pain and whirled out of the shadows to attend to Ross's bidding.

'Where the fuck have you been, you horned bampot?'

'I have been here by the stairs all this time,' Laoch answered, forced by the magic to answer the question. 'I only now heard your call.'

'Lucky for you that you did,' Ross sneered. 'The Ascendant needs us.'

'Where is he?'

'Where the fuck do you think he is? In his rooms, that's where.'

I was sure that Laoch had asked the question for my benefit. I watched from my concealed spot as he and Ross walked up the stairs in the same direction that Noah had gone.

I was alone; all the Mages were otherwise occupied. I bit my lip and gazed down at the box in my hands. From inside there was a tiny squeak. Okay, I thought. Okay. It was dangerous to try any magic inside these walls, but it could be worth the risk. I closed my eyes. It was better not to overthink this, I decided. Just do it.

I hummed a single low note. *Belsh za tum.*

My skin prickled uncomfortably.

Belsh za tum. I hummed again.

I gritted my teeth, opened my eyes and flipped open the box lid. My eyes met those of the wee mouse. *Belsh za tum.*

This time my hum barely lasted a second. All of a sudden, I was in freefall. My stomach was in my mouth. High walls surrounded me and I knew I was falling but I couldn't do anything about it. Shit! Help me. Shit. What? Shit.

There was a thud as I hit the ground. I remained where I was for a moment, faintly stunned. My shoulder felt sore where I'd knocked it as I landed. My tail hurt, particularly at the tip where it had been trapped against my body.

I froze. Wait. My tail?

I spun round in a panic and the tips of my whiskers brushed

against the sides of the fallen box. The sensation, so different to what I was used to, made me quake with fear.

There was a chink of light ahead. Body quivering, I darted towards it. As I skittered out of the small box, my paws scrabbled on the smooth floor.

As soon as I reached the lighted section of the hallway, I knew it was a mistake. I could be seen here – I could be caught. And there was no food in sight, not even a crumb.

The last thought hadn't been my own. The mouse was still here with me; I was in control but I could feel the mouse, too. Not its thoughts exactly, but feelings like hunger, fear. And above all else, the over-riding instinct to stay safe.

I whirled round, my paws surprisingly deft, then I bounded back to the dark corner. As soon as I reached it, I curled into a tight ball and assessed my situation more calmly.

Okay. I was a mouse. The fall had been because I'd been holding the box in my human hands when I'd said the magic words. My body appeared to have vanished, making the box drop at the exact moment my consciousness transferred. It was bizarre. And brilliant.

Becoming a rodent wasn't how I'd expected to end my evening, but I was nothing if not adaptable. I remembered what Laoch had said; it was indeed easier to experience than to explain.

I shivered slightly. Would I be able to transform back into my own body? I certainly didn't fancy being a mouse for the rest of my days – but I also appreciated the possibilities that were now open to me and why Laoch had gifted me these magic words.

I glanced round, suddenly worried that my transformation might have been sensed by any Mages who were nearby, but nobody was running towards me. There were no alarmed shouts. Whatever the Ascendant wanted, his summons was clearly more than enough to preoccupy the magical bastards.

I shook out my fur. In this body, I could sneak into the Ascendant's rooms and eavesdrop. Perhaps I could use my new sharp teeth to gnaw through his throat while he was sleeping and bite his jugular vein. The mouse within me recoiled at the image. Not that, then; anyway, it was an unlikely scenario.

Unwilling to waste what time I had, I took off and scampered round the edges of the hallway. I stayed close to the walls, continually checking there was a piece of furniture or a hole nearby that I could dart into if I needed to hide.

It was extraordinary how dusty the floor was. I knew how often it was cleaned because I was usually the person who had to clean it, and I didn't cut corners – not deliberately, anyway. Yet there were clumps of hair rolling around like tumbleweed, together with hillocks of mud and dirt and dust. I was grateful that Ailsa couldn't see what things were really like; she'd have had a fit.

I pattered round a corner and found myself at the foot of the main staircase. Hmm. It was some distance to the west wing and the Ascendant's rooms. I'd pinpointed them during my nightly expeditions, although I'd taken care not to venture too close in case I was discovered.

In my present form I could go where I pleased, although the staircase in front of me seemed insurmountable to my tiny rodent body. I was also painfully aware that there were long corridors and yet another staircase before I reached the Ascendant.

I'd already worked out that I could move with surprising speed as a mouse; even so, it would take me the better part of forty minutes to get to where I needed to be. Laoch had told me that I'd tire quickly. Could I stay inside the mouse long enough to get into the Ascendant's rooms and get out again? Shite. I had to try – I might never get a chance like this again.

I tightened my body and felt the mouse resist. It didn't want to go up. There was little chance of finding food upstairs; the best opportunities were on this floor near the kitchen and the dining rooms. I sent it a silent apology, promising I'd find it the tastiest morsels once this was over.

The mouse likely didn't understand because it continued to pull against me. I had no choice – I had to push it. I leapt upwards and landed on the first step. There. One down. Only sixty more or so to go.

A loud booming sound filled my ears. I paused while the mouse's mind went into meltdown mode. *Run*, it insisted. *Run!* I held my ground until I felt the ground shudder and quake, as if it were about to give away and swallow me up, tail and all. I turned, sprang off the step and darted underneath a side table.

As the booming noise continued, I squeezed my eyes shut and listened hard. It took a few moments, but then I found I could tune in. Voices, I realised: I was hearing voices.

'I hear the Ascendant has called a cabal meeting. Does that mean they've found another one?'

The words were hard to cling onto and my mouse ears took a moment to register their meaning. What was particularly distracting was that not only could I hear the words, but also the emotion behind them. This speaker, whoever it was, was very anxious.

'That would be my guess,' came the grim response. 'I reckon teams of us will be sent out tonight to find her.'

Something cold settled in the pit of my stomach. Her?

'So soon after the last one? It doesn't bode well. It's a nasty business.'

I tried to pinpoint where the voices were coming from. I needed to hear more. I swung my head round – and that was when my nose started twitching uncontrollably.

I felt the mouse's terror. Predator. Monster. Blood. The images forced their way into my consciousness.

I looked up and saw slitted eyes watching me from the other side of the room. A cat, one of several in the building that kept down the rodent population. My fear abruptly mingled with that of the mouse's. It was time to flee.

The cat crouched. It was some distance away, but I knew it was preparing to run and pounce. I had to get to safety – it wasn't just my own life I was responsible for, it was the mouse's too.

I felt a push at the edge of my mind. The mouse knew what to do and where to go, and it wanted to take over. With terrible misgivings, I let it.

We ran. I heard the cat's paws as it sprang after us. Our muscles bunched up and we pelted forward, leaving the safety of the table for the open hallway. No, I screamed in my head, but it was too late. The mouse was in charge now.

We reached the far wall. The cat lunged, one paw outstretched, and we put on an extra spurt of speed. I heard the cat hiss as it missed us. I knew that it would try again.

We were tiring already and there was nowhere else to go. The door in front of us was closed. This was worse than being attacked by one of the Afflicted. I'd end up eaten by a cat and nobody would know what had happened to me – even Laoch would never be sure.

The mouse twisted to the left. I gasped, the sound emerging as a squeak and scaring me almost as much as the chasing feline. There was a tiny hole in the skirting board by the wall. Surely it was too small and we couldn't fit through it? The mouse went for it anyway.

Splintered wood scratched my spine as it pierced the layer of fur. I heard a yowl of frustration and held my breath. Then, unbelievably, we were through. Breathing fast, I felt a surge of deep rodent satisfaction. Made it. We had made it.

The mouse yielded to me once more. The hole was dark and cramped. I knew there was no way back so I pressed forward. My only thought was to find somewhere safe and force the transformation so I could get the hell out of this body and back to my normal self.

I scuttled forward nervously. If I kept going and the map in my head was accurate, we'd end up in the kitchens. That would be safe enough. That would work.

The narrow passageway curved downwards rather than ahead and I tensed – I didn't want to go down. There would be no space for my human body if we ended up below the building. There was no choice, however; it was either down into the depths of the City Chambers or back into the jaws of the cat. No contest.

I ploughed ahead, noting that the mouse part of my mind was relaxed now. That made one of us.

It seemed to take an age. There were mothballs and dust, and I sneezed violently on more than one occasion. I could feel exhaustion setting in, not just from the surge of adrenalin wearing off but from the effort of sustaining my consciousness in the mouse's body. This was what Laoch had meant when he said it would be tiring. It was like nothing I'd ever experienced before and I started to feel like I was moving through thick sludge.

There was a corner, then another. With each step, it grew harder to keep going. There had to be some end to this, something at the other side, far below the floor.

And then I saw a pinprick of light. Praise be. I scuttled towards it as fast as my four legs could carry me.

CHAPTER TWENTY-THREE

THE ROOM WAS UNFAMILIAR; I THOUGHT I'D TRAVERSED ALL THE main areas of the City Chambers, but I'd definitely never been here. It was windowless and airless. I must have descended further beneath the building than I'd realised and was now deep in the basement.

The floor was uneven stone, which felt cold beneath my tiny paws, and the room was empty of furniture, save for a small wooden table and a chair. My nose twitched involuntarily again and I felt a thrill of fear. Had the cat somehow made its way down here and was waiting to attack again? But the image I got from the mouse wasn't of fear, it was of food. Given how tired and shaky I felt, a meal might not be a bad idea.

I nipped over to the table leg and eyed it. How hard could it be? The mouse urged me forward, keen to get to whatever delectable crumbs lay above. I swallowed and braced myself before leaping up. I expected to fall, but my tiny claws gripped the rough wood easily. I scampered up, delighted with my newfound ability. Maybe there was something to being a mouse after all. Even better, there was a plate on the table top with a half-eaten dinner roll that I knew would serve the mouse – and me – well.

I don't know whether it was the rodent's hungry enthusiasm or my fatigue but I could feel my control slipping by the time I reached the plate. I tried to cling on and maintain dominance but the mouse's desire for food was too strong. He wanted what was on that plate.

I felt a shudder and the mouse's body spasmed, then my stomach flipped and the world spun sideways. A moment later, I was looking down at the bread roll from a great height and feeling very strange. My vision swam and I was swaying from side to side.

There was a faint squeak and I looked down. A mouse – *the* mouse – was staring up at me, its cheeks filled with crumbs.

I gazed down at my human feet, then raised my hands and poked at my face. It *was* me – I was me again. As I clambered down from the table and shook my head to rid myself of the dizziness, my nose twitched in rodent fashion. Maybe it would take me some time to rid myself of a mouse's instincts.

So that was what it was like to be a mouse. It hadn't been particularly pleasant, and I doubted the experience was what Laoch had intended. The cat's slitted eyes flashed into my mind and I shuddered. I hoped not, anyway.

Now that I was back in my normal body, it was easier to get my bearings. I looked more closely round the room. It was small – only about eight feet square – and there were two plain doors made of unvarnished wood. The walls were rough-hewn and looked unfinished. I certainly wasn't in the Ascendant's chambers.

Without thinking, I grabbed the half-eaten dinner roll. My tartan dress didn't have any pockets, so I loosened the stays and shoved it down my cleavage. There was more than enough material to cover any strange bulges.

The mouse squeaked at me from the table top, not as afraid

of my human presence as it should have been. In fact, it seemed to be scolding me for taking away its meal. *Don't worry, little mouse,* I told it silently. *You're coming too.* Then I scooped it up and dropped it next to the bread.

Its warm fur brushed against my skin as it shuffled around for a moment but, after turning round a few times, it seemed to settle – save for the odd sound of chewing.

With that problem temporarily solved, I turned to the first door. It was time to find out exactly where I was and what these secret rooms contained.

I'd been expecting something surprising – or damning – so I was disappointed to find that there was nothing more than a narrow staircase behind the door. It had to lead up to the ground floor, although I had no clue where it would emerge. I'd been through every visible door on that floor, and I didn't recognise this staircase at all. I shrugged and headed for the second door.

I twisted the knob carefully and opened it a crack. There was a dim light in the room beyond but it seemed unoccupied. I opened the door wider and stepped across the threshold.

There was something in the centre of the room. It looked to be some sort of box, but I couldn't tell for sure until I drew closer. The light was coming from a single large candle on the floor that, judging by the drips of wax, had been burning for some time.

I licked my lips and drew closer. Huh. It wasn't a box at all, it was a cage. In that instant I knew exactly what I'd find inside it. I knelt, disturbing the wee mouse who let out a muffled squeak in protest. I absently patted the front of my dress to reassure it, then I peered into the cage.

Although I'd been expecting him, I still drew in a sharp breath when I saw the Afflicted man. As far as I could tell he was naked, though it was difficult to be sure because he was in a hunched, seated position, his arms wrapped round his legs and his head down. Long straggly hair hung limply from his bony skull.

I stepped back and examined the cage. It was secure. There was no chance he would escape and attack me, so I moved closer. He didn't look up at me – there wasn't a single twitch to show that he knew I was there – but I could tell he was alive. His breath was pained and rasping, as if he were struggling to get enough air into his lungs.

The cage wasn't large enough for the man to stand up in, neither was it large enough for him to stretch out, and its confines had forced him into that hunched position. Whatever reason the Mages had for taking him, keeping him like this was unnecessarily cruel. He was Afflicted, and supposedly mindless now, but once he'd been someone's son, maybe someone's brother, father, uncle. It wasn't his fault he'd ended up Afflicted, it was an unpleasant quirk of fate. He certainly didn't deserve this.

I grimaced then I squinted. There were odd marks on his arms and legs, and he seemed to be holding his right hand in a strange manner. I sniffed the air carefully. Beyond the usual reek that I'd come to associate with the Afflicted, there was the unmistakable tang of blood.

I swallowed. The marks on his skin weren't from dirt or old tattoos, they were wounds and they looked fresh. He could have incurred them when he was captured – I already knew he'd put up a fight from the screams I'd heard that night – but several of them were still oozing blood. To my eye, they'd been inflicted on him today.

I looked at the way he was cradling his hand then, with my heart in my mouth, I stretched through the bars of the cage and gently touched his arm. He flinched and recoiled with a sharp whine. As he did so, I felt sick to my stomach. Three of his fingers were missing. From the seeping cuts, they'd been sliced away recently.

I let out a small moan at the pain he must be feeling and what had been done to him. These weren't defensive wounds; he hadn't lost his fingers when he was captured. My mind drifted to the jars of body parts in Ross's study room. The Mages were experimenting on this man. They were slicing off parts of him for reasons I couldn't begin to grasp.

I shook my head in dismay. *I'm so sorry*, I projected silently. *I'm so sorry they've done this to you.* Animals were treated better than this.

As if he'd heard my unvoiced apology, the man's head lifted and he stared at me. His fingers weren't the only casualties. His left eye was also missing and, from the crusted blood around the socket, it had also been removed recently. Afflicted or not, this man was being tortured.

I glanced round the room. There were dark stains around the cage and splatters on the walls: blood. How many other Afflicted people had been brought down here and sliced up?

My gaze fell on the pile of haphazardly folded tartan in the corner. Huh. Like the dress I was wearing, I recognised it from Belle and Twister's shop. It looked like it had been used for mopping up blood, vomit and goodness knows what else. I supposed sourly that particular colour didn't suit any of the Mages, so they'd put it to another use. Typical. My familiar hatred for the Mages coalesced into something else as I turned back to the Afflicted man. God, he was in a pitiable state.

There was no decision to make. I didn't care what greater good my masters might say they were up to; this was torture for no apparent reason that I could fathom. The man might easily turn on me, but that didn't mean I could leave him. I knew what the consequences could be if I helped him but I didn't care. If I let something like this slide in pursuit of my own higher purpose, I was no better than the Mages.

I pulled back my shoulders and reached for the bolt on the front of the cage.

'And what the fuck are you doing here, lassie?'

Bish var. I hummed once, turned and attacked the cloaked Mage. My fist smacked into the side of his head and he went reeling against the wall before I registered that it was Angus.

Although I was more successful with the magic than I'd been when I'd defended myself before, I hadn't done enough to take him out. He countered immediately. *'Ins veil,'* he spat.

My body was lifted in the air and thrown against the opposite wall. Winded, I struggled to get up. My hands scrabbled on the floor, eventually curling around the lit candle. I heaved it up.

A trickle of blood was dribbling down from Angus's nose. He glared at me. 'What are you planning to do with that?' he asked sarcastically. He leaned forward and blew out the flame with a single breath.

Belzac. I hummed again. The candle spurted back to life, not with a tiny flickering flame but with a roaring jet of fire.

To my satisfaction, Angus looked stunned. *'Sel tum,'* he snarled. From nowhere, a splash of cold water drenched both me and the candle, dousing it immediately despite its strong flame.

'Crude but effective,' Angus murmured. 'The simple spells are often the best, don't you agree?' Then, to my astonishment, he held his hand out towards me.

I stared at it as if it were a weapon and made no move to take it.

'It's not a trick,' Angus grunted. 'I could have raised the alarm by now and I've not. I could have killed you dead before you knew I was here but I did not. I'm not your enemy.'

I still didn't take his hand.

Angus sighed and knelt down until we were face to face. 'You're the mute lass.' His gaze remained steady. 'You have magic. No wonder you pretend to be mute. It's a good way to hide what you are.'

I glared at him. I wasn't pretending; nobody would stay silent for twenty years by choice.

He held up his hands, palms towards me. 'Okay, okay, I get the point. You really are mute. My apologies.' There was a mocking edge to his tone, suggesting his contrition was less than sincere. 'But you have magic.' He paused for a beat. 'Right?'

This time I made no denial. Given that I'd used magic to try to kill him stone dead, I could hardly pretend that I didn't. The big question was, what was he going to do about it?

Still in his cage, the Afflicted man groaned. Angus didn't take his eyes away from me but gestured behind him. 'You were going to release him.' It wasn't a question. 'You know he'd as soon rip your throat out with his own teeth as thank you for such a dubious kindness.'

So? I could look after my own damned throat.

Angus chuckled as if he'd understood every word. 'Fair enough, lass. I understand the sentiment.'

He reached into his pocket and I tensed. When I saw what he had withdrawn, I frowned. That looked like valerian to me, a natural sedative. 'I'm not foolish enough to attempt a rescue,' he said, 'but I was hoping to ease the poor creature's suffering.' He leaned forward again. 'Is this why you came to work here? To help the Afflicted? You're not the first one who's been on their side, and you likely won't be the last. But you can't help them. There's no end to what's been attempted over the years. Once you're Afflicted, there's no way back. I guarantee it.'

I crossed my arms over my chest and continued to stare at him.

'It's quite discomfiting to be watched constantly without any attempt at conversation in return,' he said. 'A smile wouldn't go amiss. Maybe I can make you smile.' He spun round, making a full circle, while his feet tapped out a complicated jig.

I blinked in confusion. What was he doing? I looked more closely at his face. His eyes were slightly glazed and unfocused and, although he smelled much the same as he always did, there was a lingering scent of alcohol. He was drunk. Perhaps that was why he'd not killed me yet or called for the Ascendant.

I thought of the way he'd been sitting alone in the Grand Central Hotel and the way he conversed with Ailsa, not to mention his lack of care over his personal hygiene and appearance. It occurred to me that Mage Angus was more alone than I was.

He sighed, sounding disappointed. 'No smile. Oh well. At least I tried.'

The Afflicted man moaned again.

'Hush,' Angus said, distracted. He held out his hand towards me once more. 'If you're escaping, lass, you need to do it now. In less than twenty minutes there will be Mages swarming all over the building and heading out to scour the streets. I'm sure you already know who they're looking for. You know you won't get another shot like this one.'

Against my better judgment, I took his hand and allowed him to help me up.

'There now,' he said. 'That wasn't so hard, was it?' He gave me a little nudge. 'Go on, then. You're going to die and so will he, but if you go now you have a chance of a swift passing. Get caught in this place and you'll end up in a world of pain.' He shrugged. 'Your choice.'

It was a sick trick – it had to be. But I was already trapped, so I had nothing to lose. I walked slowly over to the cage bolt and reached for it.

'Wait,' Angus said, so suddenly that I jerked. I looked at him. 'Is that ... is that ... is that a ferret down your cleavage?'

The mouse's tiny nose came snuffling up and poked out from beneath the tartan. Its beady eyes appeared and blinked curiously at Angus.

'Oh,' he said. 'It's a mouse. I see.' He waved a hand at me. 'Carry on.'

I gave him a long look, but he said nothing. From the dank interior of the cage, the Afflicted man stared at me with his one good eye. I couldn't tell what he was thinking. Probably nothing. My fingers touched the metal bolt and I slid it open.

The cage door swung free of its own accord. I expected the man to rush out and attack both me and Angus, but he did nothing. He stayed where he was and continued to watch me with his single eye. I understood immediately. In the same way that I thought Angus was tricking me somehow with his lack of interference, the Afflicted man believed that I was tricking him.

'You'd better hurry,' Angus commented. He withdrew a silver hip flask from his pocket and lifted it to his mouth.

I turned back to the cage. With slow, deliberate movements, I took the Afflicted man by his undamaged hand and tugged. For a moment he resisted, then he allowed me to lead him out.

I thought he would turn on me at any moment. He was a wounded, cornered creature, and they were always the most dangerous. From the way Angus was watching us, I knew he was expecting something similar. But he didn't interfere; he was letting me orchestrate my own destruction.

I tugged the man's wrist again and led him towards the door. He followed, his head and shoulders hunched and his arms trailing by his sides.

'Wait,' Angus said.

I stopped. Here we go. This was where Angus sprang into action and called upon the other Mages to witness my deeds. He'd obviously been waiting for the perfect moment, lulling me into a false sense of security and offering false hope that I'd get away.

I turned my head slowly. Angus was unfastening the clasp at his throat and removing his black cloak. He handed it out to me. 'He won't get very far stark naked. This will make it easier.' He shrugged. 'You'll both still die, but you might get a bit further with the cloak to help.'

I stared at him before snatching the cloak as if it were a poisoned chalice instead of mere fabric and wrapping it round the Afflicted man's shoulders. He let me cover him and, although he moaned slightly when I fastened the clasp, he didn't resist. On some level, it seemed that he understood I was trying to help him. Either that or he simply had no fight left.

We shuffled together towards the door. I was still half-expecting Angus to turn on us but he remained where he was, swigging from his flask and watching our painfully slow progress.

'Tick tock,' he said. 'You'd better hurry up or every Mage in the Chambers will see you.'

I gritted my teeth. His comments weren't helping. All the same, I pulled harder on the Afflicted man and he moved more quickly. There now. We've got this.

We passed through the small room with the table and chair. The mouse squeaked and poked its head out again to check the table top for any more discarded food. I gently pushed it down again; I had my hands full enough already.

With awkward, fumbling fingers, I twisted the doorknob and opened the door to the staircase. It would have helped if I'd known where these stairs led, but I didn't have much choice. I couldn't return the way I'd come.

The stairs were old and badly maintained. Each one creaked loudly as we made our way upwards, and I winced repeatedly. I couldn't see a single chink of light at the top of the staircase and I had no idea where we would come out. I crossed my fingers tightly and prayed that somehow we'd find the exit safely.

Perhaps sensing my anxiety, the mouse stopped shuffling around. The Afflicted man by my side punctuated every few steps with a soft groan. I squeezed his hand to try and silence him, but he had to be in agony from his wounds. I could hardly blame him for making a noise.

When we finally reached the top step, I reached in front of

me and fumbled through the darkness. There was nothing there, no door, no way out. Panic clawed at my throat and I felt my chest tighten. Breathe, Mairi, I told myself. Breathe. There had to be an exit.

It was too dark to see anything. I'd hoped my eyes would adjust to the gloom, but I couldn't even see my own hand in front of my face. I steeled myself; more magic now was risky but I had to try it.

I swallowed hard. *Altush ish moy.* Cast light. I hummed slightly and drew upon all my energy and focus. The air around me stirred and I felt it bristle with my power.

A spark flared brightly for a second with such a brilliant gleam that I almost cried out. I shielded my eyes from the glare, while the Afflicted man cowered against me, whimpering. Shite. The light had been too brief and too bright to register anything beyond the solid wall in front of us.

I grimaced and slowly dropped my hand. Everything was dark again. I tried once more. *Altus ish moy.*

The air flickered around me but nothing happened. I could feel the magic stuttering and the deep fatigue that had settled in my bones and was preventing me from releasing my power.

No. Not again. I needed it to work.

Altus ish moy. There was an edge of panic to my accompanying hum. It didn't matter: the staircase remained brutally, bitterly dark.

Laoch had warned me this would happen. He'd said that using the magic he'd taught me to send myself into the mouse would make me tire quickly. It wasn't fear or overstrung emotions that were keeping my power dormant, it was sheer exhaustion. The well inside me wasn't bottomless.

I cursed to myself. There was no choice: I'd have to go back to Angus and see if his mercy, such as it was, would extend to helping us escape.

As I turned, the Afflicted man grunted sharply in my ear and yanked on my hand. I froze, convinced that he was attacking me even though he would surely kill us both. He pulled hard, his movements rough and jerky, and thrust my hand upwards. I stiffened, preparing to defend myself – and that was when my fingers felt cold metal and I realised there was something directly over our heads. A trapdoor. Of course it was.

The man released his grip while I fumbled until I found the catch. I pushed and the trapdoor swung upwards, revealing a pool of light – and the deep, earthy smell of many plants as well as the underlying reek of rotting death. The damned Mages' garden. I should have expected this. Where else would a secret staircase lead to but here?

I heaved myself out before turning back and extending my hand to the man. He took it and, with some effort, clambered out after me. As soon as his bare feet hit the soft earth, he dropped to his knees with a moan and his undamaged hand covered his nose and mouth. He smelled the rot here, too; he knew there was something wrong about this place, just as I did. The faster we got out from this accursed glass house, the better.

I looked round, searching for the path that Noah had shown me. I caught a glimpse of stone to my right and nodded. That way. Pulling the man to his feet, I took his elbow and steered him towards it. His steps were faltering, as if being in this place was making his entire body seize up, but I wouldn't allow him to give up now, not when we'd finally made some progress and there was an exit in sight.

I tugged and pulled and silently cajoled, and step by step we began to make our way out. It was only when we passed a low-lying hawthorn tree with clumps of mistletoe trailing down from its branches that the man stopped and refused to go any further.

I hissed at him. He didn't move. I yanked on his elbow, gently at first and then with more insistence. He still wouldn't go another step. If what Angus had said was true, we didn't have time for this. I clenched my jaw and turned to face him. He was absolutely still, staring at a patch of disturbed earth less than a metre from his curling, overgrown toenails.

I should have kept going. I should have used every power I had at my disposal to demand that we turned tail and got the hell out of that garden. Instead, out of bloody-minded instinct, I knelt by the spot and used my hands to dig. I didn't have to dig very far.

The body was only barely recognisable. If it were not for the grubby purple thread wrapped round her limp, already decaying wrist, I might not have been sure. Isla's skin was covered in neat lacerations that must have been performed post-mortem for reasons I couldn't fathom.

I recoiled and fell away, before choking and forcing myself to turn so I could throw up. My hands and knees sank into the dirt. I couldn't begin to understand why she'd been buried here in such a shallow grave, but there was no retreat from this gruesome knowledge. What was done could not be undone. What was known could not be unknown.

CHAPTER TWENTY-FOUR

THE BITTER IRONY DIDN'T ESCAPE ME. A GARDEN WAS SUPPOSED to be a place filled with life, and this one was nothing more than death. I brushed away the buzzing insects and overly large butterflies as the Afflicted man and I stumbled out. We located the glass-panelled door and somehow managed to make our exit.

Both of us were filthy, covered in the grim earth that fuelled the garden's plants. I longed to scrub myself clean, but there were too many other things to do first. Despite the roaring blood in my ears and the churning nausea in my stomach, I ploughed ahead, making sure the man stayed by my side.

My cheeks were wet with unchecked tears that rolled down my face, but still I kept going. There was nothing else to do. If we'd bumped into a Mage at that point, I didn't know what would have happened but the way was clear and the hallways were empty. For that I had to be grateful.

The fastest way out of the City Chambers was through the main entrance but I didn't dare use that. I might have managed it alone, but there was no way I could keep both myself and the Afflicted man hidden, even with my growing knowledge of the building's shadowed nooks and hidden crannies.

His pain was becoming almost too much for him to bear and he was groaning now with every step. Several of his wounds were leaking blood; if it hadn't been for the cloak Angus had passed over, there would have been a trail of sticky blood behind us. It was bad enough that we left dirty footprints from the soil which clung to the soles of our feet, but there was a chance that could be explained away. Blood was another matter.

I took the long way round the building, heading for the rear and the small door through which I'd forced my entrance weeks ago. On several occasions, I heard distant voices and felt certain we would be discovered but either luck was clinging to the Afflicted man for the first time in many years, or fate was smiling briefly upon me, because we made it without meeting another soul. As long as I could open the back door and get out without the ravens waking up, we'd make it.

Unfortunately, luck is an illusion that only takes you so far. We were ten feet from the door when it opened and a giggling couple fell inside. 'Are you sure this is safe?' I heard the man ask. 'The front is blazing with lights. That's a hell of a stramash oot there.'

'If it's a stramash oot there,' the reply came, 'then it'll be quiet here. Dinna fash.'

Ailsa. Oh no. It was too late to turn and hide, so I stayed where I was, with the Afflicted man next to me, and squared my shoulders. I'd attack both her and her lover, if that was what it was going to take.

She planted a long kiss on his mouth. He noticed us before she did. Comically, his eyes widened in fear while she continued to kiss him. 'Uh, Ailsa?'

'Shh. I told you. It'll be fine. The Mages dinna care about this sort of thing.' She curled one arm round his neck and pulled him so close it was a wonder he didn't smother. The Afflicted man next to me seemed to think the same thing because he chose that moment to groan once more.

Ailsa froze, then drew back from the man and glanced over her shoulder. I'd never seen anyone turn so white so quickly. 'You should go, Keith.'

'That's ... that's ... that's...'

'Go.' She reached round him, opened the door and all but threw him out. As soon as the door closed, she turned to me, her gaze steely and unwavering. 'You've gone and done it now, haven't you, lassie?'

The Afflicted man moaned and she flinched, but she held her ground. It wasn't merely disgruntled citizens and lazy serving staff whom Ailsa could stare down. I had to give her credit for her bravery – in her position, I'd likely have run a mile.

She gave the Afflicted man a long stare. Under the weight of her disapproval, he moaned once again, dropped to the floor and curled up in a foetal position. He wasn't dangerous, not like this. Even Ailsa could see that.

She sighed heavily. 'He was below? In the basement cage?'

I stared at her. She knew about that?

'Aye,' she muttered, reading my expression. 'I know what goes on down there. Some of it, anyway.'

I glared at her. So why the fuck didn't she do something about it?

'It's not like I can do anything about it. Do you have any idea what'll happen when they realise he's missing? The best thing you can do, lassie, is to put him right back where you found him. Stop trying to be a hero. You'll end up deid – and likely so will the rest of us.'

It occurred to me belatedly that, as with Angus, there was far more to Ailsa than met the eye. For one thing, she'd been out during the hours of darkness simply to get her leg over, although that was probably the best reason of all to risk your life. At least it was living.

Both Ailsa and Angus ought to stop with their dire warnings about death; there were worse things than the grave. Especially where the fucking Mages were concerned. I continued to glare at her. Then, because I had to know, I mimed rocking a baby close to my chest and raised my eyebrows pointedly.

Ailsa's eyes dropped and my heart hardened. She knew. 'There was one last month,' she said in a cracked whisper. 'Before you arrived.' She looked at me unhappily. 'It's not as bad as you think.'

I'd be the judge of that.

Ailsa sighed and scratched her skin. 'They don't kill them.'

Well, whoop-de-fucking-do. I crossed my arms. What did they do with them, then? There wasn't a damned nursery hidden anywhere in the City Chambers.

'I don't know why they take them. Last month's wee one was the first in a long while.' Ailsa's reluctance to talk to me was obvious in her every word. 'Most of the Mages were excited. A few of the other servants heard the baby crying and were aware something was up, but none of them had any real clue. The only reason I know is because she stayed for two nights and then I was ordered to take her to a couple on the outskirts of the city.'

She gave me a defiant glance. 'A young couple in a nice house who were delighted to have her. They already had a cot and clothes and toys set up. She went to a good place.'

But that didn't make sense. Why all the cloak and dagger if she was being adopted? Why bring the baby here first?

'I asked Angus about why she'd come here,' Ailsa said, answering my unspoken question. 'He told me I was better off not knowing, that it was safer that way.'

Safer for whom? I was beyond glad the little girl was alive and in a new home, and some of the heaviness that had lain in my heart since Isla's death eased. But I was still confused. And concerned.

The Gowk was looking for evidence of the Mages' wrongdoings. I'd found something, but I doubted it was enough. On the face of it they'd merely been doing charity work, though there must be more to it than that.

Isla had been executed because of that missing child, and Fee and Jane were convinced that the Mages were killing baby girls who displayed signs of magic. What if the Mages had found a way to drain the magic from those babies instead of killing them? Would such knowledge have sealed Isla's fate? And would such speculation be enough to stir a city? I shook my head. No: I had no proof.

Ailsa mistook my head shake for censure. 'Well, whit did you expect?' Her accent grew stronger as her anger increased, although whether her fury was directed at me or at herself, I wasn't sure. 'The wee girl is alive! She's in a good home! What could I do about it? Do ye think I could go up against the Mages? I'm one fucking woman! Whit could I do? Aye, I moved that wee girl. I participated in whatever was done to her, but she wasn't hurt. She came here alive, and she left here alive. And she went to a better place than she came from!'

I wasn't blaming Ailsa and neither was I judging her. Everyone did what they had to in order to survive. And if Ailsa was telling the truth, she was right: that baby was definitely in a better place. I should know.

She hadn't finished speaking and her growing anxiety was clear. 'I've worked here a long time. I've heard the comings and goings, and the strange noises in the middle of the night. I've heard the Afflicted folks screaming and seen the body bags arriving. But whit could I do? They'd as soon as set me on fire as anything. I keep my heid down and get on with my job as best as I can. I help where I can, but I'm no' a dunderheid about it. The Mages have all the power. We have none.'

She pointed a finger at the man curled on the floor by my feet. 'And let him escape today, and he'll eat you tomorrow. He's already Afflicted – the worst has already happened to him. Maybe being here is a blessing in disguise.'

There was nothing blessed about torture. I stepped towards her. I didn't know what I was planning but my feet seemed to move of their own accord.

Ailsa muttered a curse, reached behind her and opened the door again. 'Go on then,' she said. 'Off ye fuck. And ye'd better hurry. The Mages are out hunting.'

I thought back to the conversation I'd overheard. For *her* – for another baby.

My shoulders dropped, then I grabbed the Afflicted man, forced him to his feet while ignoring his sharp moan, and dragged him towards the open air.

'The ravens are about,' Ailsa said. 'You'll have to be careful. They're all oot the front right now, but they'll be moving soon and if they see you...'

I paid her no attention. Instead, I squeezed the Afflicted man's hand and looked him in the eye. Good luck. He was likely going to need it.

I nudged him through the door. He stumbled across the threshold, his battered and bruised movements showing every sign of what had been done to him. He stayed where he was for one long moment, cautiously sniffing the cold night air. At first I thought he wouldn't leave but then, without a single backward glance, he took off in a lopsided sprint.

I watched him until the night swallowed him up, then I closed the door and looked at Ailsa.

'You're not going too?' she asked, scarcely crediting that I'd go to all the trouble of freeing an Afflicted prisoner and hang around to deal with the consequences.

I folded my arms across my chest. No, I wasn't going. I couldn't leave. I was here to stop the Mages. I didn't understand most of what they were doing or why, but I was still going to do what I could to change things. I wouldn't allow anyone else to die like Isla had done. I lifted my chin. I could stop them. I *would* stop them.

'You're a fucking eejit,' Ailsa said. There was no venom in her words, only resignation.

There you are! I've been looking all over for you, Mairi. You must go back to your room. You have to stay there tonight. You're in danger, and I was worried something had gone wrong with the spell... Laoch's voice in my head stopped abruptly.

'Nicholas.' Ailsa dropped into an immediate curtsey, grabbed my shoulder and pushed me down too. Rather than make a scene, I copied her and Laoch's eyes lit briefly with amusement.

'There's a lot of commotion out front,' Ailsa babbled. 'We couldn't sleep, so we came here to keep out of everyone's way. The Mages are busy and we didn't want to interrupt them. We meant no harm, sir.'

I blinked. Ailsa was scared of Nicholas. In fact, it was more than that: she was terrified of him. Laoch was unmistakably a daemon, and his tattoos and horns and muscular body looked intimidating, but Ailsa had been here a long time. She'd got the true measure of Angus, so why hadn't she done the same with Laoch?

Laoch nodded before kneeling and examining something on the floor. I realised it was a clump of dirt, either from me or the Afflicted man. He sniffed it and his expression darkened.

'My apologies, sir!' Ailsa said. 'It's not been cleaned properly in here, and one of the messenger boys brought in lots of muck earlier. I'll make sure it's all spick and span by tomorrow morning, I promise you that.'

Ailsa was lying for me; she was trembling with fear yet prepared to lie to Laoch to protect me. I puzzled it over for a moment and then addressed him. *Why?* I asked. *Why is she so scared of you?*

Laoch rubbed the dirt between his thumb and forefinger,

then he stood up. 'Ailsa is afraid because she knows I can't be trusted.'

I stiffened and glanced sideways at Ailsa. Her face was expressionless but she didn't refute his words.

'Ailsa's been here a long time,' he said. 'And so have I. We both have long memories.'

What was going on here?

'You know I'm bound to the Mages,' Laoch continued. 'You know there was no other choice.'

My frown deepened then I realised that he was talking to Ailsa, not to me.

Her bottom lip began to wobble and for a horrifying moment I thought she would burst into tears. Instead, she inhaled deeply and lifted her head. 'There have been plenty of occasions when you've found ways around the Mages' rules, *sir*.' She might have been scared, but she didn't attempt to hide her disdain.

'There are often loopholes in their orders,' Laoch agreed. 'But I cannot gainsay a direct command.' He held up his slave cuffs. 'No matter what it is.'

'And that,' Ailsa said simply, 'is why you can't be trusted.'

I was about to open up my thoughts to communicate with Laoch again when I thought better of it. Whatever was going on here was between them; it didn't involve me. That didn't prevent Laoch from explaining aloud, however.

'Several years ago, Mairi, there was a servant here called Joshua,' he said. 'He worked in the kitchen. He was a friendly man, with a ready smile and a soft heart.' He turned his green eyes to mine. 'Too soft.'

Ailsa hawked up a ball of phlegm and spat it at Laoch's feet. 'He wasn't soft. He was just too good for the likes of us.'

'Aye.' He nodded sadly. 'He was.'

'You killed him.'

My heart turned ice cold.

Laoch didn't disagree. 'My words did.' He glanced at me again. 'I did not.'

I gazed at his face. Regardless of what he said, I could see guilt written there. Terrible guilt. I waited.

Laoch sighed and pushed back his inky-black hair. 'Joshua found out that the Ascendant was planning to cut off the water supply to several streets in the East End. There were rumours that resistance members were hiding there, and the Ascendant wanted to force them out. Denying residents water is an easy way to loosen tongues. But Joshua warned them beforehand, and they were able to stockpile what they needed while the resistance members escaped.'

Go Joshua. I didn't smile; I already knew this story wouldn't have a happy ending.

'I knew what he had done because I helped him do it,' Laoch said quietly. 'My part was discovered by the Mages and I was punished. The Ascendant asked me who else was involved and,' he gestured again to his slave cuffs, 'because of these, I was forced to tell them.'

Oh. I swallowed. But that wasn't his fault. There was nothing he could have done.

Ailsa's attitude didn't alter. 'How did Joshua find out the Ascendant's plan in the first place?' she sneered. 'Tell her that.'

Laoch looked down. 'I told him. I was present in the room when the Mages made their plans. I hoped that he could get word to those who needed to hear it. That's why,' he said heavily, 'whenever I witness any discussion between the Mages, I am explicitly ordered not to mention it to anyone else.'

'Aye, it's a fucking hard life you lead, isn't it?' Ailsa said, with sarcasm that could have cut through bone, She drew closer to me. 'Anything that daemon suspects or discovers or knows will find its way to the Mages. Remember that.'

She was telling me that if Laoch discovered I'd helped the Afflicted man to escape and the Mages ordered him to tell them what he knew, he'd have to give me up. In fact, if they asked him anything about me at all, Laoch would tell them. It wouldn't be his fault but that wouldn't change the outcome.

So far, they'd not questioned him about me. He had discovered I had magic, and the Mages didn't know that he possessed the magic to send himself into the body of another living creature. Laoch *could* still keep secrets. I was aware I was trying to persuade myself that being close to him wasn't a problem.

I wouldn't deliberately put you in danger, Mairi. His voice echoed in my head. *I didn't seek you out, you came to me. And like I said, there are often loopholes in the commands I am given that I can exploit.*

Often, I replied. *Not always.*

He was silent for a moment before he gave me a bitter nod.

Ailsa's eyes flicked between the two of us and narrowed. 'Something's going on here.'

I ignored her. *The Mages are gathering out there because they've found another baby girl with magic, right? They're going to hunt for her. What will they do when they find her?*

Strain was etched into every line of Laoch's face. I glanced down and saw that the sinews on the backs of his hands were tight with tension. He let out a growl of frustration and Ailsa took a step back.

I can't tell you anything about that. I wish I could. Believe me, I wish I could. You must go back to your room and stay there. It's not safe, Mairi. Please, do as I ask. A vein on his temple bulged with such ferocity that I thought it would burst. His tattoos flickered at the edges, licking at his cheekbones in a desperate bid to escape the confines of his skin. *Mairi, please...*

I held up my hand. It was clear he wanted to tell me something but couldn't, and this wasn't the time to push him.

'What the fuck is going on?' Ailsa asked, unable to disguise the quaver in her voice.

I pulled a face. It was too complicated to try and explain, and

I still had hundreds of questions of my own. The best thing Ailsa could do was go to her room and stay there. I had other plans.

I drew in a breath – and that was when the air was rent with the cacophony of a hundred birds cawing in alarm. The ravens were awake and they weren't happy.

Laoch stiffened. 'What? Something's wrong,' he muttered. 'They weren't to be involved during the night hours.'

Someone had already noticed that the Afflicted man had escaped. I'd thought we'd have longer, given everything else that was going on. I shouldn't have been so naïve.

Ailsa looked at me, grim foreboding in her eyes. 'They know. We need to do what the daemon bastard says and get back to our rooms before we're held as suspects.'

I could barely hear her above the birds' shrieks. It sounded like the whole of the City Chambers was surrounded by them.

'They know what?' Laoch questioned. 'What's happened?' he glanced again at the dirt on his fingers and froze. 'No,' he whispered. 'Don't tell me.'

Ailsa snorted. 'As if we would.' She looked at me and flapped her hands. 'Now, lass! We have to go!'

Shite. She wouldn't move until I did, and she would be implicated in a heartbeat if her presence here were discovered. The trail of dirt from the garden would lead the Mages here; we had to get out of this room right now. I blinked in agreement and started to move.

Mairi—

It's fine, Laoch. Don't worry, I'll find you later. Get as far away from this room as you can. And if you can think of a way to tell me—

I shook my head. If there was a way he could communicate what he knew, he'd have already found it. *Never mind.*

I reached for Ailsa's hand and we darted away.

CHAPTER TWENTY-FIVE

I DIDN'T THINK ANYONE GOT ANY SLEEP THAT NIGHT. I SAW AILSA to her room before reluctantly returning to my draughty garret. After gently removing the snoozing mouse and depositing him in a corner, I scrubbed away the grim garden soil from my body. I spent the better part of an hour systematically destroying the magical notes the Gowk had given me, and then I waited, still in my ridiculous tartan dress, for the Mages to come and take me away.

When dawn broke, the hubbub echoing around the building had subsided and nobody had come to my door. Perhaps I was safe – for now. I prayed that everyone else was, too.

I dressed in my drab uniform and, because I didn't know what else to do, I went to the kitchen for my breakfast. There were more people milling around the warm room than usual at this hour. I noted the wide eyes and hushed conversations. Everyone had been woken by the noise last night, and everyone was fearful. As far as I could tell, though, nobody knew any of the details.

I took my time picking up a dish and scooping up my porridge from the ruddy-faced cook, then walked round the room towards an empty chair. I listened in to as many chats as I could; there was a lot of speculation but nothing else. I wasn't sure whether that was a good thing or not.

'See,' Billy said to a small group that was hanging on his every word, 'I overheard Sir Alex mention the Afflicted. It can only mean one thing – those poor, diseased souls launched an attack on the City Chambers last night and the Mages fended them off. It's the only thing that makes any sense.'

Trish shook her head, her eyes wide. 'No, we'd have heard their screams if that was the case. One of the Mages turned and became Afflicted. When they come down to breakfast in an hour, check and see who is absent then you'll know who it is.'

A slim lad called Tom wrapped his arms round himself, his eyes darting from side to side. 'But – but – but if a Mage became Afflicted, aren't we all in danger now? What if it happens to us, too? What if we get infected? My ma will never forgive me if I end up Afflicted.'

Trish snorted. 'You'll have a lot more to worry about than your ma if you become one of the diseased ones, mate.'

Billy glanced up as I passed and beckoned me to sit beside him. I gave him a quick smile and a shake of my head, pretending not to see his crestfallen expression. Better that the other servants thought I was hoity-toity and too proud to sit with them than they be overly friendly with me and executed when I was finally caught.

Unfortunately, Ailsa joined me as soon as I sat down in a quiet corner. She should have known better. 'Morning, Mairi,' she said in a soft murmur that belied the hard look in her eyes.

I managed a shaky nod in response.

'Did you sleep well?' she enquired, taking a hard bread roll from the previous day's baking and biting into it. 'Did you have sweet dreams?'

I stared at her. Was she deliberately trying to draw attention to me?

Ailsa chewed noisily for several seconds then swallowed. 'I had terrible nightmares,' she said. 'Bloody, nasty violent nightmares. I was quite worried about them, but I bumped into Sir Angus and he reassured me that they were only dreams and I had nothing to worry about.' She took another large bite of her roll and leaned back, her jaws working as she chewed.

I licked my lips. I had barely touched my porridge and I didn't feel a flicker of hunger, but I forced down a few spoonfuls as I examined Ailsa's face for any minute tells. She remained impassive and silent. Apparently, she had decided her role in the matter was over.

She finished her breakfast, pushed back her chair, stood up and clapped her hands. 'Come on, you lot! The Mages will be famished this morning. It's our job to fill their stomachs and keep them satisfied. Enough of this idle gossip.' She clapped her hands again. 'Let's move!'

There were a few scowls and grumbles but almost everyone got hastily to their feet. Regardless of what else was going on, the damned Mages still had to be served.

Given all that had occurred during the night, I'd expected to see only a smattering of Mages seated for breakfast. I was wrong; they were all present long before the gong sounded and, for once, even the Ascendant deigned to make an appearance.

He took his position at the head of the long table and cleared his throat while we were still bustling around and putting steaming platters of scrambled eggs, fatty sausages and glistening tomatoes in place.

When he cleared his throat, I glanced at Ailsa, wondering if we were supposed to leave now or finish up first. She was busy pouring water for some of the more senior Mages, so I continued serving.

Out of the corner of my eye, I spotted Noah smiling at me. I managed to turn towards him and offer a weak smile in return. He winked at me.

'These are unprecedented times,' the Ascendant said, his moustache quivering. 'There have been too many failures in recent times and,' he clenched his fist, 'I will not have it. Do you hear me? I will not have it! There was a time when the Ascendants and the Mages in the other cities looked to us for guidance. They followed *our* lead. Much more of this, and we'll be the laughing stock of the country! I will not have it!'

I suspected that the Ascendant was more concerned that *he* would be the laughing stock, rather than the assembly of Mages in front of him.

I kept my eyes diverted from him and hurriedly completed my tasks. The other servants were already withdrawing to start their other chores and I had no wish to remain in this room any longer than I had to.

Unfortunately, one of the older Mages grabbed my wrist as I pulled back from his table and pointed at his plate with a frown. There was a smear round the china rim and he clearly wanted me to replace it. I nodded and picked it up. As I looked around for a clean plate the Ascendant continued.

'Mage Ross,' he said, his tone suddenly more dulcet. 'Where are you?'

I spotted the plates on the other side of the room, just as Ross pushed his chair out and stood up, blocking my path. 'Here, Your Highness.'

'You have been here for some time, have you not?'

Ross nodded. 'Six years, give or take.'

'Six years is enough time for a Mage to learn what is important, don't you think?'

Even I was starting to sense a trap. I stepped back and pressed against the wall.

'Aye.'

The Ascendant glared at him. 'Yes, Your Highness,' Ross muttered.

'Six years is also enough time to appreciate that shirking your duties, cutting corners and generally being a fucking eejit is not acceptable. Am I right?'

Ross paled and ducked his head. 'Yes, Your Highness.'

'Then why,' the Ascendant bellowed, raising his voice and sending spittle flying across the table and several platters of food, 'did you think you could cut corners with something as important as the cage?'

'I didn't cut corners, Your Highness. I took every care and—'

'If you took every care,' the Ascendant roared, 'we wouldn't be dealing with this shite now! What do you think happened? Did someone let that creature out to wander around the building and kill half of us in our sleep? Do you think Mage Angus had a crisis of faith, took pity on the beast and let him loose?'

I couldn't stop myself glancing towards Angus, who was seated at the opposite side of the table with his hands clasped and a placid expression on his face.

'I don't know, Your Highness.'

I felt a flicker of sympathy for Ross. A tiny one. It didn't last long.

'Or maybe,' the Ascendant yelled, 'one of the servants released him! Maybe, despite knowing that being in the same room as an Afflicted puts them in mortal danger, they found the entrance to the basement, sneaked inside and freed the fucker! Is that what happened? Hmmm?'

Ross cowered.

The Ascendant's eyes swept around the room, then fell on me. Oh shite.

'Maybe,' he continued, 'it was her!' He pointed at me. Every single Mage turned towards me. 'Maybe that girl did it!'

I didn't know what to do or where to look. I could feel my cheeks burning and my hands shaking.

'Did you?' he demanded. 'Did you do it?'

I shook my head vigorously, wishing the ground would swallow me up.

'Like she knows what I'm talking about!' the Ascendant shouted. He bared his teeth, then his voice suddenly returned to normal. That was the scariest thing yet. 'You fucked up, Mage Ross.'

'Yes, Your Highness.'

The Ascendant switched his bony finger from me to Ross. '*Zep tar*,' he said.

At least half the seated Mages winced. I felt the crackle of magic in the air and heard Ross scream as he fell to his knees, his head dropping so far forward that his forehead brushed the floor.

'Stand up, Mage Ross,' the Ascendant ordered.

Ross didn't react immediately.

'I will not repeat myself.'

Ross staggered to his feet. When I saw his face, I almost gasped aloud. The Ascendant's magic words had sliced into his cheekbones. There was a cut on either side of his face, slashing through his flesh to the bone. Blood dripped from the wounds like red tears. Even the wounds on the Afflicted man hadn't been as severe as this.

'No healing magic is to be used,' the Ascendant ordered. 'Your scars are to be a testament to your sloth. Perhaps you will learn something from them.'

Ross whimpered, which might have been a sign of agreement or simply from the pain. The Ascendant nodded at him to sit down and my eyes widened. He was clearly expected to stay for the remainder of the meal before receiving medical attention.

As soon as Ross sat down, I darted towards the clean plates.

The Ascendant continued talking. 'Of course,' he said, 'errant escapees aren't our only problem. What of the female? Do we know who she is? Do we have a location?'

There was a nervous cough from another of the Mages. He got to his feet. 'We were preparing to search for her last night, Your Highness, using the information that we gleaned from Farris. Our plans were cut short when we had to deal with the issue of the Afflicted.'

I swallowed. There was that name again: Farris. Whoever Farris was, he or she was on the side of the Mages.

'That's not good enough,' the Ascendant snapped. 'I expect her found by tomorrow morning or there will be more than Mage Ross requiring bandages. Find her.'

My stomach dropped. I placed the clean plate in front of the Mage as the Ascendant turned to look at me again, his beady eyes sparking fury. 'What are you still doing here?' he snapped. 'We need peace to eat and conduct our business. Get out!'

I picked up my skirts and ran as fast as my legs would carry me. It seemed inconceivable that I'd got away with helping the Afflicted man escape, and it was horrifying to witness how far the Ascendant was prepared to go to punish one of his own. But both those paled into comparison against the well-being of another child. I had to find the Gowk and enlist his help to find the baby before the Mages did.

CHAPTER TWENTY-SIX

I RUSHED THROUGH MY WORK, IGNORING THE RAVENS WHO WERE in watchful attendance at every window. I made a mental list of everything I could do to keep the anonymous child safe. I kept a continuous eye out for Laoch, but he hadn't been at the bloody breakfast, and I didn't see him in the east wing. I tried not to worry about him – he'd looked after himself for this long without my interference.

I gave a sigh of relief when I heard the Mages return to their study rooms and darted for Angus's office. The surly, complicated Mage would have to do until I could get out of the City Chambers, find the Gowk and speak to Laoch. As usual, Angus's curtains were closed. Did he keep them that way because, like me, he didn't want to be spied upon by the ravens?

I didn't start cleaning his room but sat down on one of his chairs and waited for his return. It didn't take long.

When the door opened and Angus appeared, he was whistling. His hands were in his pockets and a small smile was playing around his lips. His eyes fell on me; rather than castigating me for lounging around in his private space, his smile grew into a wide-mouthed grin.

'Wasn't that fantastic?' he crowed. 'Wasn't that bloody fantastic? When the Ascendant asked you if you were the one responsible for freeing the Afflicted prisoner, I almost laughed aloud. Fucking genius, lass. Genius!' He snorted with genuine mirth.

I stared at him. Given Ross's violent punishment for my supposed crime, I found it bizarre that Angus was so amused. I didn't find anything funny about what had just happened. I crossed my arms and waited for his chortling to subside.

When he finally registered my expression, he said, 'You need to get a sense of humour. I've not been so entertained for years. You shouldn't be glowering at me like that – you pulled one over on the Mages. I was so certain you were dead last night, and yet here you are, still breathing. I have to give it to you, you've got more luck than a prostitute on pay day!'

I remained straight faced. Angus tutted and rolled his eyes. 'You're not here to gloat, then?'

Hardly. I stood up and aped the same actions I'd performed in front of Ailsa the previous night, rocking my arms as if I were holding a baby, then I glared at him again.

He frowned. 'You're pregnant? I can assure you the child is not mine, and I will not take responsibility for it. If you're going to tell me that the father is that Afflicted fellow then—'

I stepped up to him and slapped his face. It wasn't a hard blow – I'd done it purely for effect. The sudden flash of rage in his eyes reminded me that, regardless of what else Angus had or hadn't done for me, he was still a Mage.

'You go too far,' he growled. 'My patience has limits.' He looked towards the door. 'Time for you to leave.'

I remained where I was.

'Go!'

I shook my head with dark resolution. I had too many questions and Angus had too many of the answers.

'Stubborn wench,' he muttered. He examined my face. 'You

might think, lass, that what happened last night means we're friends. Best buddies. Top chums.' He wrinkled his nose. 'You would be very wrong. You saw yourself what happened to Ross. Don't think that I'm safe because I'm a Mage. I'll be executed as quickly as you will if my loyalty is tested. The only difference is that my death will be conducted indoors, in private. You might not value your life, but I value mine.'

I didn't believe him. He'd risked his own life last night, first by allowing me to leave with the Afflicted man, and secondly by covering up my actions and pointing the finger at Ross for negligence.

'I'm not your fucking hero,' he said.

I didn't need him to be. I gazed at him unblinkingly and eventually he threw his hands up in the air. 'Fine,' he snapped. 'Although you should be on your hands and knees in gratitude for what I did, not glaring at me like I'm the enemy.'

Angus had already said in no uncertain terms that he wasn't my friend. I raised my eyebrows pointedly and he sighed, exasperated. 'For fuck's sake.' He ran a hand through his long, straggly hair. 'You've got questions?'

Lots of them. I nodded.

'I'll answer one, one fucking question and no more. After that, you'll get out of here and leave me in peace.'

One question wasn't enough. Unfortunately, Angus understood exactly what I was thinking and his glare grew stonier. 'One question or nothing. It's up to you, lassie.'

I gritted my teeth. Fine. I nodded curtly, rocked back on my heels and considered. I wanted to know why the Mages had taken the baby girl, but that knowledge wouldn't change any outcomes; anyway, it was doubtful Angus would give me any evidence that I could take to the Gowk for ammunition. Neither was there any point in asking where the next baby girl was, or what she was called. From what I'd witnessed at breakfast and last night, none of the Mages knew that. I could only presume that they sensed her magic but hadn't pinpointed her identity.

My mouth tightened. There was only one other thing I desperately needed to know. I drew in a breath and gestured towards my wrists and then my neck before using my fingers to suggest the shape of horns on my head.

Angus's eyes narrowed. 'That's what you want to know? Really? Is all this because you fancy yourself a daemon's whore?'

I was getting wise to his barbed baits and I didn't react – there was no point. I simply watched the old Mage and waited.

'What do you want to know?' he asked finally. 'How to free him?' This time there was an edge of a sneer to his voice.

Yep.

His answer was flat. 'You can't. He's enslaved to the Mages. There's nothing you, he or I can do about it.'

I wouldn't accept that. There was a way, there had to be.

Angus walked heavily over to a chair and sat down. He rubbed his hand over his forehead and met my eyes. 'He's tied to the Ascendant. Daemons always are. The Ascendant is the most powerful of us all, and your horned mate belongs to him.'

So? That didn't actually answer my question.

'If the Ascendant chooses to retire from his duties, owner-ship of the daemon passes automatically to the next Ascendant who is selected in a short ceremony. The daemon is never free, not even for a second. They are wily creatures and would take advantage of any weakness in a heartbeat.'

I snorted. As if anyone could blame them.

'So you see,' Angus continued, 'he cannot be freed unless the Ascendant himself chooses to liberate him.' He swept a hand towards the door. 'But if you want to use your silver tongue to persuade our esteemed leader to do that, be my guest. Maybe someone with the gift of the gab like yourself could force him to see sense.'

My lip curled. Ha ha. There was more than one way to get

rid of an Ascendant. I didn't need to mime for Angus to understand what I was thinking.

'Do you think the Ascendant is the leader of this city because he's a weakling?' Angus asked. 'He was proven to be the most powerful Mage in Glasgow through a series of hard challenges. He's been in charge for so long that you likely weren't alive the last time the Ascendancy changed hands. I can assure you that our current Ascendant has more magical strength than anyone else alive in this city. You cannot beat him. If you tried to give him a dirty look, he would strike you dead before you could blink. He cannot be killed. He might die unexpectedly of a heart attack, but that's only happened to one Ascendant in living memory. When the second-to-last Inverness Ascendant died, control over his enslaved daemon automatically passed to the next most powerful Mage in the vicinity. And that particular cockroach of a man was later selected as Ascendant of Inverness.' Angus shrugged. 'Like I said, there is no way out. Nicholas belongs to us until the day he dies.'

His name was fucking Laoch.

Angus regarded me calmly. 'You're young,' he said, this time with a surprising touch of kindness. 'You still believe that you can achieve anything with the right attitude and the right plans. Your life isn't fair. It's not fair that Nicholas is enslaved to us. It's not fair that we Mages control what happens to the people of this fine city, or that we can wield the power of life and death. I'm not going to pretend that you should be content with your lot, and that life is as it should be for someone like you.'

He drew out a pipe from his top pocket. Lighting it thoughtfully, he inhaled deeply before puffing out a ring of orange-tinged smoke. 'But,' he said finally, 'that does not mean that you can change anything. I can't change the way things are. Nicholas can't change the way things are – and neither can you. You got lucky last night and that has given you enough confidence to believe you can do anything. You can't. It's better to accept the life you have and get on with it.'

He smiled sadly. 'It's what I did. It's what all of us do eventually.'

I looked into his eyes. He despised the Ascendant, and he hated what the Mages stood for even though he was one of them. He knew how terribly the people of this city were treated. It wasn't laziness that prevented him from speaking out against the system and it wasn't even fear; it was resigned acceptance that this was the way things were.

Well, that wasn't good enough for me. I might have felt that way before Isla died, but I didn't now. I nodded slowly at Angus and pretended not to see the relief on his face that I supposedly agreed with his assessment. With a sniff, I turned on my heel.

'We take their magic,' he said, so quietly that I almost didn't hear him. I halted in my tracks. 'Ours has been waning for years, so we take the magic from any female child who we discover possesses it to boost our powers. It's a complicated process that only works when it is enhanced through herbs and a series of difficult magical phrases. Plus,' he added, 'it's an unnatural thing, so it requires a boost from certain other – unsavoury elements.'

I didn't move.

'Our experiments have discovered that the congealed blood from a female corpse mixed with blood from an Afflicted creature is the most effective.'

I pressed my lips together, then I left him to his silent room and his drug-fuelled pipe smoke.

I FOUND Trish in the main library, sweeping up a pile of indefinable dust and dirt and goodness knows what else. I touched her elbow; startled by my sudden presence, she yelped and started, spinning round with fear in her blue-eyed gaze.

When she saw me, she started to relax – until she realised why I must have sought her out.

It was another six days before I was due to meet the Gowk again at the Kelvingrove bandstand. I couldn't wait that long.

'You need to see him?' she whispered, though the room was empty.

I nodded.

'Can it wait till tomorrow?'

The Mages might find that baby girl before then – there were more than enough of them hunting for her. They might not be trying to kill her, but that didn't mean they should be allowed to drain away any magic she might possess. Her power wasn't theirs to take. If I could stop them I would, especially now I knew how they took such magic. I shook my head forcefully.

Trish exhaled. 'Okay,' she said. 'I'll see what I can do. Go to the same place as last time. I'll get word to him if I can.'

I took her hands and squeezed them in thanks, and she managed a smile in return. I headed out of the room to find work which would make me look busy and mindless until I could speak to the Gowk. Almost immediately I saw Laoch, walking with heavy steps and bowed shoulders.

He sensed me. His head snapped up and his emerald eyes met mine. *You're alright.* Even from several metres away, I saw his body shudder with relief. His reaction surprised me. *I was worried. I was sure that something must have happened to you.*

I'm fine, I answered. *I've never been better.*

You're lying.

I smiled. *Yes.*

Laoch smiled back, though it wasn't long before his expression settled into something darker, filled with foreboding. *Mairi, please don't use any magic today. No dramatic spells, no transforming into mice, no poultices or unconscious humming. Promise me you'll keep your head down.*

I can't promise that.

Mairi—

I shook my head. The less Laoch knew now, the better for all of us. I smiled again in an attempt to reassure him.

Matters were coming to a head, whether we liked it or not.

233

CHAPTER TWENTY-SEVEN

THE MOMENT I WAS RELEASED FROM MY DUTIES, I DARTED UP towards my room. Unfortunately, Billy was also on his way upstairs and insisted on maintaining a steady stream of chatter. I didn't want to look as if I were in a desperate rush, so I was forced to keep pace with him although I was only listening with half an ear to what he was saying.

'I've not been allowed into the garden at all today,' he told me. 'I've been assigned to other duties.'

I wondered if he was aware of the bodies buried there. He had to be; he was the main gardener. Surely he couldn't be oblivious to mutilated corpses in the soil? Did his silence on the matter make him complicit – or merely sensible? What about Ailsa? Should I hold her guilty as well for the knowledge she'd never acted upon?

'I have to be honest,' he continued, 'I've never seen the Chambers like this before. All the Mages are crabbit today. And all that noise last night! I was telling Trish and Lottie this morning that I think the Afflicted tried to attack us. It's the only explanation.'

I didn't need to hear any more of Billy's musings, I needed him to move more quickly. My time was limited.

'You know that Mage Ross has been injured? And the kitchen staff are all in a flap because the evening meal is to be served early. I heard the chef say there was roast beef on the menu and that it'll be ruined because it won't be cooked enough. Lottie said that we should get to eat it if that's the case. And before she was called away, Trish said it would do the Mages good to realise they can't change things at the last minute and still expect the best quality.'

He gave a short, slightly nervous laugh and looked over his shoulder. 'She didn't say it very loudly, though. Ailsa would skelp her lugs if she heard her.'

I patted his arm, then coughed and pointed upwards. Enough of this; I could only be patient for so long.

'Och,' he said, 'are you in a hurry? Sorry.' He stepped aside. 'On you go. Do you have another hot date with Mage Noah this afternoon?' He winked.

I'd not given a thought to Noah. If I'd been smarter, I could have put our relationship – such as it was – to greater use. If I didn't picture Laoch every time I closed my eyes, I probably would have done.

I smiled vaguely at Billy and moved past him, trying hard not to break into a run. Act normal, Mairi, for goodness' sake.

When I reached my room, I scribbled a note for the Gowk to read as soon as he arrived, grabbed my cloak and knelt to tighten the laces on my shoes. Before I'd finished, I heard a faint patter and, to my surprise, the mouse reappeared. I thought he'd have scurried away to a more familiar hidey-hole long before now. I doubted that he'd enjoyed last night's shenanigans.

I used the tip of my index finger to stroke his back and he squeaked. *Sorry, mousey*, I sent silently. *I've got to go.*

The mouse squeaked again, scrabbled forward and climbed onto my shoe. I gazed at him for a moment. I was going outside where it was cold and unfamiliar to a wee thing like him and he'd be better off here.

His whiskers quivered and his tiny, liquid eyes gazed up at mine. Shite. I reached down, scooped him up and put him in the pocket of my cloak. I was a soft-hearted fool. If this continued much longer, I'd be dressing him in tiny outfits and giving him a name. Mungo would suit him: Mungo the Mouse.

I rolled my eyes and stopped wasting time.

I WASN'T sure if Trish had been able to get word to the Gowk, so I approached the bandstand with some trepidation. The wind was picking up and there was more of a chill in the air, so there were few people about.

When I saw the stooped figure leaning against one of the pillars, a sudden weight fell from my shoulders. My luck was holding and the Gowk was here. Maybe we'd win the day yet.

Eagerness overtook caution and I nipped towards him without looking around first. He sent me a warning glance as I drew near so I kept my distance and took a seat on the bench where we'd met previously. After a few moments, he joined me. 'It wasn't easy to get here at such short notice, lass,' he growled. 'I hope this is worth it.'

Despite his words, I could hear the shiver of optimism in his tone. I hoped we'd live up to each other's expectations. I passed him the note I'd written earlier and waited while he read it.

'They bury fresh corpses inside their own home?' The Gowk gave a delicate shudder. 'Ugh. This is good, though. It would be difficult to prove without storming the City Chambers with shovels, but it's something we can use.'

He tapped the edge of the note with his mangled fingers. 'The baby they're hunting for is a different matter. If we knew who she was or where she was, we could protect her, but I don't know how we'd locate such a child. We can follow the Mages when they're out hunting for her, but they'll be spread across the city and they're likely to notice us – especially if I send lots of our people out.'

He lifted his head up and gazed across the quiet park. I tried not to grind my teeth in frustration; I understood that he was thinking aloud, rather than refusing to act. So far.

'The babe from St Mags was eight months old,' he mused thoughtfully. 'It likely takes several months before a newborn's magic is strong enough to be sensed. If we narrowed down our search and looked for female children aged from six to ten months old, we might have a chance. I've got contacts in most of the local communities.'

He straightened his back and I saw fire lighting his eyes. 'We could get warnings out to the parents. If the Mages do come for a child, not only will they be pre-warned but we might get the proof we need to show the city what the magical bastards are up to. Especially if it's true that their magic is waning,' he added with satisfaction. 'I can work with this. Good work, lass.'

I was more concerned with the child's well-being than gathering evidence to use against the Mages, but I wasn't the one with the contacts or the communication lines. I had to trust that the Gowk knew what he was doing.

I touched the note again, pointing to where I'd mentioned the Afflicted man. The Gowk shook his head. 'That information is no good to me right now. The whole city will rage against the kidnapping of a baby but nobody cares about the Afflicted, not once they're infected. They're a dangerous hindrance. We're more likely to find people are delighted that the Mages are capturing and hurting them. Fear has a lot to answer for,' he said darkly.

I wasn't surprised by his words, although I felt a flicker of disappointment. I knew the Afflicted were more beasts than men, but they were still living creatures. However, there were

237

many reasons why I couldn't argue with the Gowk on that point. I'd focus my efforts instead on eavesdropping and snooping to try and discover any salient details about the child. We might still be able to help her.

'This part here,' he said, 'about this man who's been passing information to the Mages? You think that whoever told them about the factory uprising is the same person who informed them about the child?'

I nodded. I'd overheard the name Farris twice.

'He must be someone with magic,' the Gowk said. 'Likely someone whose power isn't strong enough to be a Mage, but who sympathises with them and has enough magic to sense it in others. There have always been turncoats who seek to ingratiate themselves with the Mages for their own ends.'

He hawked up a ball of phlegm and spat it on the ground to indicate his contempt. 'If we could find him and question him, we could learn a great deal. Do you know anything about his identity?'

I glanced at the note again and realised I'd omitted the name. I wondered briefly if I was condemning someone to being tortured by the Gowk and his cronies – then I wondered if I cared.

Using the tip of my index finger, I started to spell out the name I'd heard.

'F,' the Gowk said, squinting.

Yep.

'A.'

Aye.

A voice from across the park called out. 'Farris!'

I froze. What the fuck?

The Gowk hissed. 'Shite. I know that guy. I'll go and chat to him, and make sure he doesn't see your face. Stay here. I'll be back in a few minutes.'

I didn't react; I was shocked into immobility. Stunned, I

watched as the Gowk loped towards the man. 'Douglas, how are you?' he said. 'It's been months!'

'Aye, Farris, that it has. That it has.'

I got slowly to my feet. The Gowk was Farris; Farris was the Gowk. He was the one who'd been passing information to the Mages; he'd been playing both sides all along. That was why he'd been released from the Mages all those years ago. He didn't escape and he wasn't in hiding; they let him go so he could act as their stooge.

I thought I might throw up. Did Fee and Jane and Flora know? Had they been in on this all along? I shook my head in dismay. I couldn't know for sure.

I had to get away. I had to run.

Keeping my eyes on the Gowk and his companion, I picked up the note and crumpled it in one hand. Somewhere to my left I heard the unmistakable caw of a raven, followed swiftly by a second sharper shriek. If the ravens were here, the Mages wouldn't be far behind.

I didn't think; I stuffed the note into my mouth and chewed. It made me gag. Then I started to back away. I had to get out of the park.

I spun round, still chewing, ready to flee in the opposite direction to the Gowk. That was when my eyes landed on the black-robed Mage standing ten metres away, staring at me with a nasty grin slashed across his face. His wounds had been bandaged but the white patches on his cheeks only made him look more sinister.

'It was you all along,' Ross said. 'You were under our noses all this time. We've been looking for you.'

I remembered Angus's words from the previous evening. *I'm sure you already know who they're looking for.* I'd thought that I did but I was wrong: they weren't hunting a baby, they were hunting me. They'd been searching for a grown woman with magic ability.

I gazed into Ross's face and knew it meant my death. Far behind me, I heard the Gowk shout something in panic.

Ross glanced over my shoulder and that was when I picked up my skirts and ran. Within a single breath, Ross came after me. I had a short lead on him but I knew I couldn't sustain it. Even if my clothes hadn't been cumbersome and I'd possessed the speed of a sprinter, it wouldn't have mattered. Ross had enough magic to stop almost anyone in their tracks. He didn't even have to run.

'*Kall moy*,' he shouted after me. They were the exact words he'd used when I'd first sneaked into the City Chambers.

The air rushed out of my lungs and I pitched forward onto the cold dirt. Seconds later, I felt the painful grip of large hands as he reached for me and turned me over. While I choked and tried to breathe, Ross laughed. 'You're supposed to be the most powerful female in years and look at you.' He aimed a kick at my side. 'It makes me wonder what all the fuss was about. It didn't take much to stop you.'

As I registered his dark malevolence, his words sank in. He was right: I was powerful. I was strong. I lacked knowledge and confidence and stamina, but I was no weakling and I wouldn't allow someone like Ross to beat me. If I didn't let my emotions get the better of me, I could best him.

I closed my eyes and pictured the white bird flying up towards the sky and away from the constricting effects of Ross's spell. I could do this.

I felt the magic snap and the spell break. My lungs filled with air once again and I opened my eyes to Ross's surprised – and irritated – face.

'So,' he said, 'you do have some defences, after all. It won't change anything.'

I wasn't planning only to defend myself – I could attack too. I looked at his feet and the gnarled roots of an old plant that were curling near him. *Chelta*, I hummed. *Chelta*.

This time my magic worked instantly. The roots stretched, reaching for Ross's feet and then his ankles, wrapping around his limbs. He let out a sharp cry.

I scrambled to my feet. *Bish var.* I hummed again and felt the power coursing through my veins. I clenched my fist and punched Ross in the face; with the roots wrapped round his ankles, he couldn't dodge and my hand connected with his nose with a satisfying crunch.

He bellowed in pain. 'I'll fucking kill you, bitch!' he roared. 'You're an abomination! You shouldn't be allowed to exist!' He lunged for me but I stepped away easily.

Unfortunately, I'd forgotten something: the ravens were still there. Three of them swooped down at once, their sharp beaks wide open as they plunged to attack. One caught me on my cheek and another ripped a chunk of flesh from my hand as I raised my arm to shield myself.

'Get her!' Ross screamed.

I hummed in panic. *Belzac.* Twin jets of flame shot upwards from my fingertips, singeing the birds' feathers. They wheeled upwards and away from me, cawing in corvid fury but keeping some distance.

'I don't know how you're creating magic when you can't speak, but you're not going to win,' Ross said. 'The other Mages are on their way. You won't escape. I wanted to capture you myself and prove to the Ascendant that I'm worthy to be one of his own.' His vicious smile suddenly returned. 'And I still will. This time you won't be able to fight back. *Velza ch—*'

He stopped in mid-sentence, a strange, astonished expression on his bloodied and bandaged face. His knees gave way and he fell forward, a pair of scissors protruding from his back.

My mouth fell open.

'It's lucky,' Twister said, 'that I always carry the tools of my trade with me when I'm visiting new clients.'

'Aye,' Belle agreed. The ravens circling over our heads

screeched in fury and she winced. 'Run like the wind, lass. Get the fuck oot of here while you can. Your friend has already been caught.'

My eyes switched right. In the far corner of the park, I saw the Gowk struggling with another Mage. The Mage was winning. 'I didn't betray you, lass!' the Gowk screamed. 'I didn't do this!'

I looked beyond him and saw at least twelve more Mages running towards the park entrance. I couldn't win against that many. Nobody could.

Belle glanced at her husband. 'She always was slow to react and get her work done, wasn't she?'

Twister nodded. 'Some things never change.' He glared at me. 'Fucking run, Mairi,' he ordered.

So I did.

CHAPTER TWENTY-EIGHT

I KNEW THE RAVENS WOULD FOLLOW ME, DESPITE THE THREAT OF fire from my fingertips. I had to get away from their beady eyes. I didn't want to think about what was happening behind me, or what had possessed Belle and Twister of all people to save my sorry skin. All I could do to repay their courage was ensure I got away. I'd worry about the rest later.

Vaulting over the hip-high iron fence, I landed on a cobbled street on the other side of the park and bolted towards the street opposite. It was too exposed by far, but it was my best hope for escape. There were any number of wynds and vennels nearby that I could nip down, some with overhanging roofs that might conceal me from the ravens' prying eyes. The ravens knew the city well – but so did I. Until those Mages' manacles wrapped round my wrists, there was still hope.

The commotion and noise behind me was growing by the second. Half the city must have heard the ruckus. I knew that there were plenty of people who would happily hand me over to the Mages in return for some frippery or token of reprieve from their own woes. The faster I could get out of sight from everyone, Mage or otherwise, the better. I put on an extra spurt of speed – and that was when the first front door opened.

I tensed, preparing to give whoever was leaving their house a wide berth. Nobody stepped out. Instead, a hand shot out and beckoned me inside.

My feet slowed. A second door opened, then a third and a fourth. Several more creaked open wide and, from each doorway, faces and hands invited me inside to hide. I blinked rapidly, the painful prick of tears behind my eyes. These people didn't know me and they were risking everything by offering their help.

I couldn't decline. I twisted, changed direction and headed for the nearest door.

'Quickly, lass.' It was a man in his late thirties, his hands greasy with oil and his brown eyes anxious. As soon as I was inside, he shut the door behind me and exhaled heavily. 'I dinna need to know who you are or why they're after you. But you'll be safe here for a wee while.'

No, I wouldn't be safe here and neither would he. The Mages wouldn't give up the chase; they'd work out what had happened and would start banging on doors and searching houses. The only chance I had of escaping their clutches was to get as far away from here as possible. I shook my head and pointed through the house, a question in my eyes.

The man nodded. 'Aye,' he said. 'There's a back door. But you can bide here.' He drew himself up, a sudden glint of pride in his eyes. 'I'm tired of kowtowing to those bastards. We all are.'

The Gowk had been right: the city was ripe for revolution. My heart twisted at the thought of his actions. I clenched my jaw and reached for the man's arm, squeezing it in a way that I hoped communicated my gratitude, then I pointed again.

'I understand,' he said. 'This way.'

He led me down a narrow corridor. There was an open door a few metres down. When I glanced in, I saw the frightened face of a woman, likely the man's wife, and two wide-eyed children. I stiffened. He wasn't merely risking his own life by helping me, he was risking his whole family. Aye, I had to get out of here.

I managed a smile in their direction and hurried into the small kitchen. I breathed a sigh of relief when I saw the back door.

'Wait here,' he cautioned. As he walked out, he reached into his pocket for a small bag of tobacco. I shifted nervously from foot to foot while he took his time rolling a cigarette, lighting it and blowing smoke into the sky. Anyone watching would have thought he was doing nothing more than having a crafty wee smoke.

From over the fence, I heard a hushed whisper. 'Barry? Is she—?'

'Inside. She's going to leave, but we need to make sure the way is clear.'

'Gotcha. Give us a few minutes.'

A raven wailed from somewhere above the houses and I shuddered. The seconds stretched into minutes, which felt like hours. Then another whisper drifted across. 'Okay. We're ready.'

The man nodded and summoned me. With my heart in my mouth, I stepped into his tiny garden.

'As far as I can tell, the ravens are focused on the streets beyond,' Barry said. 'The Mages are spreading out and looking for you, but they're moving slowly. All that lies between these houses and the ones opposite are the shared gardens. They're less likely to be searching here. We'll help you get to the end of the close. After that—'

'After that,' his neighbour said, 'we'll create a diversion to occupy those feathered freaks so you can get away. Dinna worry.'

I wasn't worried for myself, I was worried for these people.

There was another distant bird call. 'Go,' Barry hissed.

I swallowed hard, then scrambled over the fence and into the next garden. The whispering woman was waiting there. She thrust a scarf into my hand. 'Here. Cover your hair.'

I wrapped the scarf round my head, tucking my errant curls out of the way. The woman nudged me and I climbed into the next garden. Two teenagers were waiting there, their expressions lit with fearful excitement. 'This way,' the first one hissed, swinging open a narrow gate.

I made my way from garden to garden. In almost all of them, there was someone offering grim encouragement. One woman passed me a bag and said it might help; a man handed over a bottle filled with liquid and nodded gravely. They were risking themselves for a complete stranger.

In the second to last garden before the row of tenements ended, the young woman waiting hugged me impulsively. 'I ken who you are,' she said in my ear. 'You're the one with the magic. Right?'

I couldn't ask her how she knew that. All I could do was nod.

'Good.' She smiled with dark satisfaction. 'You get yourself away from here and you show them they cannae always win.' She pulled back. 'The house next door is empty but there's a gate that leads onto the street. Count to twenty once you reach it, then you can go. Turn left. And good luck,' she added with a feverish edge.

I licked my lips. Even if I could have spoken, I couldn't express my gratitude for what she and her neighbours were doing, but she seemed to understand.

'It's fine. We need someone to stand up to them. We need you.' She gave me a little push and I wasted no more time.

I clambered over the last fence and jogged to the final gate. As soon as my fingers touched the cold wood, I started to count. The moment I reached twenty, I yanked it open and sprinted left.

The second I started to run, I heard the commotion from the street behind me. There were shouts and screams and angry yells, followed by the cawing of converging ravens – and the crackle of sudden magic. It sounded as if the whole street was attacking the approaching Mages. The tears, which had been threatening for some time, finally spilled out of my eyes and down my cheeks but I didn't stop running. I kept going and going, with all the speed and energy I could muster.

THE SMALL WAREHOUSE by the river was dark and smelled of rotting fish. It was also, as far as I could judge, devoid of life. I checked every nook and cranny just to be sure before hunkering down behind a stack of precariously balanced barrels. I'd be as safe here as anywhere, at least for the next few hours.

I sat on the dirty floor, buried my face in my knees and allowed myself a minute to quake and tremble and take stock of all that had happened. Then I drew a deep breath and composed myself.

I opened the bottle that had been pressed on me and took a cautious sniff, relieved when it seemed to be nothing more potent than water. I took several long gulps to soothe my parched throat. Once my thirst was slaked, I undid the ties on the woman's bag and glanced inside. There was a hunk of bread, an apple and even some cheese. I felt the renewed threat of tears and forced them away. Not now. I reached for the apple and began to chew. And think.

The game was up. I couldn't return to my position as servant within the Mages' household. Ross was dead and his tongue was silenced forever, but there were others who knew my identity. The Gowk's face flashed into my mind. That bastard. He'd gone to a lot of trouble when he could have merely passed me over to the Mages and been done with it.

I paused. That was a good point. I thought about his screamed denial as I'd escaped. He'd said he hadn't betrayed me.

247

On the face of it, that was an outright lie given that he was the Farris who was passing information to the Mages, but the facts didn't stack up.

From what I'd gleaned from Ross, the Mages had known there was a woman in the city with strong magical powers and they'd been hunting for her. But Ross hadn't known her identity. If the Gowk had given me up, surely he would have told the Mages my name. I'd have been drained of magic and dead weeks ago.

The Gowk had told me that the Mages tortured and nearly destroyed him, but he'd managed to get away. What if they'd let him escape deliberately and kept tabs on him so they could observe what the resistance were doing? The Mages were canny and they played the long game.

I swallowed some of the apple. It made more sense than believing the Gowk was a traitor. I smiled suddenly; maybe he hadn't given me up at all.

Then my smile vanished. The Gowk had been captured in the park, and it was likely that Belle and Twister had been too, together with several of the residents who'd helped me escape. The Mages would show no mercy. They might throw some of the other servants onto the executioner's scaffold – Trish, Lottie. Billy, Ailsa. They might scoop up Fee and Flora and Jane.

The Mages needed to scrub out anyone who knew that I existed. There were other women who'd survived childhood despite possessing magic, but they didn't have as much magic as me. I had the potential to be as strong as the Mages themselves and they wouldn't want that information getting out. My existence disproved the Mages' claims that women couldn't wield magic.

I thought of the last woman who'd helped me escape through the line of tenement gardens. She'd known what I was – or rather, what I possessed. That young woman and others like her would be hunted down. Until I was dead, none of them would be safe. And for what? I'd achieved nothing. All I'd done was help an Afflicted man escape and run around a lot. It was hardly the stuff of dramatic heroism.

I glared at the apple. There was nothing here to celebrate. And what about Laoch? If they discovered what lay between us, what would they do to him? A stab of pain shot through my heart and I closed my eyes. I'd made things worse for everyone.

I heard a tiny squeak and froze. When I slowly opened my eyes, I saw the mouse on the floor next to me, its whiskers twitching. It had been in my cloak pocket all this time. It was a wonder it had survived. Mungo the Mouse had more lives than a cat.

He squeaked again, so I delved into the bag and broke off a corner of cheese. He took it in his tiny paws and started to munch while I watched. Huh. Maybe there was more I could do. Maybe not everything was lost.

CHAPTER TWENTY-NINE

I WAITED UNTIL DARKNESS FELL. IF I AVOIDED THE AFFLICTED AND kept my wits about me to stay out of the path of the Mages, the cover of night would make it easier to move round the city. It also allowed me time to rest and regain the strength and magical energy I'd lost during my fight with Ross.

As the mud-coloured dusk gave way to velvety blackness, I slipped out of the warehouse and moved towards the City Chambers. That should be the last place where anyone would be looking for me.

I heard the calls and shouts of Mages on the hunt, but they were distant and didn't make me falter. The only time I paused was when I passed the first poster with my face emblazoned on it. It was a poor facsimile; I was certain they'd deliberately narrowed my eyes and made my mouth and chin pointed to imply that I was both dangerous and evil. The wording on the poster was stark: *Wanted for Murder, Sedition and Kidnapping. Generous reward for anyone with relevant information. Anyone harbouring this criminal can expect the full force of the law.*

I was curious about the kidnapping accusation. Did they think I'd kidnapped the Afflicted prisoner? Or were the Mages planning to pin the baby's so-called disappearance on me? It would help them explain away a lot.

I'd not committed murder, though I supposed they would blame me for Ross's death and I'd accept that. I hadn't plunged the scissors into his back, but in my heart of hearts I knew that I'd have killed him if I'd had the chance. I left the poster where it was; strangely, its existence made me proud.

I passed Belle and Twister's shop. The windows were dark and there was clearly nobody home. I knew where they were. I nipped down the empty street, turned the final corner and finally the City Chambers were in sight.

A cluster of robed Mages stood outside the building and I regarded them dispassionately. Each Mage had a raven perched on his shoulder. They really were desperate to find me. I smiled coldly. Hello. Here I am.

As the Mages dispersed, I spotted Laoch. Even from a distance, I could see the grim look on his face. I was tempted to try and communicate with him, but I knew it wasn't a good idea. At least he looked well, which meant that nobody had discovered we shared a bond. Yet.

I sighed to myself and carefully reached for the wee mouse, drawing him out of my pocket. *I'm sorry I have to do this again to you. It won't be easy and it's incredibly dangerous, but it must be done. It's the only way.*

His tiny pink nose twitched. Part of me fancied that he understood and accepted what was going to happen, or perhaps I was merely hoping that he did.

I placed him next to my feet and gave him a moment to dart away if he wanted to. He didn't move. Okay, then. I breathed in deeply and gazed at him. *Belsh za tum.*

I'd barely begun to hum quietly when the magic crackled. My stomach lurched, my head spun, and I closed my eyes to rid myself of the dizzy, disorientating sensation. It wasn't easy to alter my body with such speed without feeling ill.

I shook out my fur and tested my paws; everything was in working order. The part of my mind that remained mouse was also relaxed. He knew where he was and where he was going, even if he couldn't quite grasp why.

I glanced up and focused on the group of Mages. Most had already left to scour the dark streets, but a few still remained. I stiffened slightly when I realised Laoch's head was turned in my direction. I could no longer discern his expression, but even so I held my breath. He turned away, moving briskly south with two Mages on his tail. Aye. It was time to go.

I scurried forward, aiming for the front door of the City Chambers. I'd never have gained access as Mairi but, I could slip inside as a mouse if the door remained ajar. If I timed it right, nobody would notice.

It took longer than I'd expected to reach the foot of the steps. I was moving as fast as my four legs could manage, but it was a long distance for a creature as small as I was. I could already feel the toll the magic was taking on me, but I girded my insides and kept going, bounding up the few stone steps until I was at the door.

Hugging the stone wall, I peered inside. I drew back when I recognised the familiar shape of the Ascendant. He can't see you, I told myself firmly. You're all-but invisible. I counted to five in my head and darted inside.

It took a moment or two to tune into what the Ascendant was saying. As he spoke, I kept moving around the edge of the skirting board, where I was less likely to be spotted by a Mage – or a cat.

'There's no chance she left the city because we have all the main routes covered. Someone is helping her hide,' the Ascendant growled. 'When I find out who, I'll rip their intestines out by hand.'

I didn't think he was exaggerating.

'She's smarter than we think.' I started as I recognised the second voice as Noah's. 'She concealed herself from us all this time. Goodness knows what she thought she could achieve.'

The Ascendant snorted. 'The bitch likely reckoned she could terrorise us into changing our ways. She doesn't know the truth of what we do, or who we are. She's not smart at all, she's the stupidest person alive.'

Considering what I was currently doing, he might be right. I nipped to my right and their voices faded away. The Ascendant could wait for now. I had other people to deal with first.

Regardless of what else was going on, the servants' routine was the same. The Mages had eaten dinner before they ventured out to hunt for me, and the dining room would be a mess of dirty plates and half-eaten platters of food. I felt the mouse rejoice at the thought of the feast and I smiled inwardly. Yes. That was where we were going.

I hurried, aware that my little paws were skittering and sliding on the smooth floor. I was making a lot of noise for a mouse, but my first goal was in sight and that boosted my confidence. I veered right into the dining room and looked around. Three pairs of feet. Shite. That was too many. There was only one person I needed right now.

I waited for a second, then darted under the table. My intention had been to examine the shoes in turn until I could identify the pair belonging to my target, but the mouse asserted its consciousness and insisted on directing me towards some dropped crumbs next to one of the chairs. Whichever Mage had sat here, he'd been a messy eater.

After several mouthfuls, I encouraged Mungo to yield to me once more. Still chewing, I headed for the first pair of feet. Nope: these belonged to a male, and one who needed to wash between his toes more thoroughly. The reek was extraordinary.

I heard the clink of plates and watched his feet plod out of the dining room. That left two, both of whom were moving silently. I frowned inwardly. I hadn't spent enough time looking at people's feet, and I couldn't identify either of these servants who were bustling around.

I nipped up to the nearest pair of shoes, whose owner had paused to clear more plates from the table, and sniffed cautiously. Could I recognise the scent?

I'd only just got a whiff of shoe leather and soap when a scream rent the air. I spun round and realised belatedly that there was a face staring at me from under the table. Well, that answered one question: it was Michelle, one of the other servants. She'd knelt to brush up the crumbs I'd not yet eaten.

'Rat!' she shrieked. 'There's a rat under here!' She screamed again and leapt onto one of the chairs.

Hardly a rat. I shook my head.

'Get down from there, you daft lass!' the other voice scolded. 'You'll mess up the upholstery with your mucky shoes!'

'But it's a rat!'

'I'll deal with it. Take the last of those plates to the kitchen and give me the broom.'

Uh-oh.

Michelle jumped down from the chair and sprinted out of the room. Ailsa got down on all fours and thrust the broom towards me with surprising force. 'Come on, ya wee bastard,' she hissed.

I concentrated hard, allowing the mental image of my bird of freedom to take over my mind. My skin juddered and, a second later, it was Ailsa who was screaming as she stared at my human form.

'What's going on here?' a male voice demanded. My stomach dropped to my feet. A Mage. Had he sensed my use of magic? Was this all over before it had even begun?

I swallowed hard and sent Ailsa a pleading look. She glared at me and pulled out from underneath the table. 'Just a mouse, my Lord. I'll deal with it.'

'A mouse? I can sort that out for you.'

Ailsa's response was swift. 'No need, sir. You have enough to be worrying about. I'll kill it. I'm used to dealing with vermin.'

My eyes narrowed. Next to my crouched body, Mungo looked up at me. I reached out and gently stroked the top of his head, then I shooed him away. He'd done enough; it would be best for him if he escaped for good.

I heard the Mage depart. Ailsa ducked underneath the table again, her mouth tight with fear and fury. 'You appeared out of fucking nowhere!' she whispered angrily. 'Can you do magic now?'

I rolled my eyes. Of course I could do magic – I thought Ailsa would have worked that out by now. But this wasn't the time for show and tell. I clasped my hands together in the universal sign for a plea. Please, Ailsa. Please help me.

Ailsa glowered suspiciously and prodded my shoulder with her index finger. 'You're really you?'

I suddenly understood: she thought I might be an illusion, a Mages' trick to trap her into betraying herself. I had no idea how to prove myself to her.

'Aye,' she muttered. 'It's you. Nobody could fake that expression of panic and frustration, no matter what magic they used.' She shook her head. 'You're here for them, aren't you? You're here for those people who were brought in this afternoon. You know they've taken Trish and Lottie too? All of us have been questioned.' She turned her head. There was a red welt on her cheek; they'd not been merely questioned. My fury sparked. The Mages didn't care who they hurt.

'They'll do more than kill you this time,' she said sadly.

I didn't bother trying to argue. We'd been through this before.

'They'll have my head as fast as they'll have yours if they find out I've helped you.' She grimaced but I knew her decision had been made. 'There's too many of them to keep in the basement cage, so they're being held in one of the storage rooms near the garden. It's normally used for Billy's tools, but it was adapted to hold people a while back.'

I knew exactly where she meant. I nodded and mouthed thank you. I wouldn't bother her any more.

I shuffled out from under the table. I was no longer a mouse but, if I were careful, I could still tiptoe unseen through the City Chambers. I knew the building well enough.

My nose twitched; a tiny part of my mind obviously remained mouse. I smiled slightly. I walked to the dining room door, peered out to check if the coast was clear – and then something brushed my shoulder.

Ailsa was right behind me, clutching the broom. 'I'll go first,' she said. 'It's safer that way.' I stared at her and she glared. 'What? If I'm going to end up on the scaffold, it might as well be for doing something useful.' She shrugged. 'Who knows? Maybe this is how we beat them.'

I blinked at her.

'Don't you dare argue with me, lass! I'm your superior!'

Okay, then. I flashed her a smile; it was her decision to make.

Ailsa stepped past me into the hallway. After a beat, I followed.

The first corridor was empty and so was the second. When we turned towards the garden, I caught a glimpse of a flitting shadow and stiffened. Ailsa marched towards it while I waited, listening to my heart thump in my ears. She paused for a moment, then ducked her head into one of the rooms. I heard the brief murmur of voices before she pulled away and quietly closed the door.

She beckoned me urgently. 'Mage Alex is in there,' she said in a low voice. 'He's working on something that can't be interrupted, even for the likes of the hunt for you.' Her tone was so grave that I blanched.

I nodded and we continued on our way.

I'd expected at least one guard in front of Billy's storage

room and I was ready to fight with whatever magic I had at my disposal. But the door was closed and nobody was posted outside. Maybe Ailsa was mistaken and the prisoners were being held elsewhere.

I touched her elbow. When she turned, I indicated that I would take the lead. Ailsa frowned but let me. I tiptoed forward until I was directly in front of the door and pressed my ear against it, listening for signs of life from inside. There were two voices, muffled but clear enough.

'You bampot. This is all your fault, you ken. You were too soft on that lass. She got delusions of grandeur, and now we're to be blamed.'

'Belle,' Twister said, 'for once in your life, hold your tongue.'

I smiled and reached for the door. The knob rattled but it was locked. I was prepared for that and I started humming. *Bish var.*

Magic surged through me and temporary strength flooded my veins. I raised my leg and kicked in the door.

'Every Mage in the building will come running now,' Ailsa muttered.

Good. Let them come.

I stepped across the threshold and looked round the grimy, tear-stained faces. Belle, Twister, the Gowk, Trish, Lottie, Flora, Jane, Fee, three residents who'd helped me escape from the street and even a few people I didn't recognise. They were all here.

I dropped a mock curtsey before using the magical strength that still pulsed through my body to yank their chains free.

CHAPTER THIRTY

NOBODY MADE A SOUND AS WE MOVED IN SINGLE FILE ALONG THE corridors of the City Chambers. Even Belle stayed quiet, though I noted several dark looks from Jane that suggested they'd 'had words' before I'd appeared.

Every time we turned a corner, I expected to see an army of rage-fuelled Mages storming towards us, but every time the way was clear. Instead of making me relax, our unhampered progress filled me with tension. This wasn't right. Even if most of the Mages were outside looking for me, some remained in the building; surely they'd sensed the wild magic I'd already conjured up. I couldn't shake the feeling that we were ploughing headlong into a trap.

When we drew close to the main lobby, I grabbed Ailsa's arm and looked at her urgently. 'Aye,' she said grimly. 'Where have they all gone?'

I pointed ahead and shook my head. We should avoid the main doors and find another way out. Thankfully, she agreed.

'We'll aim for the back door,' she said. 'It's a longer walk – but it is your favourite way of exiting and entering the building.' There was a sardonic edge to her words that made me smile.

'What's going on?' Belle asked.

'Wheesht, you!' Jane ordered. She called out in a low voice, 'Why are we running? We should stay here and burn this building to the ground.'

'That's not a bad idea,' the Gowk agreed, speaking for the first time. He looked at me. 'I didn't betray you, lass. I promise you I didn't. They were following me the whole time.' He hung his head. 'I'm sorry.'

I turned and hugged him. He stiffened in surprise then relaxed. I looked into his face and gave him a reassuring smile. *I know*, I tried to say. *I know you didn't do this deliberately.*

'I hate to break up the party,' Trish said. 'But shouldn't we be getting out of here?'

'Aye,' Fee replied. She raised her eyebrows at me. 'I knew you'd come good, Mairi. I just knew it.'

'That's not what you said to me after she vanished,' Jane muttered.

Fee elbowed her.

Lottie raised her voice. 'Let's bloody go!'

We set off again before anarchy descended, this time veering away from the main entrance and skirting towards the rear of the building. We didn't pass a soul along the way, not even a mouse. By the time we reached the final room with the narrow wooden door that led to the outside world, my earlier worries were starting to dissipate. Maybe the Mages were too preoccupied to notice what was going on inside their own home.

'If they're all out there,' Twister said nervously, 'why don't we stay in here?'

'You know,' drawled an ice-cold voice from behind us, 'I'd suggest the exact same thing.'

We all spun round.

My heart sank. I wasn't surprised to see the Ascendant. Our progress had been too easy for this to be a clean getaway, and it had been suspicious that the storage room was unguarded. He'd wanted this, I realised. He'd wanted to instil the hope of escape to make it more satisfying when we fell at the last hurdle.

Jane let out a furious roar and rushed at him. '*Belzac!*' she screamed. A jet of fire sprang from her fingers.

The Ascendant looked bored. '*Desh mar,*' he murmured. The fire was quenched immediately.

Noah stepped from the shadows. '*Silta,*' he said.

Jane was thrown backwards with such force that her body smacked against the far wall. She crumpled to the floor like a broken doll.

Bish var. I called upon my magic to imbue me with strength again, then I ran at the Ascendant with my hands raised.

'*Vaz,*' he uttered calmly.

I hit an invisible wall a metre from the Ascendant and Noah. I slammed my shoulder against it but, try as I might, I couldn't break through it. I gestured to the others to leave while they could; if they ran now, they might still have a chance.

Nobody moved. They were all too frightened.

'I have to say, Farris,' the Ascendant said, 'your little resistance movement is more pathetic now than it was the last time you attempted an insurrection.'

The Gowk snarled at him.

'Ooooh,' Noah smirked. 'Scary.'

'*Kall moy.*' The Ascendant waved his hands for effect. For the third time, I felt the air leave my lungs and the painfully familiar sensation of drowning on dry land. From the chokes and splutters, the others were similarly affected.

'You see, nephew,' the Ascendant said, 'when you want a job doing properly, sometimes you have to do it yourself.'

My knees gave way and I collapsed to the floor in almost the same spot where I had fallen when Ross had done this to me. The Ascendant strolled over and peered down at me. 'This is the girl that has everyone so scared?' He spat. 'She's nothing.'

He leaned over and gazed at my face. 'There is a reason,' he said to me conversationally, 'why we don't permit female Mages to exist, but you didn't stop to think that we might have the city's best interests at heart. You only thought of yourself.' He tutted. 'Such a selfish creature. It's because of female Mages that the Afflicted exist. Years ago, when there were more of your kind, your children were the first to be affected. You could say that state of this country is all your fault.'

His words sank in slowly. Could that be true? The thought ebbed away as I continued to struggle for breath and the Ascendant's face swam before my eyes. My vision was blurring. It was hard to focus on anything beyond the burning agony in my chest. This spell was so much stronger than Ross's had been. I tried to break free from it, picturing the bird in my head over and over again. It didn't work: the Ascendant was too powerful and I was far too weak.

'If you could have behaved yourself, you would have been on to a good thing, Mairi,' Noah said. 'I'd have treated you well. You'd have been a princess – for a while.' He shook his head. 'But you got ideas above your station. You think that you're better than us because you've got a little magic inside you. We are *Mages*, Mairi. You're nothing.'

He snorted. 'I thought fucking someone who didn't speak would be amusing – for one thing, I wouldn't have to listen to any whining afterwards. But you've ruined that. You're not only worthless, you're useless, too. You're beneath me.'

'Well said, Noah,' the Ascendant said. 'Nicholas? Come here and kill her. Let's be done with this.'

No.

Laoch appeared from beyond the doorway. His expression was grim and he held something in his hand which glittered. A knife, I realised dully. He was holding a knife.

Mairi. I can't—

I closed my eyes. Laoch couldn't fight a direct order. It was impossible. All of us had come so close and now it was over.

'Mairi,' Fee choked. 'Don't give up.'

The Gowk wheezed. 'Fight.'

Even Twister found breath to speak. 'Fucking ... get ... him.'

Laoch raised his hand. I could see the sweat on his forehead as he tried to fight the command but he couldn't do it. I stared at his face as a single tear rolled down his cheek.

I'm sorry. I'm so sorry. I heard him say. And then, *I'm in love with you.*

A voice in my head screamed and something snapped. I broke free as the imaginary bird flew upwards into an imaginary sky. I coughed as the tip of Laoch's knife moved towards my heart, and finally the word came. '*Folis,*' I said aloud. My voice echoed around the room. '*Folis.*'

Laoch looked stunned. His body jerked upwards, off the floor. His grip on the knife loosened and it fell with a clatter. I reached for it, stood up and stepped past his floating body.

'*Belzac!*' Noah yelled.

His uncle had already provided me with the words I needed to block that spell.

'*Desh mar,*' I said. And the fire ceased to exist.

I glanced curiously at my hair. A single curl of flame had reached one of the longer strands, and there was the acrid scent of burning hair in the air. I gave Noah a reproving look.

'Noah!' the Ascendant thundered.

Noah's jaw worked uselessly as he tried to form another attack. I recognised his expression; I'd probably looked much the same when the Afflicted woman had attacked me in the park. Sometimes the stress of the circumstances overtook one's ability. Noah's emotions were blocking his magic. He was weaker than I'd realised.

His uncle glowered. He knew as well as I did what had occurred and that now the fight was his alone. '*Kall*—'

He didn't get to finish the sentence. I threw the knife straight at his chest. It was a sharp weapon and it slid through his flesh, embedding itself easily in his heart.

A shocked look lit the Ascendant's face. His hands went to the knife hilt as if to pull it out, but it was clear his life was already draining away.

'You talk too much,' I told him.

He fell forward.

Noah let out a strangled cry. 'Bitch!'

Freed from their choking by the Ascendant's death, the Gowk, Belle and Flora ran at Noah, slammed into his body and knocked him flat to the ground. 'I will kill you all!' he shrieked. 'You scum! You don't know what we do for you! You should be bowing at our feet, you fuckers!'

Belle punched him in the face.

'Laoch!' Noah spat through a mouthful of blood. 'Kill them all! Now!'

I glanced up at Laoch. To my surprise, he was smiling. 'I can't,' he said, without a flicker of regret. 'For one thing, I appear to be stuck in mid-air. For another, my lord and master is dead. My ownership has passed automatically to the next most powerful Mage. I no longer have a master.' He raised an eyebrow at me. 'I have a mistress.'

My mouth dropped open. Laoch winked at me.

'You daemon wanker!' Noah screamed. 'You—'

Belle punched him again, this time hard enough for his eyes to roll back in his head. We all stared at him; he was out for the count.

I swallowed hard and released Laoch from my spell. He fell to the floor with a hard thump next to the Ascendant's body. Oops. I would have to work on that.

I reached for the cuffs around his wrists and the metal warmed to my touch. *I'm not your mistress. You're free.*

It was Laoch's turn to stare. The cuffs opened and dropped,

and so did the torc around his neck. He pulled himself up and gazed wonderingly at his bare arms. *Go home,* I told him.

He licked his lips, feverish desire lighting his green eyes. *When I said I was in love with you—*

I know, I interrupted. *It served a purpose. It gave me the boost of power and confidence I needed. It's fine. You can go.*

Laoch cupped my face and kissed me. He tasted different this time; this time he was his own person. He didn't belong to anyone else. And then, without warning, he was gone and I was left reaching for thin air. His departure was so sudden that I was left bereft, aching with the loss.

'Well,' Belle snorted, 'that's daemon gratitude for you.'

I glanced over and realised she was sitting on top of Noah, her hand clamped firmly over his mouth. The Gowk and Flora were pinning down his legs. 'Come on,' I said. 'The Ascendant might be gone, but there are a hundred more Mages to deal with. We can't fight them all. We need to get out of here.'

'How is it that now you can speak?' the Gowk asked. 'How is that a thing?'

I considered the question. 'The chains broke,' I said. 'They've gone.' It wasn't an explanation but it was all I had. 'Let's leave.' I looked at Jane. Fee was by her side. 'Is she—?'

'She's alive,' Fee said. 'Unconscious, but alive.'

Trish and Lottie moved over to her. 'We'll carry her.'

'What about him?' Twister asked. 'What about that slimy bastard?'

'We have to kill him,' the Gowk said. 'I'll do it.'

I shook my head. My voice rang out so clearly that it surprised me more than anyone else in the room. 'If we kill him, we're no better than the Mages. And we can't kill them all. Slitting his throat now isn't self-defence, it's murder.'

'Murder with good reason.'

'No. We—' I stopped. I could hear the furious caws of the approaching ravens. The other Mages were returning. Perhaps they'd sensed what had happened to their lord and highness. 'There's no time.'

The others suddenly looked as pale as I felt. Trish and Lottie scooped up Jane and, without another word, all of us fled out into the night.

I knew deep down that this wasn't an ending. It was only a beginning but, for the first time in a long time, there was real hope.

And then Laoch's voice echoed in my head. *Count on it, Mairi. I'll see you again soon. I promise.*

AFTERWORD

Thank you so much for reading Hummingbird. This book was a real labour of love and punctuated with a big house move from England to Scotland which was more disruptive than I'd planned! I truly hope you've enjoyed Mairi's story so far and would really appreciate any and all reviews. They make such a huge difference to all authors and are always so very, very welcome.

Massive thanks must go to Karen Holmes for her wonderful and patient editing, as well as to Clarissa Yeo for her gorgeous cover, and to Chrissy Vale for her beautiful illustration.

Thank you also to every ARC reader and reviewer. You're invaluable and I hope you realise how much I appreciate what you do.

The second book in A Charade Of Magic is called Nightingale and will be released towards the end of 2022.

Helen xxx

ALSO BY HELEN HARPER

The *FireBrand* series

A werewolf killer. A paranormal murder. How many times can Emma Bellamy cheat death?

I'm one placement away from becoming a fully fledged London detective. It's bad enough that my last assignment before I qualify is with Supernatural Squad. But that's nothing compared to what happens next.

Brutally murdered by an unknown assailant, I wake up twelve hours later in the morgue – and I'm very much alive. I don't know how or why it happened. I don't know who killed me. All I know is that they might try again.

Werewolves are disappearing right, left and centre.

A mysterious vampire seems intent on following me everywhere I go.

And I have to solve my own vicious killing. Preferably before death comes for me again.

Book One – Brimstone Bound

Book Two – Infernal Enchantment

Book Three – Midnight Smoke

Book Four – Scorched Heart

Book Five - Dark Whispers

Book Six - Coming Soon

The *WolfBrand* series

Devereau Webb is in uncharted territory. He thought he knew what he was doing when he chose to enter London's supernatural society but he's quickly discovering that his new status isn't welcome to everyone.

He's lived through hard times before and he's no stranger to the murky underworld of city life. But when he comes across a young werewolf girl who's not only been illegally turned but who has also committed two brutal murders, he will discover just how difficult life can be for supernaturals - and also how far his own predatory powers extend.

Book One – The Noose Of A New Moon

Book Two – Licence To Howl

The complete *Blood Destiny* series

"A spectacular and addictive series."

Mackenzie Smith has always known that she was different. Growing up as the only human in a pack of rural shapeshifters will do that to you, but then couple it with some mean fighting skills and a fiery temper and you end up with a woman that few will dare to cross. However, when the only father figure in her life is brutally murdered, and the dangerous Brethren with their predatory Lord Alpha come to investigate, Mack has to not only ensure the physical safety of her adopted family by hiding her apparent humanity, she also has to seek the blood-soaked vengeance that she craves.

Book One - Bloodfire

Book Two - Bloodmagic

Book Three - Bloodrage

Book Four - Blood Politics

Book Five - Bloodlust

Also

Corrigan Fire

Corrigan Magic

Corrigan Rage

Corrigan Politics

Corrigan Lust

The complete *Bo Blackman* series

A half-dead daemon, a massacre at her London based PI firm and evidence that suggests she's the main suspect for both ... Bo Blackman is having a very bad week.

She might be naive and inexperienced but she's determined to get to the bottom of the crimes, even if it means involving herself with one of London's most powerful vampire Families and their enigmatic leader.

It's pretty much going to be impossible for Bo to ever escape unscathed.

Book One - Dire Straits

Book Two - New Order

Book Three - High Stakes

Book Four - Red Angel

Book Five - Vigilante Vampire

Book Six - Dark Tomorrow

The complete *Highland Magic* series

Integrity Taylor walked away from the Sidhe when she was a child. Orphaned and bullied, she simply had no reason to stay, especially not when the sins of her father were going to remain on her shoulders. She found a new family - a group of thieves who proved that blood was less important than loyalty and love.

But the Sidhe aren't going to let Integrity stay away forever. They need her more than anyone realises - besides, there are prophecies to be fulfilled, people to be saved and hearts to be won over. If anyone can do it, Integrity can.

Book One - Gifted Thief

Book Two - Honour Bound

Book Three - Veiled Threat

Book Four - Last Wish

The complete *Dreamweaver* series

"I have special coping mechanisms for the times I need to open the front door. They're even often successful..."

Zoe Lydon knows there's often nothing logical or rational about fear. It doesn't change the fact that she's too terrified to step outside her own house, however.

What Zoe doesn't realise is that she's also a dreamweaver - able to access other people's subconscious minds. When she finds herself in the Dreamlands and up against its sinister Mayor, she'll need to use all of her wits - and overcome all of her fears - if she's ever going to come out alive.

Book One - Night Shade

Book Two - Night Terrors

Book Three - Night Lights

Stand alone novels

Eros

William Shakespeare once wrote that, "Cupid is a knavish lad, thus to make poor females mad." The trouble is that Cupid himself would probably agree…

As probably the last person in the world who'd appreciate hearts, flowers and romance, Coop is convinced that true love doesn't exist – which is rather unfortunate considering he's also known as Cupid, the God of Love. He'd rather spend his days drinking, womanising and generally having as much fun as he possible can. As far as he's concerned, shooting people with bolts of pure love is a waste of his time…but then his path crosses with that of shy and retiring Skye Sawyer and nothing will ever be quite the same again.

Wraith

Magic. Shadows. Adventure. Romance.

Saiya Buchanan is a wraith, able to detach her shadow from her body and send it off to do her bidding. But, unlike most of her kin, Saiya doesn't deal in death. Instead, she trades secrets - and in the goblin besieged city of Stirling in Scotland, they're a highly prized commodity. It might just be, however, that the goblins have been hiding the greatest secret of them all. When Gabriel de Florinville, a

Dark Elf, is sent as royal envoy into Stirling and takes her prisoner, Saiya is not only going to uncover the sinister truth. She's also going to realise that sometimes the deepest secrets are the ones locked within your own heart.

The complete *Lazy Girl's Guide To Magic* series

Hard Work Will Pay Off Later. Laziness Pays Off Now.

Let's get one thing straight - Ivy Wilde is not a heroine. In fact, she's probably the last witch in the world who you'd call if you needed a magical helping hand. If it were down to Ivy, she'd spend all day every day on her sofa where she could watch TV, munch junk food and talk to her feline familiar to her heart's content.

However, when a bureaucratic disaster ends up with Ivy as the victim of a case of mistaken identity, she's yanked very unwillingly into Arcane Branch, the investigative department of the Hallowed Order of Magical Enlightenment. Her problems are quadrupled when a valuable object is stolen right from under the Order's noses.

It doesn't exactly help that she's been magically bound to Adeptus Exemptus Raphael Winter. He might have piercing sapphire eyes and a body which a cover model would be proud of but, as far as Ivy's concerned, he's a walking advertisement for the joyless perils of too much witch-work.

And if he makes her go to the gym again, she's definitely going to turn him into a frog.

Book One - Slouch Witch

Book Two - Star Witch

Book Three - Spirit Witch

Sparkle Witch (Christmas short story)

The complete *Fractured Faery* series

One corpse. Several bizarre looking attackers. Some very strange magical powers. And a severe bout of amnesia.

It's one thing to wake up outside in the middle of the night with a decapitated man for company. It's another to have no memory of how you got there - or who you are.

She might not know her own name but she knows that several people are out to get her. It could be because she has strange magical powers seemingly at her fingertips and is some kind of fabulous hero. But then why does she appear to inspire fear in so many? And who on earth is the sexy, green-eyed barman who apparently despises her? So many questions ... and so few answers.

At least one thing is for sure - the streets of Manchester have never met someone quite as mad as Madrona...

Book One - Box of Frogs

SHORTLISTED FOR THE KINDLE STORYTELLER AWARD 2018

Book Two - Quiver of Cobras

Book Three - Skulk of Foxes

The complete *City Of Magic* series

Charley is a cleaner by day and a professional gambler by night. She might be haunted by her tragic past but she's never thought of herself as anything or anyone special. Until, that is, things start to go terribly wrong all across the city of Manchester. Between plagues of rats, firestorms and the gleaming blue eyes of a sexy Scottish werewolf, she might just have landed herself in the middle of a magical apocalypse. She might also be the only person who has the ability to bring order to an utterly chaotic new world.

Book One - Shrill Dusk

Book Two - Brittle Midnight

Book Three - Furtive Dawn

Made in the USA
Las Vegas, NV
09 May 2022

48673524R00163